Palisades.
Pure Romance.

FICTION THAT FEATURES CREDIBLE CHARACTERS AND

ENTERTAINING PLOT LINES, WHILE CONTINUING TO UPHOLD

STRONG CHRISTIAN VALUES. FROM HIGH ADVENTURE

TO TENDER STORIES OF THE HEART, EACH PALISADES

ROMANCE IS AN UNDILUTED STORY OF LOVE,

FROM BEGINNING TO END!

A PALISADES CONTEMPORARY ROMANCE

A CHRISTMAS JOY

PEGGY DARTY

SHARON GILLENWATER

AMANDA MacLEAN

PALISADES

This is a work of fiction. The characters, incidents, and dialogues are products of the author's imagination and are not to be construed as real. Any resemblance to actual events or persons, living or dead, is entirely coincidental.

A CHRISTMAS JOY
published by Palisades
a part of the Questar publishing family

© 1995 Snowflakes by Peggy Darty
© 1995 Love Wanted by Sharon Gillenwater
© 1995 Gift of Love by Amanda MacLean

International Standard Book Number: 0-88070-780-1

Cover illustration by George Angelini
Cover designed by David Carlson
and Mona Weir-Daly
Edited by Paul Hawley

Printed in the United States of America

For information:
QUESTAR PUBLISHERS, INC.
POST OFFICE BOX 1720
SISTERS, OREGON 97759

95 96 97 98 99 00 01 02 — 10 9 8 7 6 5 4 3 2 1

"He will be great and will be called
the Son of the Most High.
The Lord God will give him the throne
of his father David, and he will reign
over the house of Jacob forever; his
kingdom will never end."

LUKE 1:32-33 (NIV)

SNOWFLAKES

PEGGY DARTY

CHAPTER

One

It was four o'clock in New York City as Heather Grant rushed out of Saks and scanned Fifth Avenue for a taxi. Christmas music had followed her from the store onto the sidewalk, offering a cheerful message on this dreary Monday; today, however, the jauntiness of "Jingle Bells" failed to lift her sagging spirits.

What's wrong with me? she wondered. The Christmas season had always been her favorite, but this year she was as grumpy as Scrooge. She spotted an empty taxi and waved frantically, but the driver ignored her for a group of businessmen at the end of the block.

Muttering an unflattering remark about the driver, she shoved her hands in the pockets of her black woolen coat and glanced around. The sidewalk was clogged with weary-looking people, trudging to bus stops or yelling for taxis. Maybe she needed to walk the ten blocks home to vent the day's frustration. Along the way, she could gaze at Christmas decorations, try to absorb the mood of the season.

9

A light snow had fallen earlier, but only a gray slush remained to spatter from the wheels of cars as she waited to cross Fifth Avenue. Staring glumly at the dirty snow, she found her thoughts drifting toward the Colorado ski slopes, and her mind filled with a vision of pristine snow and happy skiers. Suddenly she was homesick, so homesick she could cry.

The argument that had droned in her head for months started again. *Chuck all of this, go home.* But what could she do back in Denver? She was making good money as a model, and New York was the place to be. The excitement and glamour of her job, however, had long ago faded; now she was merely tired and bored. She returned home each evening feeling empty and unfulfilled, longing to do something worthwhile with her life. But what?

The light changed and she stretched her long legs in a brisk pace, moving around and past other pedestrians. As the wind bit her cheeks, she felt more miserable with each block. At the next street corner, a man stood at the Salvation Army booth, ringing a bell. As she reached his side, she paused to drop some money in the bucket. He smiled his thanks and she walked on, hesitating before a glittering shop window which displayed a huge white tree adorned with gold ornaments. She could appreciate the beauty, but where was the joy she should be feeling?

Her eyes drifted from the Christmas tree to her own reflection in the shop window.

She stood five feet eleven inches, a height that had definitely been an asset during her climb to success in the modeling profession. Being large-boned and athletic, however, she had to work twice as hard to weigh 135 and stay a size eight. Long blond hair was neatly plaited, accenting nice features: wide-set deep blue eyes beneath wing brows, slim nose, full mouth, and prominent cheekbones.

The reflection that stared back at her was an attractive one, and yet there was was no life to her features; the light seemed to have gone out of her eyes.

Sighing, she turned away and began walking again.

Mentally, she ticked off her blessings—good health, good job, things it was so easy to take for granted. And once more, she quieted her discontent. Until she passed a church and felt a stab of guilt. She could almost hear her mother's voice whispering in her ear.

"Take Christ out of Christmas and you lose the reason for the season…"

Heather sighed, feeling even worse as a recent telephone call replayed in her memory. Her voice had been heavy with gloom as she spoke with her mother.

"No, Mother, I don't go to church…"

"Yes, Mother, I know I should go…"

By the time Heather reached her apartment building, she was frozen from head to toe, and the guilt of her backsliding had made her feel even worse, if possible. She gave the doorman a weak smile, then hurried inside, pausing at the wall of mailboxes.

Her box was empty except for one small envelope, resembling an invitation. Her eyes scanned the Denver postmark and for the first time all day, she felt a spark of interest. Stepping onto the elevator, she removed her gloves and tore open the envelope. As the elevator glided up to her seventh floor, her eyes scanned the invitation.

You are cordially invited to a five-year reunion of the Snowflakes, to be held at Snowmont in Vail. Come back to the ski slopes and reunite with your ski club on the weekend of December 18.

At first, the message was confusing; then she read the personal note written in longhand on the opposite page.

Heather, I'm now running Snowmont! Please come back for the reunion. Sam Watkins.

Heather lifted her eyes from Sam's invitation and stared at the elevator doors as they slid open. Sam was running Snowmont? She stepped into the corridor and hurried to her apartment, thinking about Sam and the lodge.

Her mind was spinning with memories as she dug the keys from her purse and unlocked the door. Snowflakes was the name of her college ski club, a non-competitive club whose members were drawn together by a mutual interest. The group hosted car washes and bake sales, and sold various items throughout the year to finance ski trips around the state. When the Snowflakes went over to Vail, they stayed at Snowmont, a small, Bavarian-style inn run by a friendly couple who had a soft heart for college kids.

Peeling off coat and boots and leaving them at the coatrack, Heather hurried to the kitchen. A smile touched her cold lips as she laid the invitation on the breakfast bar and took a carton of milk from the refrigerator. Mixing milk and chocolate powder into a cup, she began to recall all the crazy antics of her college friends. As she slid the cup into the microwave, memories drifted through her mind like wisps of fog on a winter night. And through the fog, Brad wandered back to her.

How had life turned out for him? she wondered. As she thought of him, she felt an old ache settle over her heart again. While the pain of their breakup had been dulled by time and circumstance, it was still there, distant, less troublesome, but still there, like a scar from an old injury.

The microwave buzzed just as the wall phone began to ring, and looking from one to the other, she chose the hot chocolate. Taking a bracing sip, she grabbed the phone and spoke a weary hello.

"Heather! I caught you home for once…"

"Tracy!" The voice of her best friend from college days warmed her heart. "It's great to hear your voice. How are you?"

"Fat and sassy. You?"

"A little bit homesick, but I'll be okay." She forced a note of optimism into her voice. "It's just the Christmas music and—"

"Then you must come back for the reunion! I assume you got Sam's invitation?"

"Just got it today, as a matter of fact. Tracy, when did Sam take over Snowmont?"

"In September. And knowing how everyone loves Vail, he's decided to reunite the ski club. Naturally, we pay our expenses while staying at the lodge, but he's throwing in some little perks as incentives. Lift tickets for everyone, a steak dinner to any couple who's still together. So far as I know, Steve and I are the only ones who qualify. And a ski jacket for the most loyal ski bum. Brad Barstow will get that one, for sure."

13

Brad...

Heather's fingers wound nervously around the white telephone cord. She wanted to ask about him, but she couldn't bring herself to utter the words. In any case, Tracy had just answered one important question concerning Brad's ambition. Or lack of it. Brad hadn't changed, after all. He was still the irresponsible guy she had known, caring for nothing but the ski slopes and the next adventure.

"Heather, why don't you come home for Christmas?" Tracy insisted. "If you fly in on Friday, you can ride over to Vail with Steve and me for the weekend..."

"Well...I might," she conceded. "I'd love to visit my family. And it would be fun to see all the old gang. Especially you and Steve! Any more little ones on the way?" Heather adored children. She often sauntered through the children's department just to gaze at the clothes.

"Puh-lease," Tracy groaned in response to the question. "Three kids push me to the limit!" But there was unmistakable pride in her voice.

"Twin boys and a little girl," Heather remembered. "How wonderful!"

"Three children under five years of age is not always considered wonderful," Tracy laughed. "But we adore them. So...are you coming? From the sound of your voice, you need a good dose of crazy fun. And you can depend on the Snowflakes for that!"

Heather's eyes drifted through the kitchen window to a dreary gray sky. The invitation was like a sun ray dancing on her windowsill, and just hearing Tracy's voice made her happier than she had felt in weeks.

"I'll come," she decided. "I was about to commit to a shoot in the Bahamas but—"

"Tough life, huh?"

Heather laughed softly. "Believe me, it's not as good as it sounds. I don't like the swimsuits, and I'll have to live on carrot sticks and water to stay a perfect size eight." Her mind raced over all the objections. Then, suddenly, she knew what she should do. "I'll come home instead!"

"Great. I'll meet you at the airport."

Heather thought it over, wondering what her agent would say. She had worked every holiday for the past two years; this time, she deserved to go home.

"I'll check airline schedules and let you know." Heather heard the lilt of excitement in her voice and realized she finally had some plans that excited her. "Tracy, thanks for insisting. Otherwise I wouldn't have come home."

As they said goodbye, a wistful smile crept over Heather's face. She sat down at the eating bar, sipping her hot chocolate. So Brad would get the prize for ski bum! Heather shook her head. He had been the hot dog of their ski club, taking on every challenge, and yet his daring nature was at odds with his easygoing style.

She recalled the first time she had ever seen him; even then she had felt a tug at her heartstrings. Creative Writing. An eight o'clock class that meant bolting out of bed, tugging on her sweatshirt and jeans, raking haphazardly through her long blond hair. She had trimmed her routine to twelve and a half minutes, from the time she grabbed her clothes from the closet until she raced through the ivy-covered building in the center of the campus.

On the second day of class a tall, slim guy with smooth olive skin wandered through the door. At first, he looked as though he had stumbled into the wrong class, but then he slid into the chair opposite her as though he didn't care.

"Got a pencil?" he had grinned the question, disrupting Professor Birdwell's lecture on the correct use of parallelism.

And of course he needed paper. From the look of his Nikes, sporting a hole in the left toe, he could do with new shoes as well.

After he tucked his long legs under the desk, she had ventured a curious glance in his direction. His hair was dark brown and thick, brushing carelessly against the neckline of his sweatshirt. Dark brows framed deep-set green eyes, as green as a storm-tossed sea and every bit as changeable. His nose was slim and straight. He always looked as though he needed to gain an extra five or ten pounds, and the slimness accented his long, angular jaw. He had a deep dimple in his chin; she had been fascinated by that dimple.

Heather shook her head vaguely, trying to push aside the memory of Brad. He had once been a very important part of her life, but that was a long time ago. She forced her thoughts toward a weekend of skiing, and as she began to consider the trip, she got out of the chair and hurried to her bedroom.

She opened the louvered doors of her closet, feeling a spark of excitement as she considered a reunion with the Snowflakes. Her hands flew over the coat hangers, flipping through outfits, as she pondered Colorado weather. At the far end of the rack, her slim fingers closed over the emerald green ski suit. She smiled as she pulled it from the closet. It had been two years since she'd worn it, that long since she had skied. At one point, she had decided to give up the sport she loved, for fear of adding more muscle and an extra pound as well.

Pressing the suit against her body, she took a slow, deep breath, feeling the day's tension slip from her taut muscles. She had loved gliding through the white powder, feeling the glare of the sun on her face, the beat of the wind against her body.

Tossing the suit on the bed, she reached for the telephone on the nightstand. Her fingers flew over the numbers, and it was only a matter of seconds until the familiar voice came over the wires.

"Hi, Mom." Heather smiled. "I'm coming home for Christmas…"

Brad Barstow surveyed the two flights of stairs leading up to his condominium and sighed. He was bone weary, having put in twelve hours at his ski shop. Good thing he ran his own business; he would resent the long, hard hours if he were merely on salary for someone else. This evening, he had stayed an extra two hours to help some college students select just the right equipment for their skiing holiday. But they were good kids, and he had enjoyed sharing some of his knowledge with them.

He climbed the stairs, eager to get to his sofa and play couch potato for another evening. As he reached the door and fished into his jeans pocket for his keys, his mind raced toward the kitchen. *Ah, pasta tonight,* he decided, unlocking the door and switching on the hall light. He yanked off his parka and tossed it on the back of the sofa, and there his eyes lingered.

Before he began chopping peppers for his marinara, he needed to kick back for a few minutes, rest his weary body. With that in mind, he headed for the refrigerator to grab a pint of orange juice. Uncapping the lid, he returned to the overstuffed sofa and sank down with a blissful sigh.

His eyes fell to the cluttered coffee table and Sam's invitation atop a pile of ski magazines. A smile played over his lips as he thought of Sam's clever plan. To publicize his management of Snowmont, Sam was organizing a reunion of the Snowflakes the weekend before Christmas.

A mental image of Walter Richardson, trying to balance an extra fifty pounds on skies, brought a hearty chuckle. His mind moved on to the other Snowflakes and his laughter faded, along with his smile. Would Heather come back? And bring her husband? He grimaced at that.

He took a deep swallow of orange juice and leaned his head against the cushions. Two years ago, he had summoned the nerve to call her parents' home and inquire about Heather. Her mother had gently informed him that Heather had recently become engaged. The wedding was set for Christmas. He had managed a few more polite words before hanging up. Then he had fallen into a grave of depression for several weeks.

Finishing the juice, he aimed the plastic bottle, like a basketball, and sank it into the wastebasket across the room. A fire, that's what he needed! He got up and went to the wood box beside the fireplace. Arranging the logs in the fireplace, he reached to the mantel for matches and struck one against some kindling. He watched with satisfaction as the tiny flame took hold, grew, spread and built into a cheery fire.

He sank down on the carpet, removing his hiking boots and placing them on the hearth to dry. Drawing his weary legs up and winding his arms around his knees, he stared into the dancing flames, thinking of other fires.

He drifted through memories of weekends at Snowmont.

He recalled how the ski club would rush from the slopes to the warmth of Snowmont's fireplace. Laughing at someone's antics, joking over something that had happened that day, they would collapse before the fireplace, stretching their aching bodies. Later, revived and starving, they would race down the street to a favorite Italian restaurant. It was a cozy little mecca of candle-light and red-checkered decor, with a fat jukebox wailing the latest hits.

He took a deep breath, staring into the orange flames. Three or four times a year, he wandered back to the restaurant, choosing that special table for two in the far corner, the one he often shared with Heather. And he would punch K-ll on the jukebox. Because it was a love song about Colorado, it had never been removed from the selections, while other hits had come and gone.

He would sit there, listening, remembering. In a way, it was a silly thing to do, yet he couldn't seem to resist indulging himself now and then.

She was the only woman he had ever truly loved, *the only one.* For some reason he had never quite understood, their relationship was not meant to be permanent. Over the last month, he had been thinking of her, probably because of the reunion. And because last week, walking through the snow one evening, he had spotted a tall woman with long blond hair staring through a shop window. He couldn't see her face, and he had stopped to stare. Then her male companion had come out of the shop, calling to her, and Brad had moved on. As snowflakes caressed his cheek, the woman's soft laughter had drifted to him, and he had glanced sharply over his shoulder. But of course it wasn't Heather; it would never be Heather again.

There had been girlfriends, even one to whom he almost

19

made a permanent commitment; but something just wasn't right and eventually they had broken up.

He ran a hand across his forehead, forcing his thoughts toward the weekend. Since donating his Saturdays to helping out in the ski school for the blind, he had found a joy and contentment as never before. The program was a nonprofit service offering volunteer guides at no charge for those who were visually impaired. The volunteers were all specifically trained in guiding techniques, from novice through expert.

Vail's special program was the best of its kind, and Brad felt a great deal of pride being involved in a sport so dear to his heart. It had taken only one day as a volunteer in the program to show him the enjoyment and satisfaction of helping the impaired skiers, who had taught him a lesson in courage. He especially liked working with the children, and it was in this area that he discovered his true calling.

He took a deep breath, reminding himself how his volunteer work had come about. First, he had made a commitment to God in that special little church whose members had stayed after him to attend their services. Finally, he had relented and gone to a Sunday morning service, feeling reluctant, even a bit doubtful. It had been a pleasant surprise to feel the warmth of the people, and the presence of God, touching his life. He had left church feeling as though he had swallowed all the rays of the sun. On that day he had asked God to show him what to do with his life. The next week, a friend had pressed him to be a volunteer in the ski school for the blind, and the door to a new and wonderful world had opened for him.

He sighed and stared into the fire, as his thoughts returned to Heather. What would it be like to see her again? And what could he say to her husband?

Closing his eyes, he tried to think how he would react. He wasn't sure. He was a stronger person than he had been during those reckless college years, and it was not age but rather the grace of God that kept him on course. He opened his eyes and gazed back at the fire, grateful that he no longer had to rely on his own strength to get him through difficult situations.

Two

"Heather, over here!" Tracy Whittington yelled, peering around the crowd waiting for the arriving passengers at Gate 9.

"Tracy!" Heather waved back when she spotted Tracy weaving through the crowd.

For a moment the two women merely stood and stared into each other's faces, a hundred memories crowding their minds. Then Heather threw her arms around Tracy, and they both burst into laughter.

"We're still Mutt and Jeff!" Tracy said, holding Heather at arm's length to look at her. "Only I've shrunk another inch or two while you're more regal than ever!"

They were a striking contrast. Tracy had dark hair and eyes, was five feet two with an extra fifteen pounds after having three children. Heather was slim and tall with blond hair and fair skin.

"You look great," Heather smiled down at her friend. "How are Steve and the children?"

"Rowdy as ever!" Tracy grabbed her arm. "Come on, let's get your luggage and head out."

"Tracy, I can't wait to see your family."

Tracy looked up with a mischievous grin. "Can you wait until Sunday? My mother-in-law is already installed at the house, and I've said my goodbyes. After spending the morning prying the twins from my ankles, I can't take another round of goodbyes."

Heather laughed; "Okay. I've already told Mom it'll be Sunday before I get home. So we're all set."

"And we'll pick Steve up at the office on the way out of town. Look, why don't I get the car while you head to the luggage carousel? I'll pull up to the loading zone and give you a hand with your stuff."

"Good idea," Heather nodded as Tracy turned and hurried in the opposite direction.

As Heather began the long walk to the baggage area, she glanced around the busy new airport. She had always disliked flying; ironically, her line of work had required hundreds of hours in planes and airports over the past years. Today, however, she felt good about being in an airport, for this was Denver— home. Through a glass wall, she could see a clear blue sky, promising a great weekend. Her thoughts moved from Tracy and Steve to the other friends she would be seeing in Vail.

By the time she reached the carousel and retrieved her luggage, Tracy was rushing through the door. Soon they had loaded the luggage and climbed into Tracy's station wagon.

"Have you had a lot of snow?" Heather asked as Tracy sped away from the curb.

"Actually, it's been a mild winter," Tracy replied, zipping in and out of traffic. "During our one big snow, the kids stayed home, Steve skipped work, and we played in the yard half the day." Tracy's dark eyes danced as she related the incident. "We built Mr. and Mrs. Snowman and three wild kids. Just like us! Then a snowball fight broke out, and Travis fell and cut his forehead. Had to be taken to the emergency room."

Tracy shook her head, glancing at Heather. "My life is a circus. I want to hear what glamorous models do in the Big Apple. The places you go, the people you meet. Tell me, tell me!"

Heather smiled, enjoying Tracy's bubbling personality and realizing how much she had missed her. "After hearing about your family, the life of a single woman isn't so great, Tracy. It's pretty empty, really."

"I don't believe you!"

"It's true." Heather stated, recalling how she and Tracy had made such different choices. When Tracy married right out of college, Heather felt sad for her.

"You're giving up your freedom too soon," she had admonished Tracy. "You're missing out on a lot of fun. And what about a career?"

"I'll have all the fun I want with Steve," Tracy had laughed. "And the only career I want is the one labeled *mother.*"

As Heather replayed that conversation in her memory, she glanced across at Tracy, whose sparkling eyes and easy laughter confirmed her happiness. She appeared to have made the right choice for her life. Even overweight, Tracy was lovely, possessing the kind of beauty that radiates from the soul.

"Really, Tracy," Heather leaned back against the seat and

sighed, "I think you're the one with the great life."

"*What?* Four loads of laundry a day? And I have no imagination at balancing the budget or planning meals." Her dark curls bobbed about her face, accenting her frequent gestures. "Do you know what poor Steve had for breakfast this morning? Peanut butter on stale crackers! I'm more forgetful than ever, Heather, but with hyper kids, a starving Saint Bernard, a Persian dragging four baby kittens...."

They were both laughing, but as their laughter faded, Tracy began to nod. "I know what you mean. And I am very content. Steve and I have been working with our youth group at church, and I've found a lot of satisfaction in that. The youth director wanted some role models for teenagers. Can you picture Steve and me as role models?" Without giving Heather a chance to respond, Tracy plunged on. "I don't know how seriously those kids take our advice, but I hope we provide a little bit of direction for them. I'll tell you one thing for sure: the time we spend with those kids really makes me feel a sense of accomplishment, Heather."

Heather nodded. *A sense of accomplishment.* It was a phrase that often ran through her mind; it seemed odd that Tracy was using it as well.

"I'm sure you feel a great sense of accomplishment, Tracy. You know, when I was growing up I used to think I wanted to work with children. Then I became obsessed with getting into the fashion world. Now I'm sick of clothes."

Heather paused, taking a deep breath. "As for my life in New York...well, it was exciting at first. There was the glamour of going to nice restaurants and seeing Broadway plays, and of course the great shopping. But over the past year, I find myself wanting to slow down, settle into something personal and permanent. My job is…," her voice trailed, as she tried to find the right words to describe the hectic pace she kept. "I carry my life around in a bag, going from one place to another on assignments. The friends I have are people involved in the same line of work. Our conversations center around who's working, who's got great pictures, what will happen as we get older. And of course we're obsessed with trying to maintain a size eight, while wishing to be a size six."

She heaved a sigh; just talking about it made her weary.

"Well, you shouldn't have any trouble being an eight," Tracy said, her eyes running up and down Heather's white silk jumpsuit. "So what are you saying? Are you going to quit modeling?"

The gold bracelets at Heather's wrist jangled as she pushed a strand of blond hair higher on her forehead. "I'm not sure what I'm going to do. The contentment you're talking about is totally missing from my life. I go home every day with no sense of accomplishment; none whatsoever." She turned sad eyes to Tracy. "I want to do something useful with my life."

Tracy winked. "You want to get married and start a family?"

"Eventually. But first, I want to find another line of work. Don't ask what." She threw up her hands. "See how confused I am?" She tried to laugh about it, but she wasn't kidding.

Tracy's small hand shot from the steering wheel to give Heather a reassuring pat on the arm. "You just need to come home, get back with the old crowd. Here's the building where Steve works," she said offhandedly, steering the car onto the ramp leading to an impressive office complex. "Heather, before Steve gets in the car, I want to ask you something. You never gave me the details on why you broke your engagement."

Heather sighed. "Thank God I came to my senses before we set a wedding date. He was a nice guy, basically, but he fell in love with my image, not the real me."

"Oh, he wanted to be seen with a model, is that it?"

"Something like that. He seemed to be interested in how I looked, not who I really was or what I believed. And he came from a very liberal family whose way of life was totally different from my conservative upbringing. There are certain things that I have never done and never will."

Tracy's dark eyes shot from Heather to the traffic light. "Did you know Brad has never married?"

Heather caught her breath. No, she didn't know, although she was dying to ask. Fear and pride had kept the question choked in her throat. She had suffered tormenting visions of a beautiful wife and a couple of kids with green eyes and dimples in their chins.

Tracy forged on. "Maybe you two could—"

"No! It's too late!" Heather wanted to squelch any ideas about rekindling that old flame.

"Ouch, you've got that one down pat!" Tracy's expression was serious, yet her dark eyes twinkled as she looked at Heather.

"I just want to be clear about my feelings." Heather heard the sharp edge to her tone, and she began to wonder whether she was talking to Tracy…or to herself.

Brad stood before the bathroom mirror, giving himself a long and critical appraisal. He had just stepped out of the shower, toweled down and yanked on a terry robe as a sharp wind whistled around his window. He couldn't remember the last time he evaluated his looks, but today he was curious. The lean, lanky college kid had rounded out, and his muscles were well toned from hours on the slopes.

He ran a hand towel over his head, ruffling his wet black hair. He wore it short, close-cut. It was the easiest style for him to keep with his active life. Reaching for a brush, he swept his hair back on the sides and peered at his features. Thick brows, green eyes, prominent cheekbones and a lean jaw were more pronounced beneath a wet head. And that boyish dimple still lurked in his chin.

Wishing he didn't have the dimple, he laid down the brush and sauntered into his green-and-brown plaid bedroom. He swung his arms back and forth, hoping to ease the tension in his shoulders that even the hot shower had not chased away. Why did he have this strange case of nerves about tonight's party? Was it because he dreaded having his buddies raz him about not being able to get a woman? He frowned. Or keep a woman? Of course, they knew his single status was his own choice, but they liked teasing him about it. In any case, he certainly didn't want to take a date to this particular party.

He could invite Melissa, his most frequent companion, but she would probably feel excluded, once everyone starting recalling the "good ol' days." And if she were to arch that thin eyebrow, as she sometimes did when she was bored, he would feel like taking her home. So, to spare them both, he had opted to go alone.

Opening his closet door, he studied his conservative clothes. He had the money to purchase an impressive wardrobe, but he stuck to the basics, using his money for his ski business, along with a few anonymous contributions to the blind skiers. He especially enjoyed buying things for the kids, many of whom came from families with limited incomes.

Choosing a white polo with thin red stripes and a pair of dark trousers, he began to dress. He tried not to think about Heather, or the prospect of seeing her again. If he did, he would try to act as though she were no different from the rest of the crowd.

By the time he angled his tan Jeep into a parking space, he could see from the row of Denver cars that Sam's reunion was well attended.

Hopping out and locking his car, he hurried to the front door of the quaint log lodge. Sam had added some rockers and wooden swings to the front porch, giving the place a real down-home atmosphere.

As he entered and crossed the lobby to the banquet room, his eyes took in the colorful balloons and the huge confetti sign welcoming the Snowflakes. Sam had outdone himself with detail. Old photographs of the ski club blown up in life-size posters lined the walls, and crepe paper streamers dangled from every doorway and window.

He paused in the entrance to the banquet room and scanned the spacious room where long tables held miniature Christmas trees. He began to recognize familiar faces in the crowd of about forty people, most of whom were grouped at the buffet table near the fireplace.

"Brad!" Sam rushed up, slapping him on the shoulder. "Buddy, I think you're gonna be glad you came!"

Brad grinned agreeably as his eyes roamed over the crowd, then suddenly froze.

She was crossing the room with a plate of food in her hand, and for a moment Brad felt as though someone had just punched him in the stomach.

"She just got here," Sam whispered.

She reached an empty table and pulled back a chair. He squinted at her left hand, trying to confirm what he had checked out at the beginning. No wedding rings! Had she already divorced the guy?

Frowning, he considered his options, while continuing to stare. Then suddenly she lifted her eyes from the table and looked straight into his face. Now it was too late to retreat; he had to be polite, he told himself, as he walked toward her table.

She still wore her hair long, but the style was more chic now: a cascade of golden waves about her face. As she looked at him, he noticed that the "baby fat" she used to joke about was gone. Her thinness accented huge blue eyes, apple cheeks, and a pointed chin. She was more beautiful than ever.

It had been five years; yet amazingly, as he looked at her, those years seemed to roll away.

"Hello, Heather." His tone was casual, well modulated, concealing his nervousness.

"Hi, Brad."

He looked into her eyes and saw the same eyes he remembered—wide set, deep blue, flecked with gold beneath thick dark lashes. But her words were tinged with an accent that was slightly different, not quite Colorado. That was good, he decided, for it was proof that she no longer belonged here.

But then a smile curved her lips, and he felt as though he'd just been dealt another blow. *This is crazy,* he thought, wondering how a twenty-seven-year-old guy could revert back to college boy in a matter of minutes.

"How are you?" he asked.

"Fine," she smiled. "And you?"

"Fine."

They stared at each other for a long moment, reliving the despair that had haunted both of them after the breakup.

"Who's with you?" he asked, glancing casually over the crowd.

"I came with Tracy and Steve."

His mind groped with the realization that she was not with a husband or even a date, but rather Steve and Tracy, their best friends in college.

"I see Steve occasionally, but he didn't mention that you were coming," he said, glancing at her again.

"Tracy called and insisted." Her shoulders lifted in a delicate shrug, pulling against the draped turtleneck of her dress. "Listen, you'd better grab a plate of food; it's going fast."

He nodded. "Good idea."

As he turned from her and began to walk toward the buffet, Heather grabbed a deep breath and closed her eyes. Her heart was racing, and all the old romantic feelings were sweeping through her again. She couldn't believe it.

Three

❧

B rad, come join us," Tracy yelled to him.

"Hey, man." Steve rushed up. "Haven't seen you in ages. Load that plate and come to our table." Steve was a charming guy with blond hair, vivid blue eyes and a warm smile. He and Tracy made a good pair. "Have you seen Heather?" he whispered to Brad.

"Yep." Brad got busy with the roast beef and trimmings while Steve hovered at his elbow. With his plate piled high, Brad decided: Why not? Curiosity was eating him alive. Might as well find out about her. "Save me a seat," he called to Steve.

By the time he returned to the table, a crowd had gathered. The only seat remaining was the one between Steve and Heather, obviously meant for him. He tried to slip unobtrusively into the chair, glancing around at both strange and familiar faces, as introductions were hurled right and left.

Heather was acknowledging introductions while silently marveling at what a few years had done to some of her old ski buddies.

"So, what's modeling like?" Sherry Haynes wanted to know.

"Guess you meet lots of famous people," Sherry's husband joined in.

"Do you get to keep the clothes?" Sherry rushed on.

"Please!" Tracy put up her hand. "Give the poor girl a break. How's she supposed to answer a dozen questions and chew her food?" She grinned at Heather. "Don't you just hate it when you take a big bite of food and someone asks you something?"

Heather laughed, chewing quickly. She turned to Sherry, seeing in her eyes that look of wistfulness that usually meant one assumed Heather's life was much better than it was.

"No, I don't get to keep the clothes. No, I haven't met anyone really famous, but I know some who will be one day. As for the fun of it, that could be debated. I've been to some exciting places, but then the hurry up-and-wait routine gets old."

"What do you mean?" Sherry frowned, clearly disappointed that her friend's life might not be as glamorous as she wanted to believe. She had quit college to get married, then settled into an office job where she expected to remain forever.

"Well," Heather touched a napkin to her lips, "we have to hurry to get there, hurry to get dressed, then sit and wait until the art director gets everything right. We shoot furs and winter fashions in the summer, and swimsuits in the winter."

Beside her, Brad was listening to the conversation. He turned to her, venturing a question that sprang to mind as she spoke.

"Where do you shoot winter and summer scenes?"

She glanced at Brad, thinking it was the most intelligent

question she had been asked tonight. Of course, she had always enjoyed her conversations with him; he was well read and seemed to know a little about everything.

"If I'm lucky, we go to a warm climate when shooting summer wear. If I'm not so lucky, I may be on a beach in New Jersey with goose bumps all over me and an ice cube in my mouth."

All heads turned, just as she expected. This always made interesting dinner conversation; she had gone through it a dozen times.

"I can't have my breath smoking in the cold air when it's supposed to be summer," she explained patiently. "So an ice cube in my mouth keeps that from happening."

When finally hunger overtook conversation, the crowd quieted down. Heather turned her eyes toward Brad, giving him a little smile, and he decided to be sociable.

"So you like living in New York?" Brad asked.

Sensing a note of sarcasm in his voice, Heather lifted her chin and smiled. "I love it."

He nodded. Why had he asked? In college, she always had that wanderlust gnawing at her, but then so had he.

"What are you doing now?" she asked. Even in her own ears, her tone sounded more like a challenge to a fight than a polite question. She caught her breath. Why couldn't she handle her emotions tonight?

He took a sip of tea, his eyes appraising her over the rim of the glass. "Still skiing."

She nodded. Just as she thought! He was dressed well, as though he earned a good living; but how did one make a living on the ski slopes? she wondered, toying with her food.

Accustomed to eating tiny portions, she was feeling nauseated by all the food on her plate.

A tinkling sound turned all eyes toward the center table where Sam was tapping a glass with his spoon. Once he had a captive audience, he surveyed his guests with a smile that stretched from ear to ear. He was of medium height and build, with bright red hair and a scattering of freckles across his nose. He had always been a good sport and everyone loved him.

"Hey, it's good to see all you guys!" His eyes circled the group. "I know we're going to have a great weekend."

As Sam began to detail his weeks of planning for this event, Heather felt Brad's eyes slipping over her again. She pretended not to notice. Tilting her head back, she focused on Sam as though she had to hear every word. Her mind was in a jumble, though, and she caught only a few key words: breakfast here at nine....lift tickets for everyone...a sleigh ride tomorrow night...

Then he had finished and again everyone was talking at once. At the far end of the table, someone lit a cigarette and Heather caught her breath, wondering what to do.

Brad leaned over and whispered. "Still allergic to cigarette smoke?"

She nodded, covering her nose.

"Want to get some air?"

Her eyes were blank for half a second, then she nodded and they both stood. Brad leaned down to whisper something in Steve's ear, and Steve began to nod. Across the table, Tracy glanced from the smoker to Heather and rolled her eyes.

As Heather and Brad entered the lobby, he turned to look at her. "Want to go for a walk? It's a nice evening."

For a moment, Heather wondered if that was a good idea.

Her common sense told her she had better avoid Brad Barstow, but that was not what she wanted to do.

"Look." He touched her arm, pointing to a window nearby. Outside, tiny wisps of snow were falling gently into the soft darkness.

Heather looked back at Brad and smiled. How could she resist a walk in the snow? Especially in Vail?

She lifted a black boot and pointed at it. "I had already told Tracy I wanted to go walking after dinner."

"Then you get your wish," he said, opening the door to the coat closet. Heather quickly spotted the hooded red woolen cape she had brought while Brad reached for his tan overcoat.

"One of the things I've really missed is walking in the snow," she said as they put on their coats and headed for the front door. "Of course it snows in New York, and I do a lot of walking. But this is different."

"That's why I ordered snow tonight," he said, opening the door for her.

"Oh, did you?" she laughed. "Well, thanks for being so thoughtful."

"You're welcome."

The lights of Vail glittered softly, twinkling into the breezy night around them. The sidewalk angled downward, and he slipped his hand around her arm.

"Aren't you a bit thin?" he frowned.

She lifted an eyebrow. "No."

"I guess models are supposed to be thin," he said, hoping to make amends if he had offended her. "I think I read that somewhere."

She wanted to tell him how her stomach growled almost incessantly, how there had been times she actually dreamed of hot fudge sundaes. Instead, she turned the conversation back to him.

"How are your folks?" she asked.

"Dad retired last year. He and Mom spend the winters down in Arizona to be near their grandchildren. My older brother lives there with his wife and two little girls."

The sound of his voice, steady and calm, reached deep inside her, calling up that old thrill of being with him again. She was not as nervous now as they walked along in the snow. In fact, it seemed as though the years were magically slipping away, along with the frustration and tension of the stressful life she had been living in New York.

"How's your family?" he inquired.

"They're fine. Erin married last year. She's a registered nurse and her husband is a physical therapist. They work at the hospital." She glanced at him. "Come to Vail often?" She knew he lived here, but she didn't want him to know she had already asked.

"I moved here four years ago."

Brad suddenly felt in the mood to talk, although he didn't want to be as open as he had been in college. Then, her quiet attentiveness had always pulled like a magnet, drawing out his every thought. Looking into her wide eyes now, he suspected she could still do that; he'd better be careful. *Just tell the general things.*

"I always wanted to be involved with the ski business, so I came back here, got a job and saved my money. Two years ago I opened a shop. I sell ski equipment and give lessons. It's a good life," he glanced at her, "but it must sound pretty dull compared to life in the big city."

She shook her head slowly, her eyes fixed on the mounds of snow at their feet. "No, it sounds like a very good life." She looked up. "It's so peaceful here. I can see why you would be happy."

He stared at her for a moment, certain he was hearing a wistfulness in her tone, perhaps a note of regret.

"Are you happy in New York?" he asked.

An hour ago, she wanted him to believe her life was exciting, and that handsome, important bachelors were beating her door down. But why pretend? She sensed he was still the same gentle guy who had once listened to her for hours on end. She felt the veneer of sophistication slipping from her as she took a deep breath and began to relax.

"I haven't been happy there lately," she admitted.

"Why not?"

Her eyes ran over his features, lingering on the dimple in his chin, still there though less pronounced, since his weight gain—at least ten pounds, although it was quite becoming.

"You can ask, but I'm not sure I have an answer," she said, meeting his eyes briefly before turning to scan the quaint shops and restaurants that set the mood of a Swiss village.

Brad grabbed a breath and decided he might as well ask the question that had been gnawing at him. "I thought you were engaged," he said, as they turned down a quiet street leading past shops already closed for the evening.

She bit her lip, regretting that he had learned that from someone. Probably Steve.

"Only for a short time," she said, studying an interesting hat in a shop window.

"What happened, or should I ask?"

She hesitated, wondering how to explain it. "We were just good friends, really. I came to realize that what I had with him was not meant for a lifetime commitment."

He decided to let it go at that, but he found it difficult to believe the guy had felt only friendship for her. Remembering how he'd worked so hard at forgetting her made something twist inside him, and his eyes shot back to the twinkling lights of homes tucked on the mountainside.

"What about you?" she asked.

He looked back at her. "Excuse me?"

"Were you ever engaged? Or married?"

"Nope. Never."

Her eyes pulled at him, begging for details but he looked away, torturing her curiosity. She wanted to ask a hundred questions. The weekend would fly by, and once she returned to New York she would hate herself for being so reserved. And besides, five years was a long time to hold a grudge.

"How did you like Alaska?" She decided to ease into the reason for their breakup.

He hesitated. "It was an interesting experience! I always wanted to go there, you know."

"Yes, I know." There was resignation in her voice now, but when he had announced to her that he was taking off to Alaska for the summer, she had been stunned. It had been the determining factor in her packing up her clothes and heading to New York.

They reached the center of the village, where winding pedestrian streets were filled with happy vacationers, or shopkeepers heading from one destination to another. The snow had stopped falling, but still it dripped from rooftops and flower boxes and mounded beside the walkway.

Brad and Heather were looking about, avoiding eye contact while they spoke.

"After I got Alaska out of my system, I came home," he said quietly. "I've never had a desire to leave again." He turned his head and looked down at her. "What about you? Think you'll go on modeling and breaking men's hearts?" His eyes crinkled at the corners as he grinned at her.

"Breaking men's hearts?" she echoed, shaking her head. "I don't do that."

"I beg to differ."

Her head spun around, tumbling her bangs across her forehead. She looked into his green eyes and saw a flash of pain, even though he was attempting a reckless grin.

"Brad, I know you're teasing me, but I'm sorry I was such a flighty brat."

"Flighty," he repeated, nodding his head. "We were both flighty, but at least I told you I was going." A shadow crossed his face. "I wish you had said goodbye rather than leaving a note and heading east."

"After you decided to move to Alaska!"

They both looked away from each other, fixing their eyes safely on the mountain range.

She cleared her throat. "My cousin was a flight attendant in New York. I figured it was time to try my wings."

"Well, you flew, little girl." A grin tilted his mouth though his eyes were sad.

They stared at each for a long moment, thinking back to that heartbreaking summer.

"We both did what we had to do," she said quietly.

He nodded quickly. "Yep."

Heather took a deep breath and glanced back in the direction they had come. "Sam will think we're rude, running out on his party. I think we should head back to the lodge."

"I doubt that Sam has even missed us, but we'll walk back. I have to be at the shop at six in the morning."

"Six?" she gasped. "Aren't you going skiing with us?"

He shook his head. "I can't. I've already committed to something else."

"Oh." She quickened her steps a bit, wondering to whom he had committed himself. At least he made commitments now; even better, he kept them! "So a ski bunny has snagged you, after all," she spoke in a light tone, trying to tease while struggling with a gnawing frustration over the feelings she still had for him.

He looked across at her, saying nothing for a moment. Then that taunting grin slipped over his face again. "Want to give that skier some competition?"

Of course he was teasing, but Heather had no way of knowing that. An old surge of jealousy rose up within her, and she was irritated beyond words. She had no right to be jealous now; this was absurd! She began to shore up her defenses.

"Have you heard a weather prediction for tomorrow?" she asked, nonchalantly.

He looked at the sky, orienting himself to a safer subject. "Great day. Fresh snow early, then clear skies."

"Wonderful," she said, as they reached the steps of the lodge.

Brad hesitated as they reached the front door. "I think I'll say good night now. If I go back in there, it'll be hours before I can break away."

She nodded. "Probably."

"So…good night." His strong fingers closed over hers, and he felt again that familiar cling of her fingers, and impulsively he bent down and kissed her cheek. In the process, he smelled something hauntingly sweet, like gardenias after a rain.

A sharp nostalgia pierced his senses, sweeping him back to a time and a person who had slipped through his grasp. He dropped her hand and straightened abruptly. It was an act of defiance against this haunting mood.

"Good night," she said, lingering at the door.

She watched him turn and walk away, and a feeling of sadness swept over her. Her eyes clung to him for a moment, memorizing in her mind the thick dark hair and the shape of his head, the set of his shoulders, the brisk, purposeful stride.

Well, she told herself, when she thought of him in coming years, she could remember they had made their peace; he had forgiven her, she had forgiven him. Brad had made a successful life for himself. He had channeled his adventurous spirit into a respectable livelihood, one he obviously enjoyed. That knowledge cushioned her against some of the pain. And yet, she had known that he would eventually find himself—never mind her accusations that he would not; never mind the arguments.

She stood very still, listening to the sound of his boots fading in the distance as he turned the corner and disappeared. He was gone, out of her life again, forever.

B rad sat at his desk in the shop, staring blankly at the sports page. He'd been trying to read it for the past ten minutes and still hadn't absorbed a word. Tossing the paper aside, he thought of Heather again; in fact, she was all he had thought of from the moment he awoke. Glancing at the clock—it was almost nine—he wondered if Heather had adjusted to the time change. New York was two hours ahead. Was she awake now?

He stared at the phone, fighting a temptation to call her at the lodge, invite her to join him and his little buddy, Tommy, for lunch. After all, she'd be leaving on Sunday. It might be another five years before he saw her again. If ever.

That possibility made him sadder than he cared to admit. His hand moved slowly toward the phone, as he thought through what he would say to her. He hesitated. Why hadn't he told her the truth last night? Why had he allowed her to think he was spending the day with a special friend? Well, Tommy was special, but he knew Heather had concluded he was going skiing with a woman.

He sighed, pulling his hand back. They were still playing games with one another, still letting pride get the upper hand.

That was wrong, and he knew it.

Glancing at the clock again, he came to his feet. He had to be at the cafeteria in fifteen minutes. For now, he must forget about Heather.

Sipping coffee from styrofoam cups, Heather and Tracy walked from the lodge into the sparkling morning, their skis on their shoulders.

"I'm glad Steve went on early with the guys," Tracy yawned. "I needed another couple hours of sleep."

"Me too." Heather took another sip of coffee. "Even though my system is supposed to be on Eastern time, I slept until your phone call."

"Oh, I'm sorry..."

"Please! I don't want to waste another minute."

All around her, the village bustled with activity. In the sparkling sunshine, the snow was so white that everything seemed more vivid in contrast: the reds, blues, and greens of parkas and vests on skiers hurrying past her to the slopes presented a crazy quilt of color. She was grateful she had come back; she had always adored Vail.

"So...how were things with you and Brad?" Tracy broke into her thoughts.

Heather tossed her empty cup into a trash bin and looked at Tracy. What could she say? This was Tracy; it would be insulting to lie to her, and she could probably guess the truth anyway. "It was wonderful to be with him again..." Tracy was nodding, hanging on every word. "Tracy, how can two people live totally different lives for years, then see other again and have a few fleeting moments of feeling exactly the same? When everything has changed."

Tracy frowned, thinking about the question as their boots crunched the snow. "Do people really change?" she asked slowly. "I mean, we may break a bad habit, or try to be someone we're not, but aren't we basically the same?"

"I suppose." Heather grinned. "But he's still a ski bum, in a different way, and I'm still hungering after the bright lights and big city."

Tracy touched her arm. "That's not basic and you know it. He's not a ski bum anymore, and the bright lights and big city are—excuse me for saying so—just a diversion for you. Maybe the most basic thing of all has never changed. Maybe the love is still there."

Her words were disturbing, but what had Heather expected? Tracy was nothing if not honest.

"Tracy, I think part of this feeling comes from wanting to hang onto our youth, mixing good times and good memories with someone who shared everything."

Tracy's eyebrows shot up as she glanced sharply at Heather. "You do have a point there. So is that what you were feeling when you first saw him? Memories of the good old days?"

Heather stared straight ahead, suspecting that Tracy was trying to show her what she already knew. What she had thought, when she first looked at Brad last night, was that he was the most appealing man she had seen in quite a long time. And she would have thought so even if he were a complete stranger.

The hum of the chair lift engines and chattering voices

interrupted their talk as they reached the lift lines. Heather tilted her head back, surveying the white-powdered slopes, and took another deep breath. It was going to be a great day, she could feel it. She could reflect on her feelings for Brad later. Now it was time to get her skis on and hit the slopes!

Since Brad had been serving as a volunteer guide for the blind skiing program, he had formed some deep friendships that he knew would last. He had worked with all ages in all stages of skiing. Lately, however, his special project was Tommy, a thirteen-year-old from Denver with a mild visual impairment.

Tommy had become a problem at home, for as he entered his teen years, the frustrations of adolescence had been compounded by his disability. Skiing had opened a new world for him, giving the boy an outlet for his nervous energy while building his confidence in finding a sport that he loved. The thrill and excitement of skiing had completely changed Tommy's outlook on life, for now he had something in which he could excel, a skill he would have for a lifetime.

"Get a move on, buddy," Brad teased, waiting while Tommy pulled on his orange bib.

Tommy was a handsome boy with thick brown hair, nice features, and a nose that tilted upward on the end. The freckles scattered across his cheeks gave him a wholesome look, while a slightly crooked grin hinted of mischief. When Brad had been assigned to him, he knew right away that Tommy was going to present a challenge.

Tommy had been a prankster whose antics were harmless yet distracting. Brad had been firm with him, laying down the rules of the program, then giving Tommy a choice of staying in or returning to Denver. Once Tommy knew he had to play by the rules, his eagerness to ski provided the incentive for him to get serious.

"I'm ready to ski without you hanging on," Tommy teased, tugging on his gloves.

"We'll see," Brad grinned, laying an arm around his shoulder as they headed for the slopes.

Heather's adrenaline was soaring as her skis swooshed through the deep white powder. She had begun cautiously, easing into a few turns, then picking up her tempo. But it didn't take long for her to regain her confidence and relinquish herself to the sport she loved so much. After spending the morning on the slopes, she felt wonderful, even though her legs were beginning to ache. On her last run, she forced herself to take a break. Recalling that Tracy and Steve were having lunch at a deli nearby, she decided to join them.

"Hey, how'd it go?" Tracy called to Heather as she approached them in the long line waiting for sandwiches.

"Great!" Heather responded, smiling and waving at some of her friends. "I've really missed skiing," she said, pleased with herself. "I worried about being out of shape, but I did okay, actually." She reached down to massage her right leg. "I'll probably be sore tomorrow, but I don't care. I'm having a wonderful time."

"Listen, Heather," Steve leaned over, lowering his voice, "you should take a look at what your old boyfriend is doing!"

Tracy jabbed an elbow in his ribs. "Don't be a tease! Explain what you mean by that statement."

Steve's blue eyes glowed above windburned cheeks. "Brad volunteers his Saturdays to work with the visually impaired. Maybe you aren't aware of it, but the ski school for the blind here is the largest in the world. It's great that Brad helps them out the way he does."

Heather stared into space, frowning. Last night she had automatically assumed his plans for the day involved a woman. She felt a bit guilty for that, but he hadn't bothered to correct her, either.

Heather turned her attention back to Steve and Tracy. "I remember when we came here years ago there were great facilities for the disabled. But...," her voice trailed off, as she thought about Brad donating his Saturdays for such a worthy cause. "You're right, Brad is doing a wonderful thing. Maybe I will go take a look."

She finished her coffee while Steve directed her to Golden Peak, where the blind and visually impaired would be skiing. Heather removed her skis, brushed off the snow, then hoisted them over her shoulder as she set off in search of Brad.

When finally she reached the group of special skiers, her heart wrenched. Anticipation mingled with nervousness on the faces of the kids here. She spotted Brad and his partner, and she lingered in the background, fascinated.

Brad was skiing in a reverse wedge while the boy held to Brad's poles as they slowly moved down a gentle slope. Above the boy's orange bib, lettered Blind Skier, his face was wreathed in a wide smile as Brad made some comment and the boy nodded and laughed.

Heather tilted her head to one side, studying the boy. She could see he moved with a natural grace. His face beamed pleasure and confidence.

Heather slipped over to sit down at a bench, her mind filled with awe for these courageous people. Bits of conversation drifted to her, capturing her interest. She turned and looked in the direction of the voices she had heard.

"Come on, Cindy. You have to try." A guide was speaking to a little girl who was slumped down on a bench, her face pale, her hands clenched before her.

Heather stared at the little girl, wondering if it would not be best to try and determine the source of her fear, before trying to persuade her to begin a ski lesson. Heather's eyes moved back to the pretty girl wearing a guide's vest. She appeared to be college age, and while her tone of voice was pleasant, Heather could read her growing frustration as the little girl sat glumly, unwilling to respond.

"Why don't we have a Coke, Cindy?" the guide asked.

The little girl nodded, staring blankly into the distance. Heather decided to stroll over, see if she could do anything to help. She hoped she wouldn't seem intrusive. The little girl's head whipped around, having heard Heather's steps.

"Hi," Heather called out. "My name is Heather. Have you ever tried to ski?"

The little girl shook her head vehemently. Dark brown hair fell in a straight wave about her pale face, and the eyes that stared blankly at her were a lovely brown. Her skin was translucent, her features small and dainty.

"Well, you don't have to actually ski to enjoy being here," Heather spoke gently, as she took a seat beside her on the bench. "I have as much fun sitting here, watching and *listening.*" She paused for a moment, allowing the sound of happy voices to reach out to Cindy. "You can hear how excited every-

50

one sounds, can't you? They're really having a good time."

The little girl dipped her chin in a vague little nod.

"Hi, I'm Bethany," the guide smiled at Heather.

"I'm Heather Grant. It's nice to meet you."

"Thanks. And this is Cindy Strickland. Heather, you want to keep Cindy company for a second while I grab us something to drink?"

"Sure."

"Cindy, I'll only be a few feet away." Bethany glanced back at Heather. "Want a Coke?"

"No, thanks."

The guide was grabbing cans of Coke from her backpack nearby; she had not taken her eyes off Cindy, but now she seemed to relax as she observed Heather's attempts to be friendly.

Heather took a deep breath. "It's really pretty here. Has anyone described the setting to you?"

The little girl shook her head. "No." Her voice was low and muffled.

"Then would you like for me to do that?"

The little girl turned her eyes to Heather and dipped her head in another nod, this one more emphatic.

"All right, let's see…" Heather looked around and began to describe what she was seeing: the way the sunshine sparkled on the snow, the vastness of the mountains, the majestic beauty of the pines. She paused, as her eyes moved back down the slope to the colorfully dressed skiers. She had just described a blind skier and his guide when a familiar voice spoke up behind her.

"Heather! What are you doing here?"

She turned to face Brad and his ski buddy.

"Hi," Heather smiled. "Steve told me you were working here. This is great." Her eyes moved to Tommy.

"Hey, Tommy," Brad tapped his shoulder, "say hello to my friend Heather."

"Hi, Heather." Tommy smiled right at her, as though he were looking into her eyes. *He is truly amazing,* Heather thought, wondering how impaired he was.

She turned back to the little girl seated beside her. "I've made a friend," Heather said. "We've been talking about how beautiful it is here."

Brad's brow arched as he looked from Heather to the little girl. "Hi, Cindy," he said, reaching forward to touch her hand.

"Remember me? We had hot chocolate together last week."

Cindy nodded as a tiny grin tugged at her lips.

"Hi, Brad, what's up?" Cindy's guide had returned with cans of pop. "Hey, Tommy. How's it going today?"

"Super," Tommy replied.

To everyone's surprise, Cindy's hand shot out, gripping Heather's arm. She was tugging hard. "I want you to be my guide," she spoke softly. "I want to use your eyes."

For a moment there was complete silence, then Brad spoke up. "Heather would be great with you, Cindy, but she hasn't been trained as a volunteer."

Heather was staring down into the upturned face, unable to believe the way Cindy had responded to her.

"Tell you what, Cindy," her guide knelt beside her. "Why don't we have a Coke and maybe you could talk to Heather some more? You know you don't have to ski if you don't want to."

"I know," Cindy nodded, still looking toward Heather.

Bethany glanced across at Heather and smiled warmly. "Heather, thanks for helping out today."

"My pleasure," she smiled, touched that Bethany was such a caring, concerned guide.

Heather looked from Bethany to Brad and back again. "I'm enjoying it. Mind if I stay on for a while?"

"Please do." Bethany tilted her head toward Cindy and mouthed the word *shy.* "Listen, can't I get you something to drink?"

Heather decided to join in, although she didn't really want anything. "Sure, a cold drink would be great."

"Hey, I have a great idea," Brad spoke up. "Tommy and I were on our way to get some lunch. Isn't it time you gals took a break?"

Heather could feel Cindy stiffen beside her. "Want to go?" she asked quietly.

Cindy shook her head vehemently. Heather looked back at Brad and shrugged. "I think I'll just sit here with Cindy," she replied.

Brad stared at Heather, amazed. How had she done it, he wondered? Nobody else had been able to get any positive response from the little girl.

"Want us to bring you gals a sandwich?"

Bethany nodded. "Yeah, sure. That okay with you, Cindy?"

She nodded, her head turned toward Heather, Heather's hand still clutched in her own.

While Cindy pondered the choice of sandwiches, Brad kept looking at Heather, then Cindy. "We'll be back in an hour.

Don't go away." He winked at Heather.

She nodded and smiled. "I won't. As a matter of fact, every muscle in my body is begging for rest. I think I pushed myself a bit too hard this morning."

Bethany had taken a seat on the other side of Cindy. She was sipping her drink, watching the other skiers. Heather began to talk with Cindy again, asking her questions about where she lived and where she went to school. The hour flew by, and soon Brad was back with Tommy in tow and a sackful of sandwiches.

Brad glanced at his watch. "There's a meeting over at the school in about five minutes. Everyone better get a move on," he called good-naturedly.

Before Heather could stand, Cindy's hand gripped her arm again.

"Maybe I'll just tag along too," Heather smiled at Brad.

"Good idea."

Five

How did you do it?" Brad asked as he and Heather settled into his truck. He had offered to drive her back to the lodge.

"Do what?"

"Break the ice with Cindy. Most of the kids loosen up pretty soon, but that little girl has been extremely shy."

Heather frowned, thinking about the adorable little girl who had kept her small hand tucked in Heather's throughout the day.

Finally she shook her head. "I don't know why she responded to me, Brad. I just started talking to her, and she latched on."

"Well, it's no puzzle to me." Brad looked at her thoughtfully. "It's your voice. It's a very soothing. And there's a smile in that voice."

"What?" Heather laughed. "You're putting me on, of course."

"No, I mean it. You speak with patience and warmth—"

"After all this time in New York? That's hard for me to believe, but I'll certainly take the compliment."

They laughed at her remark as Brad pulled up at a stop light. "Seriously, I've learned in my training that one's character traits come through the voice—not that Bethany isn't a terrific guide. It's just that your voice reached out to Cindy somehow. And she isn't completely impaired, you know. She has dim vision. She can probably tell how beautiful you are."

Heather's eyes slid to Brad. "Over the years I've come to realize how secondary that can be. I've met so many people whose souls do not match their faces. But I suppose that was a good experience. For a long time, I placed too much emphasis on my looks. I've learned the inner qualities are far more important."

Brad nodded, thinking it was nice to hear her say that. He stretched his arm across the steering wheel and peered at the sky. The sun was setting on the western horizon, casting a strawberry glow over the village. He had always thought that sunset was a special time of day, and he felt happy and blessed to be with Heather just now.

"Hey, before I take you back, want to stop in for coffee somewhere?"

Heather spotted a colorful ice cream parlor on the corner. Suddenly that hot fudge sundae she had been craving all year seemed like the perfect way to finish a perfect day. She turned to Brad. "How do you feel about a hot fudge sundae?"

"With lots of nuts? I feel great about it," he chuckled, whipping into a parking space near the ice cream parlor.

Before he had removed the key from the ignition, Heather was already out of the truck, dashing under the pink and white striped awning toward the door of the shop.

"Hey, wait for me," Brad called, catching up to open the door.

Laughing over her shoulder, she dashed inside and hurried to look over her choices. Just peering at the multitude of toppings was a treat, knowing she was going to break her fast. She finally chose the works, complete with a cherry on top.

"I don't how long it's been since I've done this," Brad said, poking his tongue out to grab a dollop of whipped cream before it toppled to the floor.

"I can tell you exactly when I had my last bite," she laughed. "It was two summers ago when I flew home for a family reunion. Dad dragged out the ice cream freezer from the back of the pantry and performed his special magic. We had a great day."

"That's what family reunions are for." Brad smiled at her.

"Yeah, but I don't get home often. It's another reason I hate...," she grinned over a bite of hot fudge. "I refuse to even speak the M word."

"Modeling," he said it for her. His eyes flew over her slim frame. "You never had a problem with weight. Why do you have to be so careful now?"

She dug into her sundae. "It's the nature of the profession. Every model has the same phobia. But please, I'd rather talk about something pleasant. Like skiing."

"Yeah, me too. I hope we get a chance to ski together." He paused. "It's great having you home again. In fact, I hate to think about your leaving." His green eyes were sad as he spoke, and for a moment the ice cream melted beneath their spoons as they stared at one another.

Heather turned back to the ice cream, searching for a way to move the conversation toward something pleasant. "I admire the way you donate your time to the ski school for the blind. I had forgotten what wonderful work they do."

He was nodding as she spoke. "I love doing it. The program is not for profit, of course, and everything is well organized. Each participant in the program is made to feel special. The good thing about skiing is that it's one of the few sports available to give the visually impaired a true sense of independence. They respond to the voice of their guide, but each one can set their own pace. We don't make demands on them; we want them to enjoy themselves and to gain a sense of achievement."

Heather listened attentively, nodding, marveling again at the skill of the people she had seen in the ski school. "They're all so brave and determined. I admire that."

She had finished the last bite of her sundae, and she leaned back in her chair and breathed a deep blissful sigh.

"It's been a perfect day."

Brad's eyes slipped over her face, admiring the way her eyes held a special glow when she was happy. Come to think of it, that glow had been missing when he had first seen her last night. In fact, she had not looked one bit happy when she spoke of her life in New York, although he was certain he must have looked just as miserable while staring at her like a lovesick schoolboy.

He glanced at his watch, suddenly remembering he still had paperwork waiting at the school. "I should get back pretty soon, but I'll see you for dinner."

"Yeah."

He paid the bill and they walked slowly back to the car. She stretched her arms over her head, feeling the tug of weary muscles. As she climbed into the truck and snuggled against the seat, she found herself wishing she could hit the slopes for days on end. She didn't care how sore she was. She couldn't remember when she had enjoyed herself more.

"Well," she glanced at him as they drove along, "I'm going to get a leisurely bath and a long nap."

He pulled into the driveway that circled the lodge, waving to Sam who stood out front speaking to some guests. Sam gave him a thumbs up and went back to his conversation.

"Thanks for the ride," Heather said, touching his arm gently.

He nodded, wishing suddenly that he could kiss her. But he couldn't. He had to try and keep a grip on his feelings if possible. He reached across to open the door for her.

"See you later, Heather." He winked at her as she got out and walked slowly up to the front door of the lodge. Then he forced his thoughts back to the duties at hand.

Heather was more tired than she realized, for her adrenaline had kept her going all day. Now, entering the lobby on stiff legs, she waited as Sam caught up, grinning from ear to ear.

"Hey, gal. You having fun?" Sam asked, looking her over.

"More fun that I've had in ages." Impulsively, she reached over to plant a sisterly kiss on his cheek. "You're an angel to think of this and go to so much trouble for everyone."

"Why, I'm having a blast." His eyes shot toward the window, as though he were thinking of something else now.

"How are you and Brad getting along?" he asked suddenly.

Heather followed his gaze through the window, watching

Brad's truck disappear around the corner. She felt uncomfortable, hearing Sam's tone of voice, clearly implying the old romance was burning again. She didn't want everyone staring, asking questions.

"It's nice to see him again. Well, I'm off to my room. Gotta get set for that sleigh ride."

Sam shook his head slowly, obviously taking the cue that she didn't want to discuss her relationship with Brad.

"Hope you won't be disappointed," he called after her.

She paused at the hallway, glancing back at her old ski buddy.

"Nothing about this weekend has disappointed me," she said, smiling. "Thanks, Sam."

She disappeared around the corner, leaving Sam with a wistful smile on his face.

Heather was stretched out on her bed, trying to collect her thoughts before dinner, when she heard a soft tapping on her door. Yawning, she padded barefoot across the room. Through the door's peephole, she spotted Tracy.

"What's the password?" Heather called playfully.

Tracy angled her face into a grotesque mask.

"You nut!" Heather laughed, opening the door.

"Sometimes I forget I'm with adults, not kids," Tracy laughed, as she entered the room.

She was wearing a red-and-white cable knit sweater, jeans and boots. Her eyes swept down Heather's lounging robe. "Obviously, you're not ready yet."

Heather glanced back at the clock on the nightstand. "We have another thirty minutes."

Tracy was dismayed. "You mean a glamorous fashion model takes only thirty minutes to dress for dinner?"

Heather laughed, walking across to the mirrored doors of

the closet. "Honey, I can be ready to go in ten minutes flat. In my profession, you have every detail synchronized to the last second."

Tracy tilted her head back, looking Heather up and down. "You were always that way! I had to crawl out of bed an hour early just to get my brain in gear, and you could hop up, grab your stuff and be in class before I finished drying my hair. I hated you for that!"

Heather laughed, knowing Tracy never hated her; she merely enjoyed teasing her. They had shared a wonderful friendship from the day they walked into the freshman dorm to meet as roommates, and they had remained roommates throughout college. Heather doubted she would ever have a better friend.

Heather shrugged. "What can I say? I found my niche early."

"Have you really?" Tracy asked pointedly. "I just overheard Brad bragging to Steve about how great you were with that little girl today."

At that, Heather sank back on the bed and raised wondering eyes to Tracy. "It's absolutely amazing what they're doing here to help people with disabilities. And that little girl was the most wonderful child. I could have spent days with her, Tracy."

Heather shook her head, staring into space for a moment. "Just the idea that I was helping in some small way was a great feeling. I haven't experienced that kind of happiness since…," she paused, trying to think. "I don't know; it was a different feeling," she sighed, looking back at Tracy.

"I understand. I feel the same way when I open the church door and head toward our youth department. And by the time we're finished teaching and counseling, I feel like I could walk on the moon. That may sound corny to you, but I mean it."

"Tracy!" Heather frowned at her. "What kind of monster do you think I am that I would consider church work corny? I think you're doing a wonderful thing." Heather dropped her head, staring at her red toenails. "Unfortunately, I haven't been inside a church in a long time."

"Don't tell your mother. Your family made that a priority, I remember."

Heather nodded, as her toes dug into the carpet. She didn't want to think about that just now.

"Listen, I know you and Brad still care for each other," Tracy was saying. "You both look like you're wearing light bulbs on your heads when you're together. Your faces are absolutely radiant."

"Now that one is pure corn!"

"And," Tracy continued, ignoring Heather's remark, "you can't deny your feelings any longer now, can you?"

She sank back on the bed, nestling her head against the pillow and closing her eyes. There was no point in letting these feelings get out of hand, even though Tracy and Steve were practically shoving her and Brad into each other's arms.

"Tracy," she opened her eyes and looked at her friend, "Steve was your first date, your first love. You two share common interests and are totally compatible. With that kind of foundation, love can endure. With Brad and me…well, there's nothing to build on except a college romance and some mutual friends. Really, we have little in common. He needs a woman who's interested in skiing, or knowledgeable about disabilities."

"He said you took right to it—"

"Tracy, I'd love to work in the volunteer ski program here, or even in a special program for disabled kids, but I have no training for that. All I know is clothes and fashion."

"You said you were tired of modeling, that—"

"Brad needs someone who's…"

"I know," Tracy snapped her finger. "He could place an ad in a ski magazine. Wanted: a professional skier who has a Ph.D. in special education."

"Will you stop it?" Heather swatted at her, aware of the point Tracy was trying to make.

"Well, you're being just as silly," Tracy said, shaking her head. "We might like someone to share certain interests, but a perfectly wonderful woman could answer such an ad, and Brad could admire her greatly but never fall in love with her. There's a certain chemistry that has to be there. Get my point?"

Heather reached out, squeezing Tracy's hand. "I know you mean well, and Brad and I will enjoy being together this weekend; but that's as far as it can go. Our lives are just too different."

Tracy heaved a sigh. "Okay, you win. Ready to eat?"

Heather stared at her, surprised she had given up so easily.

"Yeah, I'm starving," she said, smiling. "Want to just meet me down there?"

Tracy nodded, hurrying for the door. "Don't get too pretty," she called over her shoulder. "I don't want you breaking Brad's heart again." The door slammed before Heather could respond.

After dinner, vans loaded the group up and drove them to the stables, where horses were hitched up to bright red sleighs, complete with jingling bells.

Brad met them there, parking his vehicle beside the van. Waving to her, he pulled on his denim jacket and hurried to her side. He was dressed in jeans and cowboy boots and looked more handsome than ever, Heather thought, smiling up at him.

"How long has it been since you've ridden in a sleigh?" he asked, taking her arm.

"Not since that night we all piled into the one Grandpa pulled out of the barn. I can't wait."

Brad grinned down at her. Her eyes were glowing with excitement, and her blond hair shone like silver in the moonlight. He had rushed home, showered and changed clothes, and hurried to the stables, thinking of nothing but Heather.

"How fun!" Heather exclaimed, as they joined the group.

"Yeah, there's nothing more fun than an old-fashioned sleigh ride," Steve said, hugging Tracy. "I'm glad Sam planned this for us."

"I keep looking for Santa Claus," Heather laughed, as Brad helped her into the sleigh and they settled back for a peaceful ride.

Heather snuggled into the blanket and leaned against Brad. What a wonderful night it was, with thousands of stars, piercing the soft darkness like a million diamonds. The bells jingled softly as the sleigh glided smoothly over the snow.

"I appreciate the way you helped out today," Brad said, tucking the blanket around her.

She turned her eyes upward and smiled. "I really enjoyed it. Those people are wonderful." Her voice softened as she and

Brad looked into each other's eyes, oblivious to all the chattering around them. "Brad, I'm so proud of you."

Her eyes were glowing and her voice was warm and rich, and Brad knew, as he looked at her, that he had never stopped loving her. He had been fighting his feelings since the moment he saw her last night. Today, he had slipped deeper and deeper into the spell she always cast over him.

"Thank you," he finally responded, pulling his eyes from her face to look into the starry heavens. "There are still some areas of my life that I'm working on; but I do feel that, at last, my life has a plan."

Heather looked from Brad's face to the mountain range where lights twinkled in distant houses. In the sleighs following them, the gang laughed and teased. She was certain that she and Brad were the only members of the group who were talking so seriously.

Her thoughts returned to what Brad had told her, that he had found a plan for his life; why couldn't she?

"A plan," she sighed. "You make it sound so simple, so easy."

"No. Finding your destiny and sticking to it isn't easy for anyone. I had a talk with him," his eyes were focused upward, "and did a little housecleaning in my soul. After that, things fell into place."

"That's wonderful. So...you're saying you found what you were meant to do after you talked with him." She indicated the heavens, where Brad's eyes still lingered.

"That's what I'm saying. Want to come to church with me in the morning?"

She was more surprised by this invitation than by his previous announcement. She shook her head, clearly confused. "When I think of the times Mother pressed you to attend church with us…"

"I know. Hitting the slopes on weekends seemed more fun at the time." His voice softened as he looked at Heather. "Maybe if I had accepted one of those invitations, you and I would still be together."

Heather's breath caught in her throat. For a split second, she felt the threat of tears, and her throat ached from trying to control her emotions.

"You aren't going to respond to that?" he asked, staring into her face. As the night lights settled over her features, Brad saw the troubled expression in Heather's eyes.

"I don't know how to respond," she finally answered.

"Maybe you feel things worked out for the best," Brad sighed, looking away.

"I can't say that," she admitted quietly.

Neither had spoken for several seconds when someone in the sleigh behind them began strumming a guitar. Soon the group was invited to join in on "The Twelve Days of Christmas."

While Heather and Brad tried to follow the humorous verses, they avoided eye contact with each other, and their smiles were not as easy as before. Nobody seemed to notice, though, as the group kept up their singing until the horses returned to the stable.

Once the sleigh had come to a stop, Heather glanced at Brad. He was giving a thumbs-up to Ben, who had been playing the guitar.

"Have a good time?" The manager of the stable stood at their sleigh.

"Yes, we did. Thanks," she answered, as he extended a hand to help her down.

Tracy rushed to their side, grinning from ear to ear.

"Wasn't that wonderful?"

Heather gave her a hug. "Yes, it was. And I want to thank you again for insisting that I come back this weekend. I haven't had this much fun since…," she looked at Brad, who was folding the blanket for the attendant, while listening to the conversation. "Since college days," she finished.

Brad turned, grinning at her and shaking his head. "Tracy, I don't believe her, do you?"

"Yeah," Tracy smiled, looking from Brad to Heather, "I believe her. You two want to get a midnight snack? Or do you have other plans?"

"Actually," Brad turned to Heather, "I was going to invite you over to my place and offer you some of my special lasagna."

Heather cocked an eyebrow. "And you also cook?"

The three of them laughed as Steve walked up, grinning from ear to ear. "What a blast! Now where to?"

Tracy slipped her arm through his. "I'd like for you and me to take a walk in the snow. Maybe stop someplace romantic."

Steve chuckled, turning to Brad, ready to invite the two of them to come along.

"Just us," she said quietly, snuggling against him.

Steve's eyes shot back to Tracy. They frequently read each other's mind, and he clearly sensed that she wanted to give

Brad and Heather some privacy.

"What can I say?" He grinned back at Brad. "See you later."

Heather's eyes lingered on Tracy and Steve as they walked away, arm in arm. Staring after them, she tried to marshal her thoughts. Her instincts told her to run from Brad. *Now.*

She took a deep breath and forced herself to say and do what she must do. Otherwise, she might not be able to leave Vail as planned tomorrow. Or ever.

"Brad, I think maybe I'd better go on back to the lodge." Her voice sounded distant and strained in her own ears, but maybe she would sound normal to Brad. "My body clock is still on Eastern time, and I'm afraid I overdid it on the slopes this morning. I'm pretty tired." Her eyes sneaked up to his face and she saw the hurt in his eyes. Still, she felt she had to move forward.

He looked down at her for several seconds, saying nothing. She knew he wasn't fooled by her explanation; he knew her too well, even though they had been apart all these years. Still, they had always been able to read one another, and amazingly that had not changed, in spite of the circumstances that had so drastically changed their lives.

His eyes lifted to the crowd dispersing around them. "Okay," he said quietly, "if that's what you want. The van is about to pull out. You'd better hurry."

She caught her breath. *He's not even going to offer to drive me back to the lodge. Oh well, it's for the best, of course.* If they were going to break it off, now was the time.

She swallowed. "And maybe I'll sleep in tomorrow morning rather than going to church."

He shrugged. "Whatever you want to do."

He turned and walked away, his head high, his steps brisk and purposeful.

Staring after him, Heather felt a stab of regret. Could she really say goodbye to him again?

Seven

Heather knew that she had offended Brad. She had seen a special look in his eyes all day. Was he, too, fighting old memories and new ones as she was doing right now?

She spun around, looking toward the van. Her legs felt weak as she walked toward the group, forcing a smile. As she approached her ski buddies, their laughter filled the night, contrasting with the heavy sadness that consumed her. She stopped walking and looked back over her shoulder.

Brad was getting into his Jeep, slamming the door. In another minute, he would be driving out of the parking lot, out of her life again. The emptiness that had lived in a corner of her soul all these years spread over her, haunting her. Words of wisdom whispered quietly to her, reminding her how rare and precious her relationship with Brad had been; it was a gift, a special magic that might never come again. No man had ever taken his place; she was beginning to wonder if any man would. She couldn't let him go just yet. She couldn't.

Suddenly, she knew she had to listen to her heart. She had

no choice. Once she was back in New York, alone in her apartment, she would regret cheating herself out of a few more precious hours with him, even if these hours made her miss him more. At that moment, it was a price she was willing to pay. She turned and ran toward the Jeep.

"Brad," she called out, just as the Jeep started up.

Above the roar of the engine, he had not heard her voice, and the Jeep was backing away from the curb.

"Brad!" She ran faster, ignoring the ache in her muscles.

She caught up just in time, banging on the window on the passenger's side. Above the glow of the lights on the dashboard, she could see the look of surprise on his face.

He reached across the seat and rolled down the window. Their eyes met; she hesitated.

"I changed my mind." She didn't bother to say why, but she imagined he knew.

The door swung open for her and she crawled in, slamming it behind her.

The cold surrounded them as they looked into each other's eyes for a moment. Neither spoke.

"Okay, so I was about to run again." She swallowed hard. "This time maybe I'll just wait around and see what happens."

He stared at her for a moment, obviously weighing her words. Then a smile slowly began to form on his lips, softening the grim set of his mouth. "I'm glad you changed your mind," he finally answered.

She began to shiver, but she knew the reaction of her body was more nerves than cold. She had been much colder than this many times in her life; besides, the warm air from the heater was already curling over her feet.

"Don't want you to catch cold," he said, pulling her close.

He was leaning back against the seat, one arm resting across the steering wheel, the other around her shoulder. Just the way they had ridden together countless times, countless miles.

As she shivered and snuggled against him, it seemed as though all the years were magically slipping away once again, taking with them the heartache and pain. She was back with him, enjoying the only companionship that had ever brought her joy. She felt a childish urge to turn back the clock, be simply Brad and Heather again, trying to make their relationship work. Was it too much to hope for now? Or had she been granted a second chance?

His boot tapped the accelerator, warming the engine; neither had spoken for several seconds.

"What are you thinking?" he asked, looking into her eyes.

She wondered if he was reading her thoughts or sharing them. "I was thinking how wonderful it is to be in Vail again. With you," she added for emphasis.

"I'm glad you feel that way." He hesitated for a moment, as his eyes drifted down her nose to her lips, then returned to her eyes. "Why don't you come back to Colorado?" he asked suddenly, surprising himself as much as her.

His heart was suddenly racing, and he busied himself backing out of the parking space. He forced a casual tone as he turned onto the main road. "I've discovered that happiness is in your own backyard, or however that old cliché goes." He grinned at her, trying to appear much more nonchalant than he felt after such a bold question.

"That's how the cliché goes," she smiled, "but in my case,

Mom and Dad's backyard is now the parking lot for a dentist's office." Humor twinkled in her eyes as she looked at him. Both were attempting to lighten the mood.

"I wasn't talking about your actual birthplace, silly girl," he scolded playfully as he drove toward the outskirts of Vail.

"I know," she said and they both fell silent, staring through the Jeep window into the night lights glittering softly around them. She took a deep breath, feeling herself began to relax.

They were both on the brink of taking chances again, reverting to some of the recklessness of their youth. Suddenly, she began to think of some of the crazy things they had done during their three-year courtship.

Laughter bubbled up and overflowed as she turned her eyes from the road to his face. His head whipped around, his eyes curious as he watched her give way to deep spasms of laughter.

He laughed too, although he had no idea what was so funny. "What?" he asked, nudging her.

"Do you remember," she paused, giggling again, "our senior year when we got into a fuss, and made dates with other people for the football game? We all met up at the hot dog stand, and you almost got into a fight with…," she was laughing harder. "I can't even remember his name."

"I did not almost get into a fight," he argued good-naturedly, "I just let him know I didn't appreciate his taking you out. And I seem to remember a catty remark you made to my date, something about her hair."

"How uncouth of me!" She was laughing so hard that tears filled her eyes. "I don't remember saying anything catty." But of course she did.

As their laughter died away, she turned and looked at him.

"Now I can't imagine us behaving so badly, can you? And you're so different from the guy who was always seeking the next adventure."

"Well, something very important happened to us," he said, glancing at her with a smile. "We grew up."

"Yes, we grew up," Heather said, looking back at him, wishing again that she could turn back the clock. But she couldn't. And she had to face reality.

He was slowing the Jeep down as they approached the driveway of a condominium complex sequestered among towering pines, overlooking Gore Creek.

Heather turned her attention toward the impressive condominiums as Brad pulled into a parking space and cut the engine.

"Home sweet home," he said, turning to her.

As he looked down at her, he thought the expression on her face was one of sadness now, and he wondered again what she was thinking. He decided it was time for them to stop being so introspective; he should attempt to lighten the mood a bit.

"Something else has happened since our crazy college days," he said lightly. "Believe it or not, I've become a gourmet cook!"

"You? A gourmet cook?" She began to laugh. "You're kidding."

"You can decide if I'm kidding after you taste my lasagna."

"And you'll put me to shame. For if there's anything I'm not, it's a cook, much less gourmet." She shook her head in amazement as she tried to picture the Brad she remembered puttering around in a kitchen. She had a fleeting image of smoke curling from an oven and Brad scratching his head, as though wondering what had gone wrong.

She hopped out of the Jeep before he could come around to open the door. She couldn't wait to put him to the test on this lasagna he boasted about.

"Are you hungry?" he asked, offering his arm as they hurried up the walk that wound around a miniature rock garden.

"I'm starved, Mr. Gourmet Cook."

They climbed the stairs and approached his condo.

While they were still in a teasing frame of mind, a mood of apprehension began to creep up on her. She began to wonder if coming home with him was a mistake. She felt another spasm of nerves bearing down on her, but she couldn't go running off again. They were mature enough to handle their emotions, even if the memories brought a sharp ache later. She was leaving tomorrow—she wanted to spend more time with Brad. There was still so many things to talk about.

The lock clicked and the door swung back. Brad reached inside for a switch and suddenly they were bathed in soft lights. Heather smiled at the elegant though masculine charm of his spacious living room, decorated in browns and greens with heavy, comfortable furniture. She was quickly drawn to the glass doors opening onto a balcony that seemed to be suspended against the starry sky.

"Go on out," he said. "I'll just make us some coffee and pop the lasagna in the oven."

She lifted an eyebrow. "You've already mixed up the ingredients?"

"Yep. With all the hours I put in, I have to do a lot of preparation in advance."

"Oh, yeah. Right," she rolled her eyes. "Don't forget to show me the brand name of that lasagna and tell me which stores carry it," she teased.

"Go ahead; make fun. I'm willing to bet that I'll get the last laugh."

She stared at him for a moment. He really was serious about this. "Okay. Sorry to be a doubting Thomas. It's just a surprise to me that you've become so domestic."

Heather turned toward the glass doors, unlocking the latch so that she could step onto the balcony. The crisp pine-scented air flowed over her, and she took a deep breath. She had left the door ajar, and now she could hear him puttering around in the kitchen. An ache of regret filled her heart. Too bad their relationship had not worked out.

She tilted her head back and looked up at the sky. Soft clouds were swirling past a quarter moon, and as she looked up at the vast sky, for the first time in ages, she felt herself being drawn back to God. She had been thinking about what Brad had told her, about God revealing a plan for his life. Was it possible that God would do the same for her?

Tears filled her eyes. She regretted that she had allowed time and circumstances to lead her away from the strong faith that had once been the foundation of her life. How had that happened?

She smelled the wonderful aroma of fresh coffee and turned to see Brad stepping onto the balcony, holding two tall white mugs.

"Thanks," she said, as her palm enfolded the warm mug. "You have a nice view." She sipped her coffee and admired the clean beauty of snow dripping from evergreens.

"Yes, I do." He turned and led them to two cushioned chairs, along with a small wrought-iron table.

They were quiet for several minutes as they sat on the balcony, sipping their coffee. Then Heather turned to Brad.

"Thanks for inviting me to church with you tomorrow. And I really do want to go." She took a deep breath. "I was just thinking about how this weekend is bringing me back to my roots, and to the things that really matter." She leaned back in the chair, choosing her words. "I don't go to church in New York. Actually, I don't even know anyone who does. Most of my friends are models as well. We live a very hectic life, always on the go, often working on weekends. On the Sundays that I'm home, it's been too tempting to loll in bed and do nothing."

Brad drained his coffee and set the mug on the table. "Heather, if I'm out of line in saying this, you'll have to forgive me; but from what you've been telling me, you don't sound very happy. Are you sure you want to keep on modeling?"

She dropped her head, staring into her coffee. "No, I'm not sure. In fact, I don't think I do." She looked across at him. "I was telling Tracy that I don't feel any satisfaction or fulfillment in what I'm doing. After seeing you and Tracy and Steve so content, I may make a change in my line of work."

As she spoke those words, Brad's mind began to spin. Should he try and persuade her to come back to Colorado? No, he had no right to influence her in such a major decision. Or maybe he did. Deep in his soul, a voice seemed to be prompting him to try and help her. She was obviously confused.

The buzzer on the oven sounded, interrupting his thoughts, and he stood up. "Dinner's ready, and so am I. What about you?"

She looked at him, forcing her worries from her mind. "Absolutely. I'm dying to taste your famous lasagna."

"I never said it was famous! And you're beginning to make me nervous about my cooking. If I don't watch out, I'll burn something and then you can get prissy and say you told me so."

"I've only been teasing you," she said, shivering as she stepped back inside and closed the doors.

Brad entered the kitchen and snatched a gloved potholder from a hook over the stove. Heather tilted her head, observing him with fascination as he removed the casserole dish with expertise and brought it to the small oak table in the breakfast nook. She still couldn't believe he was so domestic.

"Can I help?" she asked, removing her coat and dropping it on a chair.

"The plates and glasses are in that cabinet," he said, pointing. "And the silverware is in the drawer below the cabinet. There's juice and soda in the refrigerator."

Heather set the table, humming softly while Brad opened the refrigerator and removed a salad. When everything was on the table and they sat down to eat, Heather hesitated, looking shyly at Brad.

"This is all so perfect," she spoke softly. "I'd like to say grace. I haven't done that in years."

"Then please do."

After her prayer, Brad scooped a generous serving of lasagna onto both plates.

"I can't believe this," she said around a mouthful of cheese. "It's the best lasagna I've ever tasted. Unfortunately, I have two left hands in the kitchen."

Brad nodded, obviously relating to that. "I did at first, then I decided if I could read, I could cook. So I did."

She laughed, sipping her pop. "Hadn't thought of it that way. Maybe one reason I can't cook is that I simply haven't been interested, nor have I had the time to learn."

The sadness she had felt at comparing her life to his began to fade. A feeling of contentment slipped over her as she ate the food Brad had prepared. She began to notice, however, that Brad had become silent. *Maybe he is just hungry or tired.* A tiny frown hovered on his forehead, and she wondered what thoughts were in his mind as they finished their meal and took their dishes to the kitchen.

Aware of Brad's lingering silence, Heather launched into a series of questions about the people they had seen over the weekend as they loaded the dishwasher. He smiled as he answered her questions and they discussed different people in the Snowflakes ski club.

Afterward, they returned to the living room and while Brad stoked up the fire, Heather settled onto the sofa, feeling warm and lazy. It was so cozy, and so completely satisfying to just have a meal with Brad, chat about friends, or say nothing at all. Her thoughts returned to little Cindy, and brave Tommy. She recalled Brad's kindness and patience in dealing with these kids.

"Brad, you were so wonderful with Tommy and Cindy. You obviously have found your niche."

When she mentioned Tommy's name, Brad smiled. "I do love working with those kids. But Heather," he took a seat beside her, "I think you'd be just as good. I suppose that kind of thing would never appeal to you," he said carefully.

She thought it over, recalling the surge of happiness she had felt when Cindy had turned to her for help.

"You know," she said, staring into the fire, "at one point, I thought about going back to school, getting a master's in a field that would bring some fulfillment. Today I realized that I might enjoy working with kids with disabilities."

His eyes lit up. "Why don't you? You would be terrific in that line of work, Heather."

She smiled, thinking of how good it had felt to aid Cindy today, even in a small way.

"I learned one thing today," she smiled across at Brad. "One reason my life has seemed so empty these past years is because it is empty. I go home every day with no sense of accomplishment. Today, watching the guides help those with disabilities tugged at my heart in a special way. In fact, I can't stop thinking about how wonderful it would be to work with those kids."

He reached over to squeeze her hand. "I hope you decide to do that. Too many people measure the value of jobs by the size of their paycheck. I've always thought that was a mistake. Of course everyone needs a decent salary nowadays, but the important thing is to find work that makes your soul a bit richer, as well. I have to do that kind of work, Heather; I have to have something that gives me a reason to look forward to each day."

His eyes slipped over her face and as he looked at her, his expression grew solemn. "When are you going to New York?"

She sighed. "I have to leave the day after Christmas."

"That soon?"

She took a deep breath, turning her eyes back to the dancing flames in the fireplace. "It does seem awfully soon, doesn't it?"

He dropped her hand and stood up. "Heather, this is getting difficult for me."

Her eyes followed him as he began to pace the room. "What do you mean?"

"When I first saw you, I felt like I'd been hit by a ton of bricks. Now, I'm beginning to feel comfortable with you again." He turned to look at her. "And that's even worse."

She swallowed hard. "I know what you mean."

Their eyes locked; neither spoke. "So what are we going to do?" he finally asked.

"I don't know."

He crossed the room, reached for her hand and pulled her up to face him. Then he lowered his head, dipping his lips to hers in a sweet and gentle kiss. They were drawn back to all the old feelings with strange new ones mixing in, and soon Heather pulled away, breathless.

"Wait...." She turned away from him, walking over to stand in front of the fire. She had deliberately turned her back to him so he couldn't see the tears that filled her eyes. It was too painful, too frightening. She had promised herself she wouldn't let her feelings get the best of her, and yet she just couldn't help herself.

"Look, we better step back and try to figure out where we're going with this." Brad spoke grimly into the silence. "You'll be returning to New York, and I have no plans to ever leave Vail. To be honest, Heather, I don't even want to come up to New York on a visit. I hate cities! I'm a mountain man through and through, and I'm sorry, but I'm afraid that's never going to change."

The tears were sliding down her cheeks as she fought for

control. He was right. They had to step back and figure out where they were going. Neither one deserved a broken heart again. They had to be realistic, stop chasing after a head full of dreams. *But is it just a dream?* A voice in her soul argued back. *Is it possible that...*

Heather took a deep breath and closed her eyes for a moment. She had never been so confused. Should she keep her job or quit and go back to school? For months, she had been tormented by a need to do something more fulfilling. Maybe she had found the answer. But what about Brad? Should she trust him with her heart or protect herself from more hurt?

"You know," Brad was saying, "I'm tempted to try and pick up where we left off years ago. Enjoy the weekend, not worry about how we'll feel next week, or next year. But I can't do that, Heather. I know how much it hurt before, and I never want to hurt like that again. Maybe it's why I've never let myself care for anyone since you."

He walked over to her side and looked down at her. When he saw the tears on her cheeks, he caught his breath. Automatically, he reached for her, cradling her head against his chest while his hand smoothed her hair. "Honey, I'm sorry."

"For what? You have no reason to apologize."

He closed his eyes, fighting the emotions in his heart. So many times he had dreamed of holding her in his arms again, and now here she was. And he could see in her eyes that she still cared, just as he did. What should he do? What *could* he do? Make promises, beg her to come home? How far should he go in a commitment when they had just found each other again? There were still a lot of missing pieces in the puzzle of what had happened to her during the five years he had not seen her.

"Look," he said gently, "let's think about this tonight and tomorrow. After church, we'll talk again."

He paused, looking deeply into her eyes. "I still care for you, and nothing would make me happier than to have you move back to Colorado, go to school, or just find a job you'd enjoy. But this has to be your decision. I know you'd be giving up a lot," he added, thinking of the glamorous life she lived. "I'm not rich and probably never will be. And I do like a simple life. You'd better think all that over before we go any further."

She nodded, saying nothing. Then, gently, she withdrew from his arms and walked over to get her coat. "We'd better go now," she said wearily.

He stared at her for a moment, wondering if he had done the wrong thing by making an issue of their problems. But he felt he had no choice. She would be leaving tomorrow. They had to think about how they would feel after they said good-bye.

Eight

❧

Heather stood in the lobby of the lodge the next morning waiting for Brad to pick her up for church. Her mind was a jumble of confusion, and she had hardly slept.

"Hey, Heather, what's up?" Sam had stepped out of his office, sipping a tall mug of coffee.

"I'm going to church with Brad this morning."

He arched an eyebrow. "Really? Boy, you two really have your heads on straight, don't you? Want some coffee?"

She shook her head. "No, thanks. I already had a cup from the urn over there."

He nodded, looking her over. "You look great."

She smiled. "Thanks." She had brought an extra dress, a simple black wool with white collar and cuffs. It was perfect for church, although she had not been thinking of church when she packed the dress, yet another black one. She was sick of wearing black.

Sam tilted his head, looking at her curiously. "Is this thing between you and Brad getting serious again?"

She took a deep breath and began to shake her head. "I really can't answer that. We're a little bit confused."

"I can understand that; but Heather, you couldn't find a better guy than Brad. He's very well thought of here in Vail."

Heather lifted her eyes, smiling at Sam. "I always teased him about being a ski bum." She felt ashamed when she thought back to her first impression upon arriving here Friday evening.

"Nope, Brad's not a ski bum. He's a successful businessman, and he's quite active in community affairs here. To be honest, I really admire the guy."

At that moment, the door swung back and Brad entered the lobby. He wore a dark suit and tie beneath his overcoat, and as Heather looked at him, she couldn't help thinking that he looked like the respectable businessman Sam had just described.

"Hi, guys," Brad called. "Sam, can I get a cup of that coffee to take with me?"

"You bet." Sam hustled off to get the coffee while Brad and Heather looked at each other, saying nothing for a moment.

"How did you sleep?" he finally asked.

She shook her head. "Not very well."

He grinned. "Neither did I."

"Here you go," Sam returned with a tall styrofoam cup filled with coffee.

"Thanks, Sam." He took a sip, focusing his attention on Sam again. "Everyone has had a great time this weekend. You've gone to a lot of trouble, Sam; but believe me, we appreciate all your hard work." He looked at Heather. "Isn't that right?"

"That's exactly right," Heather agreed, smiling at Sam.

"My pleasure," Sam grinned, looking from Brad to Heather.

Watching him, Heather guessed he was probably reflecting on their talk about Brad. He seemed to be sizing them up, trying to figure out what was going to happen between the two of them.

"Well, we'd better get going," Brad said, helping Heather into her coat.

"Brunch will be served from ten to noon," Sam called after them.

"Hope I can eat," Heather muttered under her breath.

"I know what you mean," Brad said, as they walked out into the crisp morning. "Somehow my appetite has vanished, which is pretty unusual, given my appreciation for food."

Opening the door of his truck for her, he took another sip of coffee and shook his head. "I can hardly believe this reunion has only lasted through a weekend. In a sense, it seems like you've been here for months; in another way, it's as though you just arrived."

Heather settled into the seat and smoothed her coat around her. "I was thinking the very same thing…at about three o'clock this morning."

Brad frowned. "You did have a rough night, didn't you?"

She nodded. "But I don't feel tired or even sleepy. I hope I won't be like Dad and start nodding halfway through the church service."

Brad laughed as he got in and cranked the engine. "So do I."

Heather and Brad must have looked like the perfect couple as they entered the small community church. Heather's nervousness began to disappear as Brad's friends greeted her with smiles and words of welcome. They took their seats just as the organist began playing a familiar Christmas carol. The song director announced the page number as Brad lifted a hymnal, and soon all voices were raised in the first verse of "Joy to the World." As the music swelled around her, Heather began to feel a warm wonderful joy spreading through her, touching her very soul. She joined in the hymn while her eyes drifted over the little church, admiring its beauty.

Creamy walls were enhanced by stained glass windows where the muted sunlight sifted over dark pews onto crimson carpet. It was a lovely little church, and she could understand why Brad enjoyed this place of worship, and its members, so well. He had told her how kind and helpful everyone had been, how they had established a special love offering for the handicapped kids in his ski class.

"The least I can do is show up on Sundays," he had joked. But Heather knew he would have gone to church, regardless; she could see he meant what he had said about a new commitment.

The music ended and now the minister approached the podium, smiling over the audience. Thirtyish and pleasant, he spoke with a clear, resonant voice and smiled frequently to punctuate his words.

"The message I have for you today is one of hope and joy," he was saying. "Just as Christ was born to fulfill a divine plan, so are we. Every life is a plan of God. We have a loving Father who has created each individual with a distinct purpose in mind. He knows and cares for each soul, creating you," his eyes swept over the attentive crowd, "with a knowledge of how each one can glorify him while reaching the best purpose for your life, as well...."

Heather couldn't believe he was voicing the very thoughts that had been tormenting her. It was almost as if Brad had suggested a topic for the pastor's sermon this morning. She glanced at Brad, who seemed to be hanging on every word; then she glanced back at the pleasant man delivering these words to his captive audience.

No, she decided, it was not Brad, but rather a loving God who was sending out a special message to her, directing her toward the right answers to her troubled questions.

Each word the minister spoke captured Heather's imagination as he gave verses and illustrations that seemed to soothe away the confusion in her mind.

"Just as each snowflake is similar yet different," the minister said, "so are God's people. We all have a purpose in his divine plan. But we are not run by a heavenly computer...we have freedom of choice...."

Brad reached over to squeeze Heather's hand. She smiled back at him, and now that special joy seemed to flood her heart. As she listened to the message, Heather was touched to the point of tears. She felt as though she had been on a long and difficult journey, climbing a steep mountain, climbing and climbing yet never reaching the top. Now, through the power of God's word, she had been transported to the peak of that mountain at last—swiftly, easily. She had a view of the road that lay behind her and a divine assurance about the road ahead. All the confusion in her life was swept away; she knew exactly what she wanted to do. The answer had come to her here, in this lovely little church, through words spoken by a man of God. With Brad at her side.

She could feel Brad's eyes on her, as the tears she fought to restrain brimmed up and trickled down her cheeks. His arm encircled her shoulders, and as she looked into his face, she saw tears gleaming in his eyes as well.

At the altar call, she knew she had to respond. She wanted to make a commitment to God, to turn her life around and head in the right direction now, a direction that had been clearly revealed to her. With Brad at her side, she walked down the aisle, knelt at the altar and began to pray. It was a total and complete cleansing. God's word was so simple to apply, once she was willing to listen.

Later, as they settled into Brad's Jeep and rode back to the lodge, both were filled with the deep spiritual experience that had taken place in church. Neither spoke until he turned into the driveway of the lodge and parked. Then he turned to face her.

"Heather, we've only been together a short while, but you never left my heart through all these years. I have to tell you that I still love you. And I'm sure of that now."

Again, the tears were flowing down her cheeks although she tried to hold them back. She grabbed a tissue, laughing through her tears.

"I don't know what's wrong with me this weekend. I haven't cried in years, but now I can't stop blubbering."

With a tender smile, Brad took the tissue from her hand and gently began to dab her cheeks.

"Those are happy tears, aren't they?" he asked, leaning forward to press his lips to hers in a sweet and gentle kiss. Then he leaned back and looked at her seriously. "How do you feel about me?" he asked.

She lifted her hand, tracing the curve of his chin. "When I look at you, I see a kind and caring man; honest, compassionate, gentle yet strong. I never stopped loving you either, Brad. And there's no doubt in my heart, that at this moment I love you more than ever. For now I understand what love really is."

He nodded, hugging her again. Neither spoke for several minutes as her head nestled into the curve of his shoulder, just the way it had when they were adventurous college kids, struggling to find their place in life. Now they had.

A tapping on the window behind Brad startled them. Heather peered at Steve's face on the other side of the window. Once he saw the tears, and the expression on both faces, his smile froze. He looked from Heather to Brad as though he didn't know what to say or do until Brad rolled down the window.

"Hey, partner," he said, shaking hands with Steve.

"Hey." Steve looked across at Heather. "Are you all right?"

"Never better," she smiled.

"Oh." His eyes shot back to Brad, then to Heather again. "Well...great! Heather, I just wanted to let you know that Tracy and I will be leaving at noon. We are really missing the kids and so we're ready to head back."

"I'll drive her to Denver," Brad offered, looking at Heather. "You're not ready to leave yet, are you?"

She shook her head. "No, I'm not."

Steve looked relieved. "Well, now that we've settled that point, are you two coming in to join the rest of the gang? They're all gathered around the fireplace. Sam's on the piano, and everybody's getting sentimental. Better come join us for one last rendition of 'White Christmas'...."

As Heather and Brad got out of the Jeep and hurried inside, merry voices were belting out "where the treetops glisten…" They were all giving their best to the Christmas song, smiling at one another, and particularly at Heather and Brad. Eyes glowed and twinkled; the group had been watching Heather and Brad all weekend, secretly hoping the couple would get back together after all these years.

As the music died away and everyone began to hug one another, Heather felt someone tapping her lightly on the shoulder. She turned to see Tracy, grinning like a kid who had just unwrapped a special toy on Christmas morning.

"I can tell by looking at you and Brad that things have gone very well," she said in a low, smug voice.

Heather reached out and hugged her. "I have so much to tell you, but it will have to wait until I get back home."

"Home?" Tracy echoed, her smile fading.

"Denver." Heather smiled at her. "Home is Colorado, from now on. Tracy, I'm coming home to stay."

"Great! That news will be my best Christmas present this year." Tracy hugged Heather, then Brad. "I'm so glad you two figured out what you needed to do. Now, listen. You guys are invited to dinner at our place the first evening you can come. We have lots of plans to make!" Her face was radiant as she hugged them again, then hurried off toward Steve, who was helping a friend with luggage.

Everyone was gathered around the fireplace, hugging, exchanging addresses and promising to write. Sam, wearing a wide smile, approached Brad and Heather.

"It was a great weekend, Sam," Brad shook his hand. "You did a fantastic job."

"Thanks. I had more fun than anyone." He looked at Heather and shook his head. "The bad part is saying goodbye."

"Don't look so sad, Sam," Heather reached out, giving him a hug. "You may not be getting rid of me, after all."

Sam's mouth fell open as his eyes jumped back to Brad then again to Heather; he was obviously searching for the right words.

Heather cleared her throat. "This morning in church I realized what was wrong with my life. I left a big chunk of my faith in Colorado, and I left my heart with Brad." She smiled as Brad put his arm around her shoulder. "I'm going to make some major changes in my life. For starters, I'm coming home."

Sam whooped a happy response, startling some of those lingering near the doorway. Then, realizing it was only Sam, just as rowdy as he had been in college, everyone turned and resumed their conversations.

Heather and Brad wandered toward the hospitality counter where coffee and tea were being served. Taking styrofoam cups of coffee, they found a quiet corner near the window that overlooked the ski slopes. For a moment, they stood gazing up at the slopes, watching the skiers.

Neither spoke for several seconds; then Brad turned to Heather. "So what's the next step in changing your life, Heather?"

She took a deep breath. "I'll go back to New York, cash out my savings and notify the agency that I won't accept more bookings."

Brad's eyes drifted back toward the skiers and a frown settled between his brows. "What if you change your mind once you get back?" He wanted to believe that everything would work out for them this time, but it was hard to forget how much he had missed her before. A dozen what-ifs were playing out scenarios in his mind, while he fought to squelch each one.

"I won't change my mind," she answered firmly.

She hadn't realized until Brad had come back into her life just how lonely she had been. This morning in church she had finally gotten her heart right with God; after that, a strange yet deep assurance had filled her. She was no longer puzzled about her future or afraid to take a chance. She felt a deeper strength abiding in her now; she believed she would be a better person, more tolerant and understanding. Certainly, Brad had become that way. This made it easier to focus on the important issues, with her faith as the basis of her decisions.

She slipped her hand through his arm. "You aren't planning another jaunt to Alaska, I hope?"

He grinned. "Nope, not without you." He looked into her face for a moment, saying nothing; then his grin stretched into a broad smile. "Heather, I can't wait for you to come back home. My mind is already spinning with plans for us."

She nodded. "First, I want to go back to school and get my master's in special education. I can move in with Mom and Dad in Denver while I'm going to school." She took a deep breath, feeling that this was the right thing to do. "It'll be nice to spend some time with my family again."

Brad looked at her thoughtfully, saying nothing for a moment. "But...," his voice trailed off as he glanced back out the window, and Heather sensed he was struggling with something.

"What is it?" she touched his arm.

"But you'll be there and I'll be here."

Her hand found his, squeezing gently. "There are the weekends. And maybe I can arrange my classes so that I have Fridays off." She hesitated, thinking it over. "Besides, Brad, we have to try and be sensible."

He nodded, thinking that it sounded like a pretty good plan. "I know. I'm already jumping the gun. We have to be patient, give ourselves enough time to work everything out."

She looked into his eyes. "It will work. This time we're listening to the right voice."

"Brad! Heather!" Sam was motioning to them. "Everyone's leaving. Come say goodbye."

Smiling, holding hands, Brad and Heather walked toward the front door. As they stepped outside to wave again to those getting into cars and driving away, the muted tinkle of silver bells drifted over the village. And a gentle snow began to fall.

Also by Peggy Darty:
Angel Valley
Seascape (Spring, 1996)

LOVE WANTED

SHARON GILLENWATER

One

Colin McCrea waited patiently as the airline ticket agent typed a flurry of information into the computer. When the machine beeped, the man frowned, muttered under his breath, and slowed his pace.

"We'll start to board in about ten minutes so don't wander far, Mr. McCrea," he said, glancing at several people in line behind Colin. "Since you're flying standby, we won't know if you have a seat or not until the last minute. If you aren't here within five minutes after we page you, we might have to give it to someone else."

Smiling at the harried agent, Colin took the ticket. "I'll be close by. Thank you." He tucked the folder in his jacket pocket and walked away from the counter, scanning the crowded waiting area, one of many in the gigantic Dallas-Fort Worth International Airport. This section of the American Airlines hub served passengers making flights on the commuter affiliate, American Eagle, to other Texas cities as well as nearby states.

He spotted an empty seat in the middle of a row and quickly claimed it, setting his carry-on bag and briefcase on the floor between his feet. As he straightened and leaned back, his gaze fell upon a wiggling black ball of fur on the floor across the aisle. The tiny puppy pulled diligently on a shoelace, but in spite of a mighty shake of the head and a ferocious growl, the turquoise and white tennis shoe won the tug-of-war.

A giggle brought Colin's gaze upward just as the owner of that soft laugh bent forward and a sweep of long red hair hid her face. He noted the deep vibrant color and the way it hung almost perfectly straight, then curled gently under on the ends. When he found himself analyzing the condition of her hair instead of simply admiring the soft, shiny locks, he frowned.

I've been cooped up in the lab way too long. He'd never been a ladies' man, but he wasn't a recluse, either. Not exactly. He just hadn't dated in a while. His work in the research department of Bosman Pharmaceuticals kept him busy, occupying his mind even when he wasn't in his office or the lab.

"I'm wise to your tricks, Shade, my girl," the woman crooned, tickling the puppy's tummy. "I tied the bow in a double knot. You won't be tripping me today." She picked up the puppy and set her on her lap. As she straightened, Colin noted that her hair fell several inches past her shoulders. She met his gaze and smiled.

She had beautiful green eyes, and a pretty face with well-defined cheekbones, a nice nose, full lips—and a fading smile. He realized he was probably staring at her with his scientist-studying-a-microbe look. Embarrassed, he smiled, holding her gaze long enough to see a glimmer of warmth return to her eyes before he looked away.

Real smooth, McCrea. He tried to remember the last time he'd taken a woman out but drew a blank. Then it came to him in a flash. Natasha, the company picnic two summers earlier. An attorney, she had worked in the corporate legal department. One afternoon of hamburgers and softball and she'd invited him to spend the night. He didn't think he'd ever forget her shocked expression when he politely declined. For several months afterward, he went to great lengths to avoid her until she moved on to some big Dallas law firm.

It occurred to him that perhaps he had been avoiding women ever since. He watched the redhead surreptitiously, wishing he could think of something clever to say, but nothing came to mind. It seemed that his self-imposed isolation had left him sorely lacking in the light flirtation department. She dangled an old knotted sock in front of the puppy, sometimes letting the little animal grab it, sometimes playfully pulling it back just beyond her reach.

Shade captured the sock and shook it viciously, flinging it across the aisle right at Colin's feet. The puppy tripped all over herself in her haste to retrieve it, but he was quicker. He picked up the sock and wiggled it in front of her, laughing as she jumped up, trying to grab it. Then she stopped, tipped her head to one side, and gave him a beseeching look.

"You're quite the little charmer, Shady lady." He leaned forward and patted the puppy on the head, laying the sock on the floor in front of her. She looked at him for a second then picked up her toy and returned to her game. Colin straightened and smiled at the redhead. "She's a character. What kind is she?"

"Little, I hope."

Colin laughed, delighting in the mischievous twinkle in the woman's eyes.

"Actually, I don't have the foggiest. She's a grocery store special."

Colin nodded in understanding. "A little kid standing outside with a long sad face and a cardboard box of adorable puppies?" The man sitting beside the redhead left, and Colin debated moving across the aisle to sit next to her. He decided against it, not wanting to seem too forward.

"You got it. Only this one had two kids. Bless their hearts, they knew what to do, too. The little boy explained how the puppies had to go to the pound *that* day if they couldn't give them away. Then the little girl looked up with great big crocodile tears and asked, 'You know what they do to puppies at the pound, don't you?'"

"Oh, man." Colin shook his head. "I probably would have taken the whole bunch."

"I came close," she said with a smile. "Thankfully, a couple of other softies were there at the same time. Otherwise, I don't know how I would have gotten them all home. Uh-oh." She jumped up, but a young boy wearing earphones and carrying a large bag walked in front of her, blocking her way.

Colin followed her worried gaze. Shade had abandoned her knotted sock and was stalking the precisely tied shoelace of an immaculately dressed gentleman two seats down from him. Colin lunged for the puppy, scooping her up half a second before she launched a full-fledged attack. The startled man peered over his newspaper with a scowl.

Handing Shade to her mistress, Colin grabbed his things and moved over next to her. "Maybe we'd better fence her in."

"Good idea. If someone complains, I'll have to put her back in her cage." She pulled her large purse and the doggie travel crate around to form a semicircle with his bag and briefcase.

The makeshift kennel didn't quite reach the chairs on Colin's side. When Shade headed for the open spot, he blocked her way with his foot. "Good thing I decided to wear my loafers."

She laughed and dug a leather chew stick out of her purse. "Here, Shady, lay down and chew on this for a while." The little dog obeyed with a happy wag of her tail. "Well, that's a first. Maybe she's starting to understand when I tell her something."

"How long have you had her?"

"Two days. I've been in Dallas all week on a buying trip for my dress shop. I stayed with a friend, otherwise I never would have found her," she said, meeting his gaze.

He noticed tiny flecks of gold in her eyes. "So now you're headed back home?"

She nodded. "Buckley. It's a little town in West Texas. My store is in Sidell, which is considerably bigger. How about you? Are you going home?"

"No, I live in Dallas. I'm spending the weekend in Springfield, Missouri, at my aunt and uncle's place. My cousin is there from Seattle. He had a business trip to St. Louis that ran longer than he had planned so he decided to stay the weekend with his folks." He glanced toward the gate. "They'll be boarding in a few minutes. The flight was sold out so I'm on standby."

She made a face. "That can be a pain. What if you don't get on this one?"

"I'll have to try the one in the morning. I haven't seen him in about a year and I really hope this one works out. We've had a hard time matching up our schedules."

"You're close?"

He nodded. "A year apart. When we were kids, he'd come here and stay a couple of weeks, and I'd go up to his place for a couple of weeks. We even roomed together in college. Now he's a geologist and travels all over the world for months at a time."

"What do you do?"

"I work for Bosman Pharmaceuticals in their research department. Right now I'm working on developing a new antibiotic."

"That must be fascinating."

"It is. Sometimes frustrating but always a challenge. When we finally make a breakthrough, it's very rewarding."

She glanced at his briefcase. "Do you always take your work home?"

"Seems like it. I'm not married, so there's no one to mind. I don't figure I'll do too much this weekend, but I brought along some notes on a particular problem. Sometimes the solution comes when I least expect it." He shrugged, feeling sheepish. "I guess I'm a workaholic. I get caught up in the hunt, searching for answers. I'm afraid I fit the old saying—all work and no play makes me a dull boy."

"I don't think you're dull."

Her sweet smile made Colin's heartbeat quicken. He took a deep breath and released it slowly. "Well, that's nice to hear." He returned her smile. "Running a store must take up a lot of time." He glanced at her left hand—no wedding ring. "Does your, uh, significant other mind?"

She grinned. "Nope. Don't have one. No husband, no boyfriend. Just a little ol' grandma who fusses over me like a mother hen."

"Well, grandmas are nice." He paused, then blurted, "The men out your way must be nuts or blind."

Her soft, musical laughter seemed to float between them. His fingers twitched as he stifled the impulse to reach out and try to capture it. He should have been embarrassed by his brash statement, but the gentle acceptance in those enchanting green eyes instantly banished his discomfort. He grinned. "Not very subtle, was I?"

"No, but that's the nicest compliment I've had in a long time." She held his gaze for a moment before glancing down at the puppy, who had fallen asleep with the leather chewie trapped between her front paws.

The delicate pink warming her cheeks made Colin wonder what she was thinking, but he was too polite to ask.

A garbled statement came over the loudspeaker, announcing the last call for passengers on the flight to Springfield.

"Uh-oh. That's my plane. I didn't realize they were boarding."

"Do you think they called you?"

"Probably not. The ticket agent said they wouldn't know if I had a seat until everyone else had boarded." He thought ruefully that it was entirely possible he hadn't heard his name if it had been announced. He had been completely focused on the woman next to him and in quite an unscientific way. That in itself was a pleasure and something of a relief. Perhaps he wasn't as far gone as he had feared.

The loudspeaker crackled and a muffled voice declared,

"Mr. Colin McCrea, please come to the ticket counter at Gate A-7."

"Well, that's me." He grabbed his bag and briefcase and stood, waking the puppy. "Oops. Sorry, Shady lady." He waited while the woman picked up the yawning dog. "It was nice talking to you. Sometime when you're in Dallas, give me a call at Bosman."

"Mr. Colin McCrea, please report to the ticket counter at Gate A-7 immediately."

"You'd better go." She smiled and patted Shade on the head. "Thanks for helping me with my rambunctious friend. Have a safe trip."

"Thanks. You, too." *She's one special lady,* Colin thought as he hurried toward the ticket counter. The agent assigned him a seat, and seconds later the computer printer screeched like a parrot with a sore throat as it cranked out his boarding pass. Suddenly experiencing a tremendous sense of loss, he glanced back at the redhead and caught his breath. She was watching him, and though she smiled when she met his gaze, her expression held a trace of sadness. *I don't even know her name!* He grabbed the ticket and boarding pass from the agent's hand and started back toward her.

"Mr. McCrea, you have to leave right now! They're holding the shuttle bus to take you to the plane."

Colin hesitated, his gaze lingering on the lovely face of the lady from Buckley as she looked down at her puppy.

"Mr. McCrea, please," cried the exasperated agent. "They're already ten minutes behind schedule."

He whirled around. "The flight in the morning?"

"It's overbooked. You'd never get on it."

Colin knew it might be another year before he had a chance to see his cousin. With a sigh, he turned toward the open door.

"Thank you," said the ticket agent, watching him warily.

Colin climbed aboard the crowded shuttle bus and hung onto the overhead railing as they sped toward the waiting plane. He should have been glad to get on the flight. Instead, he felt as if he had just made the biggest mistake of his life.

Two

It had been over two weeks since Colin's flight to Springfield. He'd had a good time with his relatives, laughing, joking, and catching up on their lives. Yet his thoughts had often drifted to the woman he'd met at the airport. Even his cousin, Nick, noticed his distraction. Colin had been surprised when he didn't scoff at the intensity of his attraction to her, until Nick reminded him that his father had fallen in love with his mother the first time he saw her.

Colin didn't think he was in love, but he certainly couldn't get her out of his mind. He estimated that he thought of her at least once every waking hour, and she'd made so many guest appearances in his dreams he figured she should have top billing in that theater of the mind. He had even asked the Lord to help him forget her so he could concentrate on his work. Nothing changed. That's when he began wondering if God didn't want him to forget her.

On the Monday afternoon before Thanksgiving, Colin sat at his kitchen table. Restless, he had gone to work early that morning but instead of staying late as usual, he came home mid-afternoon.

A map, folded to display West Texas, was pushed to one side of the butcherblock table. A bright red circle marked Buckley. Since Sidell was the only city close enough to it for a reasonable commute, he called Directory Assistance and asked for the names and numbers of the dress shops. He was told he needed the store name to obtain the number. The operator suggested he call the Chamber of Commerce.

He did, only to get a brief message stating the office was closed until the following Monday because the roof was being repaired.

It was probably just as well, he mused. If he started calling dress stores asking about a redhead, they might think he was a weirdo. He could imagine half a dozen frightened women calling the police department. They might trace the next call and before he knew it, his house would be surrounded by cops. It was not a pleasant picture.

"Now what?" Colin muttered, drawing squiggly shapes on a notepad. He stopped and stared at them. "Good grief, now I'm drawing viruses and bacteria."

His gaze fell on the Sunday newspaper he had tossed by the back door. One corner of the classified section was exposed, and his heart began to beat a little faster. "Why not an ad in the Buckley paper? If there is one." He shook his head. "Stupid idea." Slumping back in the chair with a grimace, he threw his pen on the table. It bounced onto the notepad. *Doodling in Dallas. That's me.*

The thought of using the paper nagged him. If there was a Buckley paper, or even one in Sidell, wouldn't she probably read it? Or if she didn't, surely someone who knew her would see the ad. Excitement zipped through him. "It might work. All

I've got to lose is some pride." He paused and prayed. "Lord, please give me wisdom on how to word this thing. I have to try to see her. If she tells me to get lost, then I won't bother her again. But I have to know if she's interested in me, too."

Half an hour later, he called Directory Assistance once more and asked for the number of the Buckley newspaper, silently praying that there was one. When the operator told him to hold for the number, he calmly said, "Thank you," but he wanted to shout it instead. He wrote down the number, took a deep breath, and dialed.

A pleasant woman answered the phone. "Buckley *Chronicle.* How may I help you?"

"I'd like to place an ad in your classifieds. I'm from out of town, though, so would a credit card be all right?"

"Certainly. Could I have your name, address, and the credit card number, please?"

Colin gave her the information and listened as she explained the charges.

"Now, which section do you want the ad in, sir?"

Love wanted. He shook his head with a wry smile, thankful he hadn't voiced the thought. "The personals."

There was a long pause. "Did you say the personals?"

"Yes, ma'am."

"Oh."

"Your paper does have a personals section, doesn't it?"

"Not since I've been here." She laughed. "And that's going on fifteen years. But that's only because nobody ever asked about it. Don't see why we can't put one in, as long as what you have to say is decent."

"It is but it's a bit long."

"Fine with me if you're willing to pay for it. I'll type while you dictate. Just don't go too fast. How do you want it to start?"

"Desperate in Dallas." He heard the faint tap of keys as the woman typed his words. "Can't get her out of my mind."

Sudden silence.

Colin held his breath until she resumed typing. When she paused again, he continued, "Please help me find the wonderful young lady from Buckley that I met at the Dallas Airport, Friday, November third, American Eagle waiting area. She has beautiful long red hair and green eyes. Didn't get her name. She had a black puppy named Shade and owns a dress shop, maybe in Sidell. If you recognize her, please call or ask her to call Colin in Dallas." He listed his home number. "Work for a pharmaceutical company. Was flying standby to Springfield, Missouri, to visit a cousin. Helped corral puppy with my luggage. Very anxious to talk to her."

The woman finished typing. "Are you for real?" she asked quietly.

He laughed. "Yes, although I'm feeling a little strange at the moment. I've never done anything like this before, but she's the most incredible woman. I can't stop thinking about her. I'd really like the chance to get better acquainted." He thought he heard a sniff. "Do you know her?"

"Maybe." A definite sniff. "We'll have to let her read the ad and see what happens. I'll say one thing for you, honey, if I wasn't an old, happily married woman, I'd give my eye-teeth to be in her shoes. Don't think I've ever heard of anything more romantic. I hope she calls you."

111

"I hope she does, too." He waited while the woman blew her nose. "When will the ad run?"

"On Wednesday. Paper only comes out once a week. Want to run it a couple of times?"

"Yes, please. If I hear from her before next week, I'll let you know."

"I'll be rootin' for you."

"Thanks." He hung up the phone and grinned as exhilaration replaced his nervousness. "Whew!" Jumping up from the table, he walked over to the back door and threw it open, taking a deep breath of fresh air. "Me...romantic." He laughed, thinking of what he had just done. It felt good.

And it felt right.

He looked up at the clear blue sky, enjoying the special crispness in the air that comes with autumn. Thanksgiving was just a few days away, with Christmas nipping at its heels. Colin came from a loving, close-knit family and usually spent those holidays with them. The last few years, he had felt lonely even in the midst of all the joy.

"I don't want to be alone this Christmas, Lord," he said softly. "Is she the one you've chosen for me?" He closed his eyes, picturing her sweet smile. Shaking his head, he looked up at the heavens. "Love is a big present to wish for. If you do get us together, Father, give me wisdom. Don't let me go where you aren't leading."

But please let her call.

Three

As Michelle Lane stepped through the back door of her house on Wednesday evening, her grandmother thrust a folded newspaper under her nose.

"Read this," ordered the tiny, delicate woman.

Michelle took the paper and set her purse on the kitchen table. "What did the city council do now?"

"Nothing to speak of. Look at the paper, dear. Read where I've circled."

Michelle sat down at the oak table, kicking off her low-heeled pumps, and absently rubbed her feet on the rung of the wooden chair. "Grandma, these are the classifieds." Her gaze fell on the heading of the section circled in red. "The personals? When did they start having a personals section?"

"Today. Sally Williams from the *Chronicle* called this morning to tell us to be sure and read it," her grandmother said impatiently. She pulled out a chair and eased into it.

Michelle frowned and began reading silently. *Desperate in Dallas. Can't get her out of my mind.* "Oh, brother," she muttered, but as she read the next three sentences, her mouth fell open and her heart started pounding. "Oh, my..." She continued to read, picturing the nice, good-looking man who had helped her with Shade. The same man who had wandered into her thoughts countless times since she left Dallas.

"Well? That's you, isn't it? You didn't say anything about meeting someone."

Dazed, Michelle looked up. "We only talked a few minutes before he caught his plane. He was nice but seemed a little shy. I never dreamed he'd do something like this."

"So is he a hunk or what?" A sparkle lit the elderly woman's eyes.

Michelle laughed. Hetty Lane delighted in surprising her granddaughter with a bit of contemporary slang now and then, usually something she picked up during her weekly visit to the beauty parlor. "I'd call him that. He's about five foot ten and in good shape. I expect he does some weightlifting or something and maybe jogs because he was tan, even though he works indoors. He has ash blond hair, cut short on the sides and back but a little longer on the top. He combs it to one side with a little wave on his forehead. His eyes are blue with a gray rim, and he has a nice smile."

Hetty chuckled. "Sounds to me like you were lookin' mighty close."

"He was nice to look at."

"Shall I hold supper while you call him or do you want to eat first?"

"I'm not sure I'm going to call him."

"Why not? You said he seemed nice."

"Well, he did," said Michelle. "But we only talked about ten minutes. How can you find out what a person is really like in that short a time? Maybe he's a kook or something. I mean, who'd take out an ad in the personals column of a newspaper?"

"A lonely man who met someone he truly liked but didn't know how else to contact her. Goodness, child, you'd think you lived in the sticks."

"I do, Grandma. I've been reading the Buckley paper since I was a kid, and I've never seen such a thing in it." Michelle pushed away from the table and went to the cabinet near the sink. Taking down a glass, she filled it with cold water and drank half of it. "Half the people in town who read that ad will know he's talking about me."

"And you're embarrassed."

Michelle shrugged, uncomfortable beneath her grandmother's penetrating gaze. "I guess so. I'm also flattered and dumbfounded."

"As well as interested and excited?"

"That, too. But it's so risky. Dating a man I met in an airport just isn't normal."

"Humph! It's time you did something a little unconventional, otherwise they'll bury you young with 'died of boredom' on your tombstone."

"I like my life just fine, Grandma." Michelle slipped an arm around the older woman's thin shoulders. "I'm happy and content living here with you and running my store."

"Then you should have your head examined." Hetty's expression grew stern. "Don't you dare let life pass you by because you feel obligated to take care of me. If you're at all interested in this young man, you pray about calling him. See what God leads you to do." She laid her hand lovingly on Michelle's cheek. "Remember that God doesn't always do things in ordinary ways. Why did this particular man help you with Shade and strike up a conversation? Why not someone's grandfather? Old men like playing with puppies and talking to pretty girls, too. Perhaps God intended for you to meet Colin McCrea. At least think about getting in touch with him."

By choice, they spent a quiet Thanksgiving at home, enjoying each other's company, sharing a small turkey, and eating too much corn bread dressing. That day and the next, Michelle carefully considered her grandmother's words, often talking to her heavenly Father about the situation. On those rare occasions when she wasn't thinking about Colin, others seemed determined that she should be.

Her friend Dawn called both Wednesday and Thursday evenings to see if she had contacted him, cheerfully scolding her when she admitted she hadn't.

At the post office Friday morning, the clerk wanted to know all the details about him and how they met. When she tried to brush off the man's inquiry, saying she really shouldn't make the other customers wait, the congenial postman declared they wouldn't mind. A quick glance confirmed that the three people behind her were actually leaning forward in anticipation. Blushing furiously, Michelle stammered something about Colin being nice, grabbed her roll of stamps, and fled.

When she stopped by Greene's Grocery that evening, three people cornered her in the produce section and asked about him. Another one caught her in the dog food aisle, and two more hemmed her in with their carts by the frozen foods. She was covered with goose bumps by the time she satisfied their curiosity.

She decided she had to call him, if for no other reason than to tell him what a stir he'd caused. Her heart pounded and her hand trembled slightly as she dialed his number after supper. When he answered, his voice sounded warm and mellow. Welcoming.

"Colin?"

"Yes."

She wondered how such a small word could hold so much anticipation. "This is Michelle Lane in Buckley. Shade and I met you at the airport in Dallas."

"Michelle..." He spoke her name as a sigh, and a shiver danced down her back. "I was afraid you weren't going to call."

"I had to think about it. Then I decided I'd better talk to you before half the town called you."

He laughed softly. "I don't know how big Buckley is, but I've already had eight calls, half of them on Wednesday. Most people just left a message on my answering machine, telling me your name and phone number, but one elderly man talked for ten minutes last night, singing your praises and pumping me for information."

"Oh, dear." She tried to imagine who it had been.

"Do you have a grandpa to go along with your little ol' grandma?"

"No. Did he give you his name?"

"Ralph something. I didn't catch the last name. He said he sees you sometimes in the mornings at the grocery store when you run in to get a cinnamon roll on your way to work."

"It was probably Mr. Hamilton. He and several of his cronies hang out at Greene's in the bakery every morning having coffee and discussing the latest news. That ad is the most

117

excitement this town has had in a couple of months."

He was silent for a long moment. "I've never lived in a small town so it didn't occur to me until I started getting calls that the ad might cause a lot of talk."

"It's been interesting," she said with a laugh. She related the incidents at the grocery store and post office, chuckling again when he groaned. "But it's also had a plus side. All of my regular Buckley customers suddenly decided they needed something new to wear, and a few others dropped by the shop for the first time. As far as sales go, it's been one of my best weeks."

"But it hasn't been so good otherwise." He sounded as if it truly bothered him.

Michelle sat down on her bed, propped a pillow behind her back, and leaned up against the headboard. Shade napped beside her in the special spot she had claimed since her arrival at the house. The little dog opened her eyes, yawned, and stretched, then rolled over on her back so Michelle could scratch her tummy.

"I've been in a stew trying to decide whether or not to call you," she said. "I guess I'm a little prudish when it comes to men. Grandma says I'm too conventional. If it hadn't been for Shade, I probably wouldn't have even talked to you at the airport."

"I'll have to send her a box of doggie treats."

"She'll be your friend for life."

"I'm sorry if I've embarrassed you," he said quietly.

"It really hasn't been awful. Not nearly as bad as when I was running for student council secretary and tripped on my way to the podium to make my campaign speech. Did a great belly flop in the middle of the stage."

"Oh, no!" Colin leaned his head against the back of the couch, picturing her face, her twinkling eyes. "But you won the election anyway, right? I can't imagine the guys voting for anybody else."

"Nice thought," Michelle said lightly. "But I couldn't live that one down."

"That's too bad. At least you gave it a try. I was never interested in running for office. Went to a big school here in Dallas and didn't even know all the people in my class. Did you grow up in Buckley?"

"I lived in Houston until the seventh grade. My folks were killed in a plane crash that summer, and I moved here to live with my grandmother."

Colin thought of his family and how painful it would be to lose any of them. To lose one's parents at such a tender age must have been shattering. "I'm real sorry to hear about your folks." The words sounded lame, but he didn't know what else to say. "Do you have any brothers or sisters?"

"No. Grandma is all the family I have. How about you?"

"I have kinfolk all over the place. Several aunts, uncles, and cousins, both sets of grandparents, my parents, two sisters and their husbands and kids. Four nephews and two nieces. Except for my cousin in Seattle and his folks in Springfield, we were all at my parents' house for Thanksgiving. It was fun but a little wild because we had people eating wherever they could find a spot. I had a great time with my nieces and nephews. The boys are full of mischief and the girls are little angels."

"And you're a doting uncle who spoils them rotten."

He laughed. "Afraid I do. They live within an hour's drive and I never miss a birthday party. I'm a glutton for cake."

"So you do get out of the lab now and then."

"Not enough." He paused. "I'm hoping that will change soon." Colin absently wrapped the phone cord around his finger, unwound it, and started all over.

"Why didn't you call me after you found out my name and number?"

"I started to at least a dozen times, but I didn't want to push you. I kept telling myself I had to let you make the next move, that if you were interested, you'd call. I've been praying a lot though."

"So have I," Michelle said. "Will you cancel the ad before it runs next week?"

"Might bring in more business."

"I think I can live without it."

They discussed her store and his research. Michelle told stories about her grandmother, and Colin kept her laughing with tales about some of the things he and his cousin had done while growing up. When they finally hung up, they'd talked for two hours.

He canceled the ad on Saturday and called her that evening to let her know. This time they chatted about music, sports, and houses. He liked the blues and she loved country, both conceding that sometimes the two blended nicely. They both rarely missed a Dallas Cowboys football game, but she watched them on television and he usually went to Texas Stadium when they played at home. Colin caught a Rangers game now and then, but Michelle thought baseball was boring. He'd been on the tennis team in high school and college and tried to play a couple of times a month. She'd never even held a tennis racket. Her house was old-fashioned, filled with her grandmother's things and lots of memories. His was a cookie-cutter rambler with minimal furniture and decoration.

Colin glanced at the clock and saw it was almost eleven. They'd been talking for three hours, but it only seemed like a few minutes. "I'd better let you go. I have to get up early tomorrow and hit the first service at church before I go to the stadium."

She yawned. "Now see what you did? Mention how late it is and I get instantly sleepy. Do you go to church often?"

"Most every Sunday. I don't usually make the midweek service since I work late a lot of the time. I try not to miss on Sunday mornings. I love the Lord and really need that time of worship and renewal to help me keep on track."

"I know what you mean. I'm a believer, too."

Yes! Colin felt like shouting but somehow managed to keep his voice mellow. "I'm glad." He paused, then plunged ahead. "That strengthens my belief that God had a hand in our meeting."

"Mine, too," she said softly. "Colin, that trip was the first time in years I'd flown to Dallas. I usually drive even though it takes several hours. My car hadn't been running right so I was afraid to take it. I left it in Sidell in the repair shop while I was gone. Normally, I wouldn't have gone near the airport."

Again, it was easy to see—or at least imagine—God at work. "It's too bad you had to go to extra expense, but I'm sure glad you were there. I almost didn't get on that plane. Even as I walked up the steps, I wanted to turn back. When I called the newspaper to place the ad, I felt foolish. But afterward, I knew it was the right thing to do. I want to see you again, Michelle."

"I'd like to see you, too. Talking on the phone is a nice way

121

to spend an evening, but it would be better in person."

"Much better. Would it be all right if I drive out next weekend?" Colin noticed his palms had suddenly grown moist.

"Of course it would be all right."

"I'll be tied up at work late on Friday so I can't make it until Saturday. Is there a motel in town?"

"Yes. It's not fancy, but I understand it's clean and comfortable. We're having our first annual Country Christmas Arts and Crafts Fair on Saturday. That night several of the churches are sponsoring a soup supper and pie social at the high school to supplement our regular Christmas toy drive. A lot of toys have been donated but we need cash to buy some things for the teenagers. It should be fun."

"Dibs on your whole pie, no matter what it costs."

Michelle laughed. "You're out of luck. I'm afraid Grandma is the baker in this family, and she's not up to it anymore. But I'll guarantee you won't go hungry. Since I work in Sidell, I was assigned the job of picking up the things we need from the Grocery Warehouse. My job will be all done long before you arrive."

"Sounds good to me. I'll call you tomorrow," said Colin.

"Even if the Cowboys lose?" she teased.

He growled into the phone, smiling when she giggled. "Hush your mouth, woman. Don't even think such a thing."

"Yes, sir. Don't yell too much tomorrow."

"I won't. Have to be able to talk to you. See you on Saturday." He had the feeling she didn't want to hang up any more than he did.

"I can hardly wait," Michelle said softly.

"I don't know if I can. I wish I could show up a day or two early."

"I'd put you to work sticking on price tags. We have a big shipment coming in on Thursday. I'll probably have to work late."

"Think I'll pass. I'd rather chase bacteria."

"That shouldn't be too strenuous. They can't run far."

"But they're fast." He laughed and said goodbye, wondering how he would make it through the next week.

As Colin pulled into Buckley on Saturday, the town bustled with a festive air. The street lights looked like big candy canes, and above Main Street at the east end of downtown, near Greene's Grocery, hung a bright red and green banner welcoming visitors to the Country Christmas Arts and Crafts Fair.

He smiled, remembering what Michelle had said about the old gentleman who had called him about the ad. Sure enough, although it was afternoon instead of morning, he spotted four elderly men sitting beside the grocery store, holding white Styrofoam cups. They had evidently abandoned the bakery and taken their coffee outside to keep track of the activity. Two were dressed as cowboys, with Western shirts, faded jeans, and boots, while the others wore khaki work shirts and pants. All kept the sun out of their eyes with beige felt Western hats.

Colin wondered if they had brought their own chairs or if the grocer had provided them.

The weather was a balmy sixty-five degrees, not bad for the first weekend in December, and a good thing since the arts and crafts booths lined the sidewalks on both sides of the street. The area teemed with people.

He drove slowly through the three blocks of downtown, noting several empty buildings as well as three antique shops, a drugstore, and a museum. Most of the stores, the museum, and even some of the empty buildings were decked out for Christmas with twinkling lights and painted scenes on the windows. Memory Lane Antiques had a life-sized, straw-filled wooden manger in the window. Several white and gold angels hovered above it. Another banner stretched across the street between Jackson's Hardware and Feed Store and the back side of a farm implement company lot containing green John Deere tractors and other machinery.

Turning around at the intersection, he drove back through town, wanting another look at Findley's Apothecary. The building, with its dark red brick walls and faded green awning, looked nearly a hundred years old. Colin smiled, thinking that if the old building could talk, it would probably have some tall yarns to spin. He felt drawn to it, as if wonderful secrets waited there for him to discover.

Laughing at his whimsy, Colin took a spin around a couple of blocks to see the sights—the post office, library, Citizens Bank, fire station, City Hall, and Police Department. Catching a cross street, he drove out to Eleventh Street and found Michelle's house.

It was just as she had described it the night before, a turn-of-the-century gray two-story with white gingerbread trim and white wrought-iron railing on the wraparound porch. It was the complete opposite of his sleek brick rambler, but he loved it instantly.

A frail, white-haired lady opened the front door and walked out onto the porch. She peered at him with a slight frown until he opened the car door and climbed out, then a delighted smile lit her face. "You must be Colin," she called.

"Yes, ma'am." He shut the door, automatically locking it, and hurried up the red brick walkway. "And you must be Grandma Hetty," he said, returning her smile.

The old woman chuckled. "Well, I'm not Michelle's sister, that's for sure."

"Oh, I don't know." He studied her for a minute. "The eyes and smile are the same."

"Hair was red once upon a time, too." She winked at him. "I was a looker in my day, just like my granddaughter."

"You still are, ma'am." He meant it. Time had left its mark, but her bright green eyes sparkled with mischief and her face glowed from within.

"You're quite the charmer for a scientist." She opened the screen door, leading the way inside. "Michelle said you were good lookin', but I kept wondering if you'd show up in a white lab coat and thick glasses."

Colin laughed. "Thankfully, I don't need glasses. I admit I practically live in a lab coat, only it's blue."

She stopped and turned, running an assessing gaze over his green cotton shirt and casual beige slacks. "You wear blue because it looks good on you?"

"Not exactly, although I guess it does. The company provides the coats in either blue or ugly green. I tried the green once and felt as if I should scrub up for surgery."

Hetty laughed and led him into the living room. "Would

you like something to drink? I usually brew up some hot tea about now, but you probably would rather have something cold."

"Actually, I'd enjoy a cup of hot tea."

"Then let's go into the kitchen. I took some banana cookies out of the oven a little while ago. Michelle is on her way. She should be here any minute." As they walked through the dining room, Hetty stopped suddenly and grabbed the back of a maple chair, closing her eyes.

Colin put his arm around her and felt her body shift to lean against his strength. "Are you dizzy?"

"A little." She took a deep breath and opened her eyes, blinking a few times. "There, that's better."

"Do you need to sit down?"

"Not here, but I'll sit and watch while you make that pot of tea."

Colin peered at her face. The delicate color had drained from her cheeks, making her skin appear paper-thin. Her eyes had lost their luster. "Are you in any pain?"

She met his gaze. "No. There's never pain, thank the Lord. Just weakness. It comes more often these days. Doc says my heart's gettin' old like the rest of me. One of these days it'll just quit tickin'."

"Are you on medication?"

She managed a smile. "Oh, yes. Lanoxin. Take it faithfully."

"Are you sure you shouldn't lie down?"

"And miss having you all to myself for a few minutes?" A tiny glimmer lit her eyes. "Not on your life, young man. A cup of tea, a few cookies, some good conversation and I'll be fine."

Colin laughed. "I think I can manage that."

"Good. Now give me your arm."

Her hand shook as she curled it around his arm, and they made their way slowly into the kitchen. He was concerned about the weakness in her step but decided not to say anything.

"Too bad you aren't a doctor. You have a much better bedside manner than that ol' coot I go see in Sidell. Better looking, too."

He smiled and eased her into a chair. When he was certain she wouldn't keel over, he went to the sink and filled the teakettle. "There's no doctor in Buckley?"

"Nope. Haven't had one here in over thirty years. We've got some good paramedics at the fire department, and the home health care nurses visit quite a few folks that need checking on once a day or so. We count on Mr. Findley down at the drugstore a lot, too."

She pointed toward the counter between the sink and the stove. "Tea bags are in that ceramic canister. Mr. Findley is good to listen to our complaints and offer advice. Sometimes he suggests trying something that he has on hand; other times he tells us to hotfoot it to the doctor. Mugs are to your left."

Colin took down two mugs and set them on the table. He'd already placed the tea bags in the pot, noting with approval that she was drinking decaffeinated. If she'd been drinking regular, he would have felt compelled to say something. "Since you've been sitting for a few minutes, I'd like to check your pulse."

"Go ahead. Feels like it's behavin' now though." She rested her arm on the table.

Colin gently placed his fingers on the inside of her wrist,

finding the pulse. Timing the seconds on his watch, he counted the beats and lifted his hand. "Nice and steady, fairly strong and running about normal." He glanced at the pile of cookies on wire racks in the middle of the table. "I suspect you overdid it."

"Could be. I didn't take a very long rest."

Colin reached for a cookie. "Did I wake you?"

Hetty shook her head. "Don't usually sleep in the afternoon anyway. Just lie down for a bit. How's the cookie?"

"Great. I'll have to get the recipe for my mom. She likes to bake." He picked up another one and walked back over to the counter. "Sugar?"

"To your right." She smiled. "Trying to sweeten yourself up?"

He nodded. "Need all the help I can get." The kettle whistled and Colin took it off the burner, pouring the boiling water into the teapot.

"Spoons are in that first drawer."

He withdrew a spoon and tucked it in his shirt pocket, then carried the teapot and sugar bowl to the table and sat down. When Hetty reached for the teapot a few minutes later and poured them each a cup, Colin noticed her shakiness had passed. They chatted for a while and drank their tea until Michelle came through the back door, juggling two bags of groceries.

Jumping up, he took them from her. "Hi, lady," he said softly, smiling into her eyes. It was odd—they had talked so much over the past week that they seemed like old friends, but he hadn't realized she was only about four inches shorter than he was. *How can she be even prettier than I remembered?* Her

129

rust knit shirt and matching floral skirt were flattering, but he decided the welcoming warmth in her eyes and her happy, excited smile made the real difference.

"Hi. Sorry I wasn't around when you got here. I decided I'd better stop by the grocery store on my way home." She grinned. "Guess that's obvious. You can set those on the counter over here." A sharp bark sounded at the back door. "Oops, forgot the boss."

Colin set the groceries on the counter as she opened the back door, and Shade scampered in. "Running the place, is she?"

"Got us wrapped around her paw." Michelle picked up the puppy and rubbed her face against the dog's black head, then dodged as Shade tried to lick her. "Sweetie, look who came to visit us," she said, running her hand down the dog's back to calm her.

Shade gazed intently at Colin.

"Hi, Shady. You've grown a little."

She wagged her tail excitedly.

"Hey, I think she remembers me." He patted the dog on the head, and she wiggled, leaning toward him. "Sure, I'll play with you while your mama puts the groceries away." As he took Shade, his gaze met Michelle's. He hoped they didn't wind up spending all their time in the company of others, even a lovable pooch. He had the feeling she was thinking the same thing, even though she looked away first.

"Did you get settled in at the motel?"

"Sure did." Colin sat back down at the table and shared a cookie with Shade. "It's cozy and comfortable. I'm glad you made the reservation Sunday, or I might not have gotten a room. The manager said they were all filled up because of the arts and crafts fair."

"The turnout is even better than we'd hoped," said Michelle. "There are a lot more people in town than usual." As she put a bag of dog food in the bottom cabinet, Shade's ears perked up. Michelle grinned when Colin laughed. "Yes, she knows it's hers. But we already have an open bag. And a very special box of goodies." She smiled as she took several small bone-shaped biscuits from the box of doggie treats he had mailed to Shade and handed them to him. "Here, you can spoil her some more."

He fed them to Shade, who took them daintily, looking up at him with total devotion as long as he gave her the crunchy biscuits. Finishing her chore, Michelle folded the paper bags, tucked them beneath the sink, and sat down next to him.

Shade wiggled again and he set her on the floor. She immediately went to the cabinet containing the dog food and sniffed before wandering over to her food dish to eat. "Doesn't miss a trick, does she?"

"Not a one." Michelle picked up a cookie and took a bite, turning to her grandmother with a frown. "These are good, Grandma, but what are you doing baking?"

"Don't fuss. I enjoyed myself. Didn't hurt me a bit, either. Besides, I rested while Colin made the tea. Get changed so you can go have some fun."

"You're sure you don't want to come with us?"

"I may be old but I still remember that when you're dating, three's a crowd. Rosemary and Harold will be by later to give me a ride to the soup supper. Now I'm going to sit outside and enjoy the sunshine." She poured herself another cup of tea and went out the back door, calling Shade to accompany her.

"She's a real sweetheart," Colin said after Hetty closed the door.

"Yes, she is. Gets a little cantankerous now and then—like with these cookies. The doctor told her that she should just do the bare essentials and really take it easy, but she doesn't want to give in. She's slowed down, of course, but she still overdoes it."

"She had a weak spell after I got here. Had me worried but she snapped out of it before long. I checked her pulse after she rested a few minutes and it was steady."

"That's usually the way it happens. She just needs to let her heart catch up. Sometimes it's worse and she has to go to bed for a while. Thankfully that doesn't happen very often. I worry about her and try to do as much of the work as I can, but she'd go crazy if she couldn't putter around the house some."

"If you think we should stay here, I don't mind."

She laid her hand over his on the table. "That's sweet of you but we'd never hear the end of it. If she even suspected we were hanging around because of her, it would upset her."

He turned his hand over, clasping hers. "It's hard to believe this is only the second time I've seen you. I feel like we've known each other for years."

"That's because once we start talking, we forget how to hang up the phone," she said with a laugh. "But I know what you mean. I'm happy you're here."

"I am, too." He glanced down at their joined hands and smiled. "Now that I can actually touch you, I don't want to let go."

"Well, you'll have to for a little while. I'm more than ready for a pair of comfy jeans and tennis shoes."

Five

Michelle was surprised to discover Colin drove an immaculate but older maroon Chevrolet. When he caught her glancing at the license plate, she laughed. "I was checking to see if you had one of those license plate holders that says 'My other car is a BMW' or something equally fancy."

"This one not yuppie enough for you?" he asked dryly, opening the car door for her.

"I think it's wonderful. I just figured the head of a research team would own something newer."

"And more expensive."

"Well, you would in the movies," she said, grinning as she slid onto the seat. "But I really do like this one. What year is it?"

"It's a '70 Chevelle Malibu. My dad helped me buy it when I was in high school. We spent a lot of time together fixing it up." He shut the door, went around to the other side, and got in. "It runs great, and I can do the maintenance on it myself if I want to."

"Ah, the man has a practical streak."

He smiled. "Only when I'm in the mood. These days I usually let someone else get their hands greasy."

They drove downtown and parked, then spent the next couple of hours strolling through the arts and crafts displays and antique shops. Michelle bought some crocheted snowflake Christmas ornaments, a couple of aprons for her grandmother, and a sweatshirt decorated with painted poinsettias. She was so impressed with the woman's artistry on the shirts that she asked her to bring some by her dress shop. Colin bought a pen-and-ink sketch of a hawk and a painting of the West Texas prairie for himself, then picked up a teddy bear dressed as a cowboy for each of his nieces.

At Memory Lane Antiques and Collectibles, Michelle introduced him to her friend, Dawn Adams, who owned the shop.

Dawn smiled at Colin. "Well, looks like you got my message."

He laughed. "Yours and several others. I expect if Michelle hadn't called Friday, I would have taken your advice and phoned her."

Smiling, Michelle shook her head. "I should have known you'd try to play Cupid."

"Hey, I just want everyone to be as happy as I am." Dawn looked at Colin. "Got married last summer, and I'm madly in love. After reading that ad, I figured you deserved a chance to talk to Michelle but might need a little help. Sometimes she's as cautious as a bobcat on a barbed wire fence." A customer asked a question, and Dawn edged away. "Better get to work. It's nice to meet you, Colin."

Michelle and Colin browsed through the displays, admiring

the antique furniture, laughing at an old tin bug sprayer and a windup monkey that played a drum. A porcelain nativity scene caught his eye, so he bought it.

As they walked back toward the car, Colin glanced across the street at Findley's Apothecary. "Would you mind dropping into the drugstore? I'm curious to see if it's as quaint on the inside as it is on the outside."

"Don't mind a bit." They stashed their purchases in the car and walked across to the drugstore. Colin held the door for her as she went inside. When he followed she heard his sharply indrawn breath.

"Did we just step through a time portal?" he murmured, staring at the high shelves running down each wall and across the back of the store. All kinds of old bottles, canisters, boxes, and gadgets from early in the century filled them.

"In some ways. Keep going. It gets even better." Michelle followed him down the aisle, grinning when he stopped in front of a long counter with high red stools and shook his head slowly.

"It has a soda fountain!" Colin turned to her, grinning broadly. "Want something?"

"Thought you'd never ask."

He cupped her elbow to help her climb up on the stool and slipped his arm around her waist, giving her a tiny hug. She glanced up at him as a tingle zipped through her.

"I've always wanted to take my girl out to a place like this," he said softly. "But the few times I've run across a fountain, I was alone."

He slid onto the next stool, and she instantly missed his closeness. "We used to come down here a lot when I was in high school, especially in the summer."

"Then I guess sharing a malt would be boring."

Michelle caught a hint of disappointment in his expression. "Nope. The guys preferred going to the drive-in so they could show off their cars as well as their dates. I was usually here with a girlfriend or two. There were more stores downtown then." She leaned closer and said softly, "Besides, competing over a malt with you couldn't possibly be ho-hum."

His blue eyes sparkled with pleasure and laughter. "I don't think the object of sharing is to see who can drink the most."

"Oh." She gave him a wide-eyed innocent look.

Colin chuckled and gave their order to the young man behind the counter. A few minutes later, he set the chocolate malt and two straws in front of them. Colin stuck the straws into opposite sides of the fluted glass and motioned for her to go first. She complied and when he leaned forward for a sip, their heads almost touched. They cast a sideways glance at each other and burst into laughter. "I think the previous generations were smarter than we give them credit for," he said.

"Definitely a form of dating that should be revived."

They had just about finished the malt when the druggist sat down next to Michelle. "I can tell you two have been watching old movies," he said with a smile.

"And listening to stories," said Colin. "One of my dad's favorite tales is about how he used to meet Mom at the drugstore for a soda before Grandpa would let her go out on a real date. My dad was pretty sly."

"I know of several old married couples who started out right here at this counter, including me and my Izzy. Two bits your father stole a kiss or two when the owner wasn't looking."

Colin laughed and winked at Michelle. "Yes, sir, he did." He held out his hand to the pharmacist. "I'm Colin McCrea. You must be Mr. Findley."

The man shook his hand firmly. "That's right. And you must be the young man who put the ad in the paper."

"Guilty as charged."

"Smart, if you ask me. I respect a man with initiative."

"Colin works for Bosman Pharmaceuticals as a researcher," Michelle said.

"That so?" Mr. Findley sat up a bit straighter as a gleam appeared in his eyes. "Working on anything interesting?"

Colin nodded. "A new antibiotic. We should have it approved for hospital testing in a week or two. I'm rerunning some tests now to confirm our earlier findings. It looks very promising. Should be effective against a couple of bacteria that resist everything else."

"Sure hope it works. Some of these new strains are frightening. You must have gone to school for quite a while to get into research." Mr. Findley glanced at Michelle. "Usually takes at least a masters these days."

Michelle thought Colin looked a little uncomfortable.

"Actually, I have a doctorate."

"In pharmacy or something else?"

"Pharmacy."

"Good for you. The more knowledge the better; gives you better opportunities. You goin' to the soup supper and pie social?"

"We'd planned to." Michelle looked at the clock on the wall above them. The dinner started in a couple of hours. "Now I'm

137

not sure I'll be hungry."

"Stop by anyway and let folks meet your young man." The pharmacist grinned at Colin as he stood. "You're something of a celebrity."

When he walked away, Colin groaned softly. Michelle patted his hand. "Told you that you'd caused a stir. I'd like for folks to meet you, but if you don't want to go tonight, I'll understand."

He stood and squared his shoulders like a fighter going into the ring. "I'm game if you are."

She spun around on the stool and hopped off. "I wouldn't miss it. I want to prove you're real."

"Someone has doubts?"

"Marge at the beauty shop said a few of her customers were speculating that I'd placed the ad myself. They just couldn't imagine a man actually doing it."

He pushed open the heavy glass door, holding it as she walked through. "Maybe I should wear a sign saying 'I'm glad I used the classifieds.'"

Michelle grinned. "If you did, the paper would probably refund your money."

"Got any cardboard?"

She looked at the mischievous twinkle in his eyes and laughed. "I expect I can scrounge some up. You want a big piece or a little one?"

"Big enough to make a full-sized sandwich sign. When I do something, I go all out."

A swell of tenderness caught her by surprise. Linking her arm with his, she said softly, "So I've noticed."

Colin drove as Michelle showed him the sights. He decided Buckley was a nice place, although like many older towns it was a little run-down around the edges. There were several churches and a well-maintained park with an outdoor pool and amphitheater. Michelle explained that the Chamber of Commerce was planning to have their first annual Old Fiddlers Contest there the next summer.

They passed a couple of cotton gins and the auction barn where local ranchers bought and sold livestock almost every Saturday. Teenagers milled around the Lazy Day, the local hamburger joint, just as other generations of teens had done. An oil field supply outfit was located north of town with a welding shop nearby. Near the freeway and the hotel were a Pizza Hut and a newly built Mexican restaurant.

"I didn't notice any ranches on the way into town. It seemed to be farmland from way on the other side of Sidell," said Colin.

"It is. Actually the area for several miles around town is all farmland. The ranches are farther out. It's getting too dark to see anything now. We'll have to take a country drive the next time you're here."

"I'd like that." He also liked the silent invitation to visit again. "Do you want to stop by and check on your grandma before we go to supper?"

"It's probably a good idea. I need to pick up a heavier jacket, so we have an excuse to stop."

As they drove up, Hetty was walking out the door with her friends, Rosemary and Harold. She introduced them to Colin on the front porch. "They're practically newlyweds. Rosemary taught high school English, but she's retired now. Harold is our local undertaker. And he's heard all the jokes." She smiled at Colin. "Even made up a few himself, I expect."

After they exchanged pleasantries, Rosemary folded her arms, clearly studying him. "Hetty says you're a scientist."

"That's right. Pharmaceutical research."

"Makes sense," she said, nodding.

"What?" asked Michelle.

"How he found you, dear. He has an analytical mind so he studied the problem, came up with the best solution, and had the gumption to follow it through." She winked at him. "And the packaging isn't bad, either. You're very fortunate, Michelle."

Chuckling, Harold ushered the older women off the porch and down the walk before Colin could think of a comment.

He glanced at Michelle. She was staring after them with her mouth hanging open. He gently pushed up her chin with his knuckle. "What's wrong?"

"She was flirting with you."

"Women do occasionally."

"Not Miss Atkins—er, Rosemary. After having her for senior English, I have a hard time calling her by her first name." She shook her head. "Something tells me this evening is going to be very interesting."

On their arrival at the high school cafeteria, they received plenty of curious looks along with the expected murmuring. A few of the women sighed dreamily when they learned who he was, but most were calm and friendly. Most of the men were cordial, although he sensed a hint of reservation in some. He figured they considered him a smart-aleck city slicker who wanted to waltz in and steal away one of the prettiest women in town. Since that was exactly what he wanted to do, he couldn't blame them.

"Uh-oh," Michelle mumbled, looking across the room as they stood in the food line.

"What's up?" Colin followed her gaze. An attractive blonde in a clinging scarlet jumpsuit moved purposely toward them. "Red alert?"

She giggled. "Man your battle stations and prepare for attack."

He edged closer to Michelle. "At the ready, captain."

"Hello, Michelle." The woman's gaze stayed on Colin as she

gave him a coquettish smile. "Where did you find this hand-some man?"

"In Dallas," Michelle said.

"At the airport," Colin added. "Thankfully, I tracked her down."

The woman's smile faltered. "You mean you really...." her voice trailed off as he nodded.

"She swept me off my feet." He met Michelle's glance and held it. "I was prepared to knock on every door in Buckley until I found her."

"You can't be serious!" exclaimed the blonde.

"Oh, but I am," he said quietly, gazing into Michelle's eyes, watching as amazement softened to tenderness and longing. "Very serious." He finally forced himself to look away, noting that a big gap had formed between them and the next person in line. "Excuse us, we need to move on." He smiled benignly at the woman and casually rested his hand on Michelle's low back.

"Nice evasive maneuver," Michelle said as they stepped forward. "Although next time, make sure I'm sitting down before you say such sweet things, or you may find yourself holding me up."

Colin grinned and leaned close to her ear. "I'll make sure there's not a chair in sight."

She laughed and shook her head. "Beneath that shy, serious exterior lurks a rogue."

"I'm not shy. Too serious sometimes, but I've never been shy."

"That wasn't my first impression in Dallas."

He grimaced. "I'd forgotten how to talk to a pretty lady."

"Well, you can relax, 'cause you've got it down pat now."

A few minutes later, they joined a group at a long table. Baskets of rolls were placed in the center of it, along with a pot of coffee and a pitcher of water. After they were seated, a high school girl came by with a pitcher of milk, pouring some for two small children sitting with their parents.

Michelle introduced Colin as a friend from out of town, avoiding any hint of where he was from or how they met. Although he caught a few speculative glances, no one pressed the issue.

He ate his vegetable beef soup quietly, making a comment now and then, but mostly listening to the friendly conversations going on around him. He quickly deduced that the tall man across from him, Coach Peters, ran the high school basketball program, and the shorter, husky man at the other end of the table was the football coach.

"We gonna win district again this year?" asked a middle-aged man two seats down. Colin thought he'd said his name was Bill. He worked at the auction barn. The owner sat next to him.

"We should," replied the basketball coach. "Only lost two starters last year, and we've got a good crop of new boys in the program."

"I'm slipping them weight gain formula on the side," the football coach said with a grin. "Put some meat on 'em and recruit them for football next year. We might even have a winning season." He glanced at the man sitting at the other end of the table, then winked at Colin. "These ranchers may know how to fatten up their cattle, but they sure seem to raise tall, skinny youngsters."

"Now, Hank, you can't go holding a grudge because my boy preferred roping steers to running down a field with a whole passel of hombres chasin' him," said the rancher.

"I think you're doing a fine job, Coach," said a young woman, carefully monitoring her son as he drank some milk. "It takes time to turn a football program around."

The others nodded in agreement, and the talk turned to a recent city council meeting and plans to pave some of the outlying streets. "Should have done it a long time ago. Those folks put up with mud when it rains and blowing sand the rest of the time."

"Don't know why they have to raise my taxes to do it," grumbled someone.

"They're not raising them much."

"Still don't like it."

"Then run for the city council."

Colin listened to the agreement and disagreement, the ebb and flow of talk punctuated by laughter and friendly teasing. He envied their camaraderie and the sense of belonging so obvious to an outsider. They were a diverse group, but there was no distinguishable rank among them. They were neighbors, concerned about their town and each other.

"Why so thoughtful?" Michelle asked quietly.

"I was trying to remember the last time I paid any attention to what the city government was up to or had an idea of how the neighborhood high school team was doing. Other than at church or family reunions, I'm rarely around folks from various walks of life. I spend all my time with people in my field." He shook his head as the feeling of dissatisfaction with his life took a giant leap. "I hope you all realize how good it is here."

"We do, but don't paint too rosy a picture. We have our squabbles. Sometimes things get downright nasty, but eventually it all blows over and for the most part, life falls back into a routine."

A shrill laugh in the serving line behind them drew their attention. A slim young woman in her late twenties was talking up a storm to an elderly gentleman about the aerobics class she just started attending. "Us newbies must be a riot to the others. Just a riot. What a workout." She took a long drink of diet pop, practically pouring it down her throat. "I'm starved. Are you starved? I'm so hungry I could eat a...a...oh, I don't know, just about anything."

Colin frowned as he watched her lift the can of pop to her lips. Her hands shook badly and her face was flushed. On closer inspection, her whole body appeared to tremble.

"She must have really overdone it," Michelle said, glancing at the basketball coach. "Isn't she one of the new teachers?"

"Karen Anderson, the high school librarian. Always been pleasant but seemed a little shy. I've sure never seen her act like this."

"She came into my store last week. She seemed shy then, too."

As the line moved forward, the young woman followed, stumbling slightly. She glanced around, her expression fearful. "Sorry. I'm really tired."

"Looks like she may have something a little stronger than pop in that can," noted one of the men.

Colin didn't notice who made the comment. He was far more concerned about the woman's fading color and other symptoms.

145

"Hope none of the parents or school board sees her, or she'll be in big trouble," said the football coach.

"She's in trouble but I don't think it has to do with alcohol," Colin said, noting her pallor and the sheen of sweat that suddenly appeared on her face. He was afraid she might be unconscious in a matter of minutes.

He grabbed several sugar packets and ripped them open, emptying them into a glass of water. "Is she diabetic?" Colin glanced around the table, but everyone shook their heads, murmuring that they didn't know. Dropping a spoonful of blueberry filling into the glass, he stirred briskly as he stood.

"If she's diabetic, shouldn't she stay away from sugar?" asked the young mother.

"Normally, but her symptoms indicate insulin shock. Heavy exercise and missed meals can lead to low blood sugar." He looked at the rancher. "See if you can find Mr. Findley."

"Should we call the paramedics?" asked the football coach.

"Not unless she passes out," said Colin. "That shouldn't happen if she drinks this." He glanced at Coach Peters and Michelle. "I'd appreciate your help." When they both nodded, he handed her the glass of blue sugar water.

They were one step behind him as he rushed to the young woman's side. Michelle noted that as he grew closer, he slowed his pace so he wouldn't startle her.

"Karen, my name is Colin. Coach Peters and I noticed you seem ill," he said, placing his arm lightly around her shoulders.

"Need to eat," she said weakly.

"Are you diabetic?" Colin gently guided her into the chair the coach set behind her and knelt on one knee in front of her.

"Yes."

"Do you take insulin?" When she nodded, he asked, "Did you take your regular dose today?"

"Yes," she whispered, looking down at her wrist as Colin checked her pulse. "You a doctor?"

"No, a pharmacist. Do you feel faint?" When she slowly nodded, he held out his hand for the glass, never taking his gaze away from Karen.

Michelle handed it to him, admiring his calm and caring manner. Even though her heart pounded like a jackhammer, his very presence seemed soothing to Karen and those gathering around them. *What a waste for him to be in a lab.*

"Did you eat before your workout?"

"No."

"Karen, I brought you some juice. It's fake blueberry so it may taste funny, but I want you to drink it all down, okay?"

The young librarian slowly looked up, meeting Colin's gaze for the first time. Michelle watched as the light of trust slowly chased away some of the dullness in her eyes. Karen didn't object as he slowly lifted the glass to her lips. She drank several swallows, then made a face.

"I know it's probably not very good, but it was the best I could do on short notice," Colin said with a smile, holding the glass to her lips again. She drained it without another protest.

When the school principal worked his way through the crowd to her side, Michelle turned to him. "Is there someplace she could lie down?"

"The nurse's lounge has a bed."

Colin glanced up and nodded, indicating he heard them.

147

"Karen, I'm going to carry you to the nurse's lounge so you can rest a bit." When she nodded, he looked up at Michelle. "Would you come, too?"

She was surprised to see a plea in his eyes. "Of course." After he carefully lifted Karen, Michelle moved beside him and they followed the principal toward the cafeteria door.

Mr. Findley fell in step with Colin. "Couldn't have done better myself."

The nurse's lounge was only a short distance away. Colin settled Karen gently on the bed and pulled a blanket over her. "Feeling better?"

"A little."

Colin, Michelle, and Mr. Findley stayed with Karen, chatting casually and keeping a close eye on her. A short while later, the crisis had obviously passed, although the young woman was not back to normal.

As Karen sat up, Michelle was surprised to see Clint Marshall, their thirty-something pastor, come rushing into the room. Without a glance at anyone else, he sat down beside Karen and gently put his arms around her. "Are you all right?"

"I'm getting there."

"I'm sorry I was late. I had a flat tire. Do you need to go to the hospital?"

Michelle smiled at the tenderness and concern on Clint's face as Karen explained that she just needed to rest a few more minutes and then go home.

"She should get something to eat, and someone should stay with her until she's back to normal," said Mr. Findley, with a wink at Michelle.

"I'll take care of her." Holding her close, Clint took a deep breath and exhaled slowly. "What happened?"

As Mr. Findley explained the situation, Colin slipped out the door. Michelle followed and found him leaning against the wall, suddenly appearing drained. "Now I know why I didn't become a doctor," he said quietly.

Michelle put her arms around his waist in a hug. When he wrapped his arms around her, holding tight, she closed her eyes for a second, then pulled back minutely to look at his face. "Hi, hero."

"Not me." He held out one hand to show her it was trembling.

"Yes, you. You were wonderful. Are wonderful." She rested the side of her face against his. "I think I'll just stay here for a while."

"Please," he murmured, his voice thick.

They were still standing there several minutes later when Clint and Karen walked out of the nurse's lounge. Karen looked much better. She reached for Colin's hand. "A simple thank you doesn't seem like enough since you may have saved my life."

"I'm just glad I was here. You take care of yourself. Be sure and eat before you exercise."

Karen managed a smile. "I think I'll skip aerobics and stick to walking. I'm used to it. I don't want to get caught like this again."

As Clint and Karen continued down the hall, Mr. Findley squeezed Colin's shoulder. "You very well may have saved her life, son, and you know it. You've got a good eye for seeing a problem. I saw you tonight when you first noticed something was wrong. It took me a few minutes to see who you were looking at. By then you already had the situation sized up."

"Why didn't you take over? I'm sure you've had more experience at this type of thing than I have."

"I was standing by, but you didn't need me." The druggist looked Colin squarely in the eye. "I expect you're a brilliant scientist, Colin McCrea, but the good Lord has given you a special touch when it comes to people. If you ever decide you want a life outside the lab, let me know. I'll give you a fair price on my drugstore. I'd like to retire while I still have plenty of good fishing days left. Tomorrow wouldn't be too soon."

"No thanks. It's scary out here in the real world. If I make a mistake in the lab, the only thing I'll kill is a cell or two."

Mr. Findley smiled and patted him on the back. "Things like this don't happen often, and the hospital is only a phone call away. Those folks have talked me through plenty of things I wasn't sure about. After all, we aren't doctors."

"No, but I have the feeling some people think differently."

"Could be," said the older gentleman with a grin. "Some folks think I buy half the fish I catch, too."

They watched him walk away with a jaunty gait. Michelle caught Colin's hand. "There will be a fuss if we go back inside. Would you like to leave? Mr. Findley will make sure they know she's all right."

He heaved a sigh of relief. "Yes, ma'am." He drew her closer, putting his arm around her shoulders as they started down the hall. "Let's go someplace quiet. There's too much excitement around here for me."

"I know the perfect place, but we need to stop by the house and get my car."

"What's wrong with mine?"

"It doesn't have a sun roof."

After trading cars, Michelle drove out of town about five miles, then turned onto a dirt road. They followed it for another ten minutes until she stopped at a metal gate in a barbed-wire fence. "I'll be right back."

Colin watched as she walked to the gate, framed in the beam from the headlights, and unlocked the padlock on the chain holding it closed. She pushed it open, then scampered back to the car. "Where are we?" he asked.

"The old home place. Or what's left of it. Grandma grew up in the country, and Grandpa figured she wouldn't be happy in town, so he bought this farm as a wedding present." Michelle drove through the gate and a short distance down an overgrown road, stopping in front of an old tumbledown house. "He owned the lumberyard and didn't know a thing about farming." She laughed softly and turned off the engine. "But he loved his woman. And because she loved him and didn't want him to be disappointed, it took her two years to tell him that she had always wanted to live in town."

Michelle opened the sun roof, smiling when moonlight drifted in. "Here you are, sir. Quiet, moonlight, and stars to boot. Of course, we'll also freeze in about half an hour."

"Not if we snuggle." He laid his arm across the back of the seat.

"True." She slid across the seat to his side and leaned her head against his shoulder. "Bet you can't see a kazillion stars in the city."

Colin settled his arm around her and looked up through

the sun roof, resting the side of his face against her hair. "Nope. Only the biggest and brightest. So your grandparents moved to town. Did they sell most of the farm then?"

"Yes, but they decided to keep twenty acres in case times got bad. They figured they could survive if they had a bit of land to raise a cow, chickens, and a garden. Grandma said they never used it except for picnics. The house wasn't much to start with and fell apart before long. But I love it here. Sometimes I bring out a tent and camp overnight."

"By yourself?"

"Hey, I can put up a tent." Michelle tried to tickle his ribs but gave up when she discovered it didn't affect him. "Someday I'd like to buy a little trailer. Maybe build a cabin."

He had spent considerable time thinking about where this relationship might lead. Marriage was the ultimate possibility. He was tired of being alone, ready for love and a wife. Michelle touched his heart in a way no one else had. The time he spent with her, whether on the phone or in person, only strengthened that feeling, almost as if second by second their hearts were bonding into one.

Worry nudged him. Living in Dallas and continuing his job with Bosman was a logical part of his plan. He had an excellent salary and benefits, with many advancement opportunities. She could move her dress shop there and do well, probably better than in Sidell. Now Colin realized he had never once really considered her feelings or needs. He had looked at everything from his perspective. From her point of view, moving to Dallas might not be logical at all.

"Don't you get lonely out here?"

"Sometimes. But it can be the same at home or in a crowd.

Loneliness is not a place but a condition. It's being without someone."

Shifting so he could see her face, Colin trailed his fingers along her cheek. "When I'm with you—even when I talk to you on the phone—I don't feel alone."

"I know. It's the same for me."

He lowered his head slowly, giving her time to turn away, but Michelle closed her eyes and lifted her face to his. He kissed her gently, reverently, awed by the depth of longing welling up in his heart. When he raised his head, the moonlight caught the sparkle of tears on her lashes. "Sweetheart?"

"You make me feel..." She looked away and shook her head.

"Loved?"

"Yes," she whispered. "But how can you be in love with me? It's too soon."

"I'm not so sure about that." When she met his gaze, he smiled ruefully. "I'm not sure about much of anything. You've turned my whole world upside down."

"Ditto."

He laughed, relieved to see her smile. "I'm not complaining."

"Neither am I."

Even in the moonlight, he saw the yearning in her eyes, the need to love and be loved, the reflection of his heart. "Michelle, do you believe in love at first sight?"

"I don't think so. Attraction on several levels, certainly. After talking to you in Dallas I couldn't get you out of my mind, either. Now it's worse. I find myself daydreaming right in the middle of helping a customer."

"Good. I don't feel so bad about the two experiments I botched this week." He brushed her lips with his, then deepened the kiss. Elated by her response, he held her close, sharing the wonder of blossoming passion. Several minutes later, he reluctantly drew back. Holding her tenderly, he whispered, "How about love at second sight?"

"Maybe," she said, slightly breathless. "A definite maybe."

"I can live with that." Colin smiled. *For now.*

Seven

Michelle decided that Colin truly was a romantic, even
though he denied seeing himself in that light. He had dis-
creetly held her hand at Buckley Community Church
Sunday morning as he listened intently to the sermon. On
Monday, he sent her roses—eleven red and one white. On
Tuesday, it was chocolates. Wednesday, a blues album.
Thursday, a teddy bear wearing an "I need a hug" button. Plus
he called every night and sometimes during the day. No man
had ever showered her with such attention. She delighted in it.

He planned to drive out Friday night, so she was happy and
excited about seeing him. He didn't call during the day, nor did
any special gift arrive. She hadn't really expected him to send
another present, but she was disappointed he hadn't called
because she didn't know when to expect him.

As Michelle closed the shop, melancholy settled over her.
She locked the door and walked down the block toward the
parking lot where she had left her car. With the hood of her
winter coat pulled forward to shield her face against the sharp,
cold wind, she almost didn't see the maroon Chevelle sitting

beside a little corner park. Her heart leaped when she thought she recognized the car, but disappointment instantly followed when she realized Colin wasn't in it.

She scanned the area. There was no one around except a cowboy leaning against a building sheltered from the wind, hands jammed in his pockets, the collar of his sheepskin-lined leather coat turned up, and his hat pulled low against the cold. Her gaze skimmed past him, then halted. There was something very familiar about that cowboy. She looked again, and he edged the front brim of his hat upward. "Colin?" she whispered.

When he smiled and moved forward, she ran to him. He met her in the small park, sweeping her up in a hug, then set her down on the ground without saying a word. She started to speak, but he touched her lips with one cold finger and looked upward. Her gaze followed his. Above them in a leafless mesquite tree grew a huge clump of mistletoe. "'Tis the season of joy and gladness," he said softly.

Her heart singing with happiness, she slid her arms around his neck and kissed him with a swell of emotion that went far beyond joy and gladness. *Love? No, it can't be. But it is.*

In spite of the cold, the kiss lingered. Finally, Colin raised his head and grinned. "You're glad to see me."

"You know I am." Michelle stepped back and gave him the once-over. "But look at you. I almost didn't recognize you." His clothes were clean but not new. "What did you do, go to a vintage Western wear store?"

He laughed and propelled her toward his car. "No, ma'am. I bought it all new, way back when. Cousin Nick was a farm kid who knew the advantages and comfort of jeans and a good pair of boots. Some of it rubbed off on me. Not that I 'go country' every weekend, but the mood strikes occasionally." He opened the car door and helped her inside, then hurried around to his side. "I thought your last customer was never going to leave. My fingers are about frozen." He started the car and turned on the heater full blast, rubbing his hands together.

"Here, let me." Michelle pulled off her gloves and rubbed first one of his hands then the other. "Why weren't you wearing gloves?"

"Didn't think I'd be out there that long. I've got a pair in the back seat, but I don't like wearing them when I drive a long way. Besides, I figured gloves would hamper my style." He leaned over, framing her face with both hands, kissing her tenderly.

"I do like your style," she murmured when he straightened. "And your clothes aren't bad, either. Do you want to follow me home?"

"Anytime." He grinned mischievously. "I called your grandmother when I got here. She said pizza would be fine with her as long as I got one with everything on it."

"She loves the stuff."

He pulled in next to her car in the parking lot. She started it, then hopped back in his until hers warmed up. They drove to Buckley, stopping at the Pizza Hut to pick up their supper. After they ate, Michelle built a fire in the fireplace insert while Colin tossed a ball to Shade. They spent the next hour chatting with Hetty until she picked up a novel from the table beside her easy chair and headed for her bedroom.

"I'm going to read awhile, dears, but it won't bother me if you have the television on." She winked at Michelle. "And it won't bother me if you leave it off, either. Good night."

They laughed and settled down on the couch side by side. Colin flipped the TV channels with the remote, but they decided there wasn't anything interesting on. Turning off the lights, they watched the flames dance through the glass in the insert. With his arm around her and her head resting on his shoulder, Colin stretched his legs out on the wide hassock. Michelle kicked off her shoes and curled her legs up on the couch.

"This is nice," he said quietly. "Sure beats being home by myself."

"And working on whatever you brought home from the office."

He chuckled softly, sifting his fingers slowly through her hair. "I haven't done that much these last couple of weeks. My evenings are spent on the phone."

"Is it causing a problem at work?" She cuddled a little closer, resting her hand on his chest. *This isn't nice; it's heaven.*

"No, although my boss asked if I was feeling all right. Seems he'd noticed me daydreaming a few times." He smiled and dropped a tiny kiss on her forehead. "Several times, actually. So I told him about you."

"Oh?" She looked up at him with a teasing smile. "What did you tell him?"

"That I'd met the most beautiful, intelligent, wonderful woman in the world, and that she's crazy about me. He didn't believe it. Said no woman like you would be interested in a nerd like me."

"Well, a lot he knows. The big dummy. You're not a nerd."

"So does that mean you're crazy about me?"

Michelle blinked, then laughed. "You crafty character." She ran her finger lightly along his jaw. "I guess you could say that."

"So will you tell him?"

"Me? When?"

"Next Saturday night when you go to the company Christmas dinner with me. It's actually a banquet. They give out employee awards and make speeches. It's a fancy affair. I don't always go, but I'd like to show you off and have you meet the people I work with. I'll pay your way—airfare, motel, meals, anything you need."

It was clearly very important to him. *And it should be,* she reminded herself. *He has accomplished so much, and his work can benefit so many.* If their relationship was going to lead to something lasting, she had to be willing to share his interests, his world. She loved Buckley, but she had lived in a big city as a girl and knew life could be good there. It would be hard to move her store, yet she could do it.

But what about Grandma? This concern was troubling her more and more. Hetty wouldn't want to move. She had lived in Buckley all her life. If she did agree to go, she wouldn't be happy, which wouldn't be good for her health. No matter what Michelle felt for Colin, she would never leave her grandmother in the care of someone else. Michelle loved her too much, owed her too much. *If only he could be happy here.* Judging from his reaction to helping Karen at the soup supper and his quick rejection of Mr. Findley's suggestion about buying the pharmacy, she feared that was an impossible dream.

She swallowed hard, her mind in turmoil. She could do this

much for him and pray that God would show her a way to resolve the situation so that no one else would be hurt or have to make sacrifices. "I'd be honored to go with you," she said, forcing a smile, but she had to look away as his face filled with joy.

Colin arrived at Michelle's the next morning at eight, bringing fresh cinnamon rolls from the bakery at Greene's Grocery. She scrambled eggs and they ate a leisurely breakfast before driving down to the church to help distribute the things collected in the toy drive.

A line was forming outside the building when they arrived, although the doors weren't open yet. Colin was amazed at the array of items available. No age group was overlooked, from rattles and small stuffed crib toys for the babies all the way to makeup, earrings, T-shirts, and baseball caps for the teenagers. Many of the toys were used but in excellent condition; an equal number of gifts, especially those for the older kids, were new. Most things were displayed on several long tables, but the bigger items, such as tricycles and bikes, were set up in an area off to one side.

Unsure of the procedure, Colin stood in the background to watch and see how he could help. Some of the church members were outside to keep an eye on the small group of children who had come with their parents. Michelle's friend Dawn and several others were stationed behind the display tables to replace items as they were taken, and still others stood casually a short distance from the door.

Michelle gave him a smile as she walked over to open the main outside door to the fellowship hall. She paused, glanced back at those inside the room to make sure they were ready, then pulled it open.

Trying not to be obvious, Colin watched the people as they came into the room. Generally, they moved quietly, their expressions hesitant but with a glimmer of hope in their eyes as the desire to give their children something special for Christmas outweighed their pride. Michelle greeted each person warmly, directing them to those who could help find the things they needed.

Colin soon found his niche, carrying boxes and some of the larger items out to the cars. Loading a bike in the back of a beat-up station wagon, his heart was touched by the tears of joy brimming in the mother's eyes as she thanked him for at least the fourth time. He received the same kind of blessing over and over during the morning and knew this was a type of project he wanted to be involved in again.

A new work crew came in around one, so Michelle and Colin took their leave. As they walked to the car, they shared some of their experiences of the morning. He opened the car door and pulled her against his side, holding her close. "Sometimes we don't know how blessed we are."

When she met his gaze, his heart did a double back flip at the tender glow in her beautiful green eyes. The golden flecks seemed to sparkle in the sun. "I have a good idea," she said softly.

After a drive in the country, Colin dropped her off at her house so she could rest a little and change clothes. They were going to dinner in Sidell, then they planned to come home and decorate the Christmas tree. He looked forward to joining them for church in the morning, too, but for now, he had something else on his mind. He drove downtown and parked in front of the drugstore, staring up at the old building.

Going inside, he took a seat at the soda fountain counter and ordered a Dr. Pepper. Sipping his drink, he swiveled on the stool and let his gaze skim over the store. It was much smaller than the drugstores he was used to, yet seemed well stocked with non-prescription medicines and other health aids, cosmetics and grooming supplies, and a small section of gift items and greeting cards. There were plenty of customers, just as there had been the other time he had dropped by.

Colin looked up, reading the labels on various old bottles and jars lining the upper shelves, smiling at some of the touted benefits. He listened to talk of crops and cattle, aches and pains, minor illnesses and a few major ones. Mingled in were Christmas plans and anticipated visits from children or grandparents. He heard the customers greet the druggist as they neared the back of the store, and heard Mr. Findley call them each by name and ask about a husband or parent or if Johnny or Susie was home from college yet.

An ache filled Colin's heart, a desire to be so intertwined with others' lives that he would know about Uncle Joe's bunions or Henry's upcoming heart surgery or could suggest a specific cough syrup for Mrs. Smith's chest cold. His research was important but it was too impersonal. Being counted on to fill in for a doctor sometimes was frightening but not necessarily beyond his capabilities. The incident at the soup supper had shaken him, but he realized later that such a thing could happen at a park or in a grocery store or in a traffic jam. And he would have responded the same way.

He hung around the store, checking inventory, letting ideas run through his head, waiting until the other customers and even the employees left.

Mr. Findley locked up the pharmacy section and met Colin by the fountain. The older man sat down on a stool and took off his glasses, rubbing the bridge of his nose. "Somethin' on your mind, Colin?"

"Would you consider a short-term partnership?"

Mr. Findley slowly slid his glasses into place, his expression thoughtful. "Maybe. What do you have in mind?"

"Fifty-fifty for six months to a year so you could train me in running the place and help me get to know the people and their needs. Then I'd buy you out."

"I'd consider it. We'd have to talk numbers, of course."

"Think you could give me some idea this week of how much we're talking about?" asked Colin.

"I suppose I could. You plannin' on doing this soon?"

"I'm still thinking on it. If I decide to go ahead, it would be soon."

Mr. Findley slanted him a glance and smiled. "Let me know what she says."

Eight

❧

Colin led Michelle through the crowded banquet hall. "I think everybody who ever worked for Bosman must have come to the Christmas party. But you are by far the most gorgeous woman here. With your hair and eyes, that green velvet dress is perfect."

She smiled and squeezed his hand. "Thank you. But if one more drooling lab assistant or file clerk comes up and bats her baby blues at you, cooing about how fantastic you look—even if it is true—I'm going to dump a drink on her head." She wondered if his suit was custom-made; she didn't know how else he would have found one that exactly matched the gray rim around his dark blue eyes.

He laughed and stopped, pulling her close. "Jealous?"

"Yep. They're with you every day. I only see you on the weekend." She smoothed a stray lock of hair on his forehead.

"Sweetheart, I don't even notice them. I'm too busy thinking about you."

Michelle raised an eyebrow and looked back at a curvaceous

blonde who had practically embraced him. "You can't tell me you don't notice her."

He followed her gaze. "Who?" Then laughed when she poked him in the stomach with her finger. He leaned close. "Well, she doesn't wear that getup to work. Lab coats are big and loose, you know."

"Somehow I doubt if hers are."

He smiled and cradled her face in his palm. "I may appreciate another woman's beauty, but you're the only one I want to kiss."

And he did. Gently and sweetly. She forgot all about the sultry blond and everybody else. When he slowly raised his head, she was too dazed to be embarrassed.

"You have no reason to be jealous, my love," he said softly.

A man walked up and slapped Colin on the back, breaking the spell. Michelle wanted to kick him in the shin with the pointed toe of her shoe.

"McCrea, I wouldn't have believed it if I hadn't seen it with my own eyes. How did you ever find such a beautiful woman?"

"He put an ad in the paper," Michelle said sweetly, batting her eyelashes at Colin and tucking her arm around his. Colin grinned. "And his natural charm did the rest. Bye." She gave the man a saccharine smile and tugged Colin away.

He followed, chuckling. "Michelle, that was my boss."

"Oops." She giggled and looked over her shoulder at the man's puzzled expression. "Well, he's got lousy timing."

"True, but he's not a bad guy. Let's go back and I'll introduce you."

"Guess I have to, huh?"

"It would be polite." Colin escorted her back and introduced her to his boss. "Jack is head of the research department so I report directly to him."

"When he remembers to report, which hasn't been often lately." He smiled at Michelle. "Now I know why. Did he really put an ad in the paper?"

Michelle laughed and gave him the short version of how they met, then deftly changed the subject. "Colin told me a bit about his project. It must be very gratifying to know you've developed a drug that will save lives."

"It is, but mostly I'm grateful we came in under budget. This was Colin's baby, from the idea right down to the final formula. He's worked night and day to make it happen. I only wish I had more devoted employees like him. Colin is our golden boy, brightest scientist we have." He glanced toward the head table. "Oh, excuse me, I'm needed by the bigwigs. Don't leave early," he said, his tone serious.

Michelle glanced at Colin, surprised to see him frowning as Jack walked away. "What did he mean by that?"

"I don't know." He shrugged. "They're probably giving me a plaque for finishing up the project. Come on, let's find a seat."

A short time later, the master of ceremonies greeted the employees and guests and told corny jokes while the waiters served dinner.

Michelle noticed Colin seemed distracted and wasn't eating much. "What's wrong?"

"Huh? Oh, nothing." He poked the tasteless baked chicken. "Don't like rubber chicken."

"Try the veggies. They aren't bad."

He ate a couple of bites and put down his fork, his gaze focused on the people at the head table.

Michelle looked, too, watching the company president and another man glance at Colin as they talked intently. "There's something brewing."

"I vaguely recall hearing something about Jack moving up, but I was so busy finishing up the project and making plans for tonight that I didn't pay any attention."

"It's not Jack they keep staring at."

Colin squirmed, looking as if he were ready to make a quick getaway.

She leaned closer and took his hand. "Honey, what is it?"

Tenderness warmed his eyes. "That has a nice ring to it." His brow wrinkled in a light frown. "If Jack moves up, his job is open."

"Do you think you might get it? Do you even want it?"

"I don't know. I have as good a shot as anybody. It would be a lot different from what I'm doing now. More paperwork and administration, less time in the lab, although I could personally handle projects if I wanted to. The head of the department decides what projects to take to the board. Usually what he pushes is accepted.

"I have an idea for a pain reliever that I've wanted to work on for a couple of years. If I'm right, it'll be about as effective as morphine but with fewer side effects. If I were head of the department, I could probably get it on the agenda. I might not actually be in charge of the team, but at least someone would be working on it." He took a deep breath and exhaled slowly. "And being department head would mean a big raise in pay. A very big one."

He straightened and smiled, although she thought it seemed forced. "I'm probably worrying over nothing. Even if Jack does move up, there are a couple of other people who are a more likely choice."

The president stood and walked to the microphone. For the next fifteen minutes, he handed out plaques for various accomplishments, including one to Colin and his group for finishing the antibiotic project in record time and under budget. As Colin stood, he smiled at Michelle, his expression relieved, but she thought she caught a hint of disappointment in his eyes.

He walked up the steps to the head table, accepted the plaque from the company president, and thanked him as well as the team for a job well done.

As he turned to go, the distinguished, silver-haired president grinned at the audience and clamped his hand down on Colin's shoulder. "I'm not done with you, boy." A murmur of laughter flowed through the crowd.

Colin looked surprised and faced him, his expression growing wary.

"As most of you know, every year we choose an employee of the year. It is not an honor given lightly, especially since they also receive a five thousand dollar bonus. Employees are nominated by their department heads with detailed reasons for their recommendations. The final decision is made by the officers of the company. It was a unanimous decision this year. Ladies and gentlemen, Bosman Pharmaceuticals' Employee of the Year, Colin McCrea."

Michelle stood along with the rest of the crowd, clapping as hard as she could, her eyes brimming with joyful tears as her heart overflowed with pride and love. Stunned, Colin took the second plaque from the president, finally smiling when he handed him the bonus check.

The president moved aside, allowing Colin access to the microphone as the audience sat down. "Thank you, sir, and the other officers. I'd also like to thank my boss for nominating me." He stopped and caught his breath. "This is a big surprise, especially since it usually goes to a salesman." Everyone laughed. "I put in a lot of time on the project this year but I wasn't trying to win an award. I did it because the antibiotic was desperately needed and I believed in our product."

"You're my next sales rep," hollered one of the marketing supervisors, evoking more laughter.

Colin merely grinned and held up the check. "This will just about pay for all those extra hours." He looked straight at Michelle and winked. "And I think I know how to spend it. Thanks again."

Once more the president clamped a hand on Colin's shoulder. "Folks, we don't normally do things quite this way, but since Colin is already up here, and we're having so much fun, we decided to give him another surprise. Most of you have probably heard the rumor that Jack Forbes is moving up to vice president."

While he waited until the applause for Jack died down, trepidation slowly crept over Michelle. In a tiny corner of her heart, she had harbored a secret hope that Colin would fall in love not only with her but with Buckley as well.

"With Jack gone, we need someone to run the research department. Someone with vision and drive, who's not afraid of hard work. Colin, you're the one we want as head of research."

At Colin's grin, her hope died.

He said something to the president, causing the man to frown slightly, but his words were drowned out by applause. Michelle clapped, too, and plastered a smile on her face. Only God knew that her tears were both of joy and sorrow. Joy for recognition of his worth and the opportunities that lay in front of him. Sorrow because now she must choose between the two people she loved most.

He did not reach the table for several minutes because so many people wanted to shake his hand and congratulate him. When he finally got to Michelle, she gave him a big hug and a kiss. "I'm so proud of you."

He absently set the plaques on the table and searched her eyes. "But are you happy?"

"Of course. You deserve the award and the promotion." She looked away from his penetrating gaze. "It's a wonderful opportunity."

"Michelle, I told him—"

A waiter stepped up beside them, his expression solemn. "Excuse me, Mr. McCrea, ma'am. Are you Michelle Lane?"

"Yes." Michelle's heart lurched. Her fingers convulsed around Colin's hand.

"There's a long distance call for you, ma'am. If you'll follow me, I'll take you to a phone."

Michelle nodded, unable to speak, and automatically reached for her small handbag.

"I'm with you, sweetheart." Colin scooped up the awards, keeping a firm grip on her hand.

They followed the man to a small office where he showed

her the phone and quietly left the room. Trembling, Michelle punched the button beside the blinking light and picked up the receiver. Colin stood beside her, his arm around her shoulders, giving her strength. "This is Michelle."

"Michelle, dear, this is Rosemary Garner. I thought I should let you know that Hetty fainted while she was here tonight." Michelle sank against the side of the desk, and Colin's grip tightened on her upper arm. "She wasn't unconscious long, but the paramedics felt she should go to the hospital for observation. We're here in Sidell with her at the hospital. The doctor wants to keep her here for a few days and run some tests. He said it may only be a matter of different medication, but he can't be sure at this point."

"Can I talk to her?"

"She's sleeping, dear. She's quite weak, I'm afraid, but she didn't want me to call you. She was afraid it would spoil the party. I told her of course it would, but that you needed to know."

Reaching for Colin's hand, Michelle choked down her fear and swallowed her tears. "Rosemary, is she going to be all right?"

"I don't know, Michelle. The doctor said he didn't believe her condition was life-threatening, but he did think she would do better if you were here."

"I'll get a flight as fast as I can."

"We'll stay here with her. If you can't get here until morning, I'm certain it will be fine."

"Thank you, Rosemary. Bye." Michelle dropped the receiver onto the phone.

Colin drew her into his gentle, yet firm embrace. "How is she?"

"She fainted. She's in the hospital. The doctor thinks he may only need to adjust her medication, but he's not sure." Michelle could no longer hold back the tears and buried her face against his shoulder, drawing comfort in his touch. He held her close, whispering encouragement as he rubbed her back and let her cry. A few minutes later, she drew in a shuddering breath and straightened. "I need to call the airlines."

"Let's go to my house. It's not far and it's quiet. We'll call the airlines and stop at your motel on the way to the airport. I'm going with you."

"But your new job—"

"Can wait. I have six weeks of vacation stacked up so it's not a problem. Come on, sweetheart, let's get you home." On the way out, Colin saw one of the chemists on his research team. He explained the situation and asked her to relay the information to Jack.

At his house, Michelle paced around the living room in her stocking feet while he called the two airlines that flew into Sidell. Neither one had another flight out that night. "We can catch a flight in the morning, but it won't get us there until almost eight." He glanced at his watch. It was a quarter past eleven. "If we drive, we can get there a good three hours sooner."

Michelle started for her shoes, but he put his hand on her arm, halting her. "Give me ten minutes to throw together some clothes and let my folks know where I'm going."

She nodded and sank down on the couch, closing her eyes, praying fervently. *Please God, let her be all right. Don't take her from me! I won't desert her, I promise!*

Colin came out of his bedroom a few minutes later, wearing casual clothes, carrying a suitcase and pillow. He grabbed a blanket throw from the couch and tossed it in the back seat with the pillow. When they stopped at the motel, he checked Michelle out while she changed clothes and gathered up her things.

He made the trip to Sidell over an hour faster than the speed limit allowed.

CHAPTER

Nine

❧

When Hetty woke up the next morning, Michelle and Colin were sitting side by side in two uncomfortable plastic chairs, holding hands, her head resting on his shoulder, his head nestled against her hair. Michelle dozed but Colin smiled as the elderly lady looked at them.

Hetty shook her head slowly and pushed a button, raising the head of her bed. "You two look like you've been rode hard and put up wet."

"Feel like it, too," Colin said. "Good mornin', Grandma."

Michelle opened her eyes and blinked, flinching as she straightened. When she saw her grandmother sitting up in bed, she jumped up and hugged her. "How are you feeling?"

"A little puny. Never could sleep worth a hoot in a hospital bed."

Michelle smiled. "You've been sleeping fine since we got here." She took hold of her grandmother's hand. "You gave me a scare, lady."

"I didn't want Rosemary to call you, but you know how

stubborn she can be." Hetty blinked back a tear. "Guess I scared myself, too. I'm sorry I spoiled your weekend but I am glad you're here." She looked at Colin as he joined Michelle by the bed. "Both of you."

"I wasn't about to let her come by herself." He patted Hetty's hand and winked. "Besides, I don't let just anybody drive my car. Not that far, at least."

Hetty smiled and closed her eyes. "I'm a little tired. Think I'll rest until they bring breakfast."

Michelle sent Colin a worried glance. "We'll be right here, Grandma."

"Thank you, dear. Makes me feel better already."

Hetty perked up after breakfast and insisted that Colin and Michelle should go down to the cafeteria to eat. When they returned, the doctor was there and Hetty introduced them to the medical center's new cardiologist.

"Miss Lane, I was just telling your grandmother that things are looking good, except for her potassium level. Her body isn't assimilating it from her food so I'm putting her on potassium supplements, four capsules a day. It's very important that you take them, Mrs. Lane. Potassium is crucial to keep the heart functioning properly, especially one as weak as yours. If the level drops too low, your heart will stop."

"I reckon I can take some pills without too much trouble."

The doctor smiled. "Most people think I'm giving them horse pills, but I'm sure you can get them down. If I dismiss you this morning, will you promise to go home and rest? No work. No stress. Otherwise, I'll keep you here."

Hetty snorted. "All I've done for months is rest."

"Now, Grandma, that's not quite true," Michelle admonished.

"Close enough."

Colin laughed and tugged lightly on a bouncy white curl. "Not nearly close enough from what I've seen. We'll keep her in line, doc. Won't let her lift a finger except to eat and take pills."

"Good. Take her home before she drives the nurses crazy." The doctor winked at Hetty and smiled at Michelle as he left the room.

Wanting to catch Rosemary before she left for church, Colin called her from a pay phone down the hall with the good news while Michelle helped her grandmother dress. Before noon, they had Hetty home and in bed asleep.

Colin pointed Michelle toward her bedroom. "Go get some rest. I'll catch a snooze here on the couch. We'll hear her if she needs anything."

Hetty improved rapidly, and by Wednesday, Colin felt he could go back to Dallas for a few days without causing a strain on Michelle. He was actually more worried about her than her grandmother. Since bringing Hetty home from the hospital, the love of his life had been trying to distance herself from him. And he thought he knew why.

He loaded the breakfast dishes in the dishwasher and cornered Michelle in the laundry room as she threw a load of towels in the washer. Sneaking up behind her, he put his arms around her waist and kissed her cheek. For a heartbeat, she relaxed against him as if cherishing his touch, then she straightened and reached for the box of detergent. Colin moved to one side, leaning against the dryer. "How are you holding up?"

"Fine. The girls at the store are handling everything without me. Grandma's so frisky this morning I figured I'd better get the wash going before she decided to do it."

"I'm glad she's still improving. I'm heading home this morning for a few days. Need to talk to Jack and pick up some clothes and Christmas presents, but I'll be back by Christmas Eve. Sooner if you need me."

She studied the back of the detergent box as if it were the first time she'd ever seen it. "There's no need to come back right away. Your family will be expecting you for Christmas."

"I'd rather spend Christmas with the woman I love."

Her gaze shot to his, and his heart almost broke at the agony he saw there. "Colin, don't talk of love."

"Why?"

"Because we can't be together." She turned away and hung her head, her fist pressed against her lips as if she were trying to hold the pain inside.

He reached for her, but she pulled away. "Michelle, I love you. We *can* have a wonderful life together."

She shook her head. "Your life is in Dallas. Mine is here. Grandma could never leave Buckley. The stress of moving might kill her. Even if it didn't, she'd be miserable." Michelle looked at him, her eyes bright with tears, her expression fierce with determination. "And I won't leave her, not ever. I was lost after my parents died. In spite of her own grief, she saved me. With her love, understanding, and patience, she pulled me out of that black hole and gave me a life worth living. She needs me now and I won't desert her." Her voice broke and she looked away. "Not even for you."

"I'm not asking you to, sweetheart. We can make it work."

She shook her head. "No, we can't. Your home, family, and job are in Dallas. Mine are here. You can't tackle a new job there during the week and commute out here on the weekends. It would doom our relationship before we even had a chance to make it work."

"I told Jack on Monday that I'm not taking the promotion."

"Colin, how can you turn it down? I saw your face when they offered it to you. You were overjoyed."

He smiled. "I was pleased because they offered it. It's nice to know they think I'm capable. But I told Mr. Bosman that night I'd have to think about it."

"Colin, it's a great opportunity, not only because of the money. You could get your pain reliever developed and help guide the direction of the company. You have a vision for what people need, not just for what will make money."

"If I took the promotion, I'd have to work even more hours than before. I don't want that. I don't care about money, and I can always give them my notes on the pain reliever and let someone else research it. I want a life outside of Bosman Pharmaceuticals." He put his arms around her, thanking God when she didn't move away. "I want a wife and kids and to spend my evenings with them instead of locked up in a lab or an office. I've done my good deed for mankind; now I want to do a good deed for myself."

"You can't just walk away from the opportunity."

"Watch me. I have other projects in mind." He drew her into his embrace. She held him as if she couldn't bear for him to go. "Michelle, do you love me?"

"Yes." She raised her head, meeting his gaze. "With all my heart. But I can't see how—"

He interrupted her with a kiss, one meant to be light and quick that became passionate and lengthy. When they finally broke apart, he leaned his forehead against hers. "Sweetheart, you're tired and a bit distraught. Do you trust me?"

"Yes," she replied with no hesitation.

"Then relax. Go shopping or soak in a bubble bath or anything else you want to do. Now send me off with another kiss. The sooner I leave, the quicker I can get back."

"Michelle, dear, why don't you just go sit on the porch and wait for him instead of peeking out the window every two minutes?" Hetty smiled at her granddaughter from her easy chair. "He said he'd be back on Christmas Eve. It's only noon."

"I know, Grandma, but I can't wait to see him. I want to hug and kiss him until he can't stand up."

Hetty laughed. "I'd like to see that. I take it you're thinking a little straighter since you got some sleep?"

Michelle plopped down on the couch. "In some ways. I love him and want to marry him, but I'm not convinced that moving you to Dallas is such a good idea, even if you did volunteer to do it."

"I'll manage fine."

Michelle noticed the strain in Hetty's smile. "Well, I'm not sure I want to do it. I like Buckley and having my store in Sidell. I don't know. Maybe we could make a marriage by commute work."

"Perhaps Colin would like to live here. He seems to enjoy

the people and the town."

"The night he helped Karen at the soup supper, he was so adamant about preferring to work in the lab rather than with people that I didn't hold out much hope. When I saw how admired and respected he is at Bosman, I gave up hoping."

"Never give up hope, child. If you seek God's will in all things, you'll be surprised how he will bless you."

"I know, Grandma, but I forget sometimes." Michelle heard a car and ran to the window. "He's here!" When she ran outside to meet him, he swept her up in a bear hug.

"How's my woman?" he asked, setting her feet lightly on the ground.

"Fine now that you're here. How's my man?"

He grinned and gave her a kiss. "Wonderful. Terrific. Fantastic. Shall I go on?" He laughed and opened the trunk of his car, filling her arms with presents.

"Goodness!"

"I'm in such a great mood, I bought anything that caught my eye. Got a good discount on some of it." He grinned. "I know the owner real well." He helped her carry the packages inside and put them under the tree, adding the nativity scene he'd bought at Memory Lane on his first trip to Buckley. He looked at it for a minute, smiling tenderly. When he glanced up at Michelle, his eyes were misty. "The greatest gift of all," he said softly.

"Amen," she whispered, knowing he wasn't talking about the porcelain figures but the living Savior.

He walked over and gave Hetty a big kiss. "How's my number two girl today?"

"Feeling like I want to get out of the house. How about taking me and your number one girl around town to see the Christmas decorations?"

"Be glad to. Grab your coat and I'll be right with you after I get a drink of water."

Michelle looked from Hetty to Colin, noting the sparkle in their eyes. They were up to something, but she decided not to say anything that might spoil their fun.

Since his car was a two-door, Michelle climbed in the back seat, giving the front one to Hetty. They drove around the residential part of town admiring all the Christmas lights and decorated trees shining joyfully through the windows.

Colin stopped near a house practically covered with lights. "Anybody want a snack?" He leaned over the back seat and pulled three boxes of Cracker Jacks from a paper sack on the seat. "I don't know why I bought these crazy things. Guess I was hungry for popcorn balls." He handed Michelle a box. "Closest thing I could get."

She laughed. "I haven't had these since I was a kid but I used to love them."

"Then be a kid again and enjoy." He smiled tenderly and turned back around in the seat, giving a box to Hetty.

They drove downtown, munching on Cracker Jacks and laughing about some of the prizes they found when they were younger. "I saved some of the tin ones," said Hetty. "Now I understand they're quite valuable."

"We'll have to save these. Who knows, maybe someday they'll be worth something," Michelle said. When Colin choked, she frowned and pounded him on the back. "You all right?"

He nodded, blinking the moisture from his eyes. "Okay," he wheezed. He coughed again and cleared his throat. "Lots of last minute shoppers."

"What's going on at the drugstore?" Michelle pointed to the crowd of people on both sides of the street. Two men were up on ladders in front of the pharmacy. Mr. Findley was standing down below. "Looks like they're hanging up a banner or something."

"I'll park and we can go watch."

Michelle glanced at Colin, catching the twinkle in his eyes. Something was definitely going on. *Oh, Father, if only…no, I can't wish for selfish things. I'll only be disappointed.* She laid her box of Cracker Jacks on the seat as she climbed out of the car.

Colin appeared at her side seconds later.

"Must be a sign of some kind," said a man standing nearby.

Michelle looked up as the workmen stepped back and tossed Mr. Findley a rope. He tugged, pulling off the plastic cover that hid the sign. Michelle gasped as she read the large black letters edged in gold: *Findley-McCrea's Apothecary.*

She stared at Colin. "You're his partner?"

"I am." His grin turned to laughter as she threw her arms around his neck. "And in six months or so, it will become McCrea's Apothecary."

Mr. Findley walked up and shook his hand. "Hopefully there will be two or three generations of McCreas to carry on the tradition."

"Hopefully." At the sound of a small airplane, Colin glanced up. "Here comes our big community announcement."

"There's more?" asked Michelle.

His expression grew tender. "Yes."

The plane circled overhead pulling a banner that read: *Shop Findley-McCrea's Apothecary for after Christmas bargains.* The crowd laughed and pointed at the sign.

"Oh, look, there's a second plane," called a bystander.

Michelle shaded her eyes with her hand as traffic slowed to a crawl and the other plane and banner came into view: *Love Wanted. One soul mate. Lifetime Contract.*

"And another one!" cried a woman across the street. The traffic stopped completely.

Tears pooled in Michelle's eyes and cascaded down her cheeks as she read the last banner: *Michelle, I love you. Will you marry me?*

Her heart overflowing with love, she looked at Colin, certain that God had brought them together. "Yes, my love. I'll marry you."

Everyone around them burst into applause. Horns blared and people cheered. Hetty and Mr. Findley beamed.

Colin wrapped Michelle in his embrace and touched her lips in a kiss filled with love. He looked into her eyes and smiled. Stepping back slightly, he handed her the Cracker Jack box. "You didn't get to your prize."

Michelle felt the grin start at one side of her face and slowly spread to the other. "You didn't."

"I did." He laughed as she dug in the box, tossing Cracker Jacks all over the street.

Michelle found the prize packet and eased it from the box. "It's all sealed up," she said in amazement. "How did you do that?"

"I went to the company. The manager had no problem

substituting a real engagement ring for a fake one." His voice grew husky. "Open it."

"No, you'd better. I'm so weepy and shaky, I'd probably drop it."

Colin chuckled. "You don't think I'm shaking?" He carefully ripped open the packet and slipped the diamond ring on her finger. "I do love you."

"I know. And I love you, too." She looped her arms around his neck, kissing him with all the love in her heart until Hetty stepped up and hugged them both.

"Sorry to interrupt, but I just couldn't wait any longer. I'm so happy for you!"

"Grandma, did you know about this?"

"Just about the drugstore." She smiled first at Michelle, then at Colin, patting his cheek. "Such a clever boy. I didn't have a clue about the rest of it."

"Me, either," said Mr. Findley. "Come on inside, Hetty. I'll buy you a cup of coffee."

"Make that tea, and you're on."

"Decaffeinated," Colin and Michelle said in unison, watching them walk away.

Michelle grinned at Colin and looked up as the three planes circled the town again. "Afraid I might miss it the first time?"

"I wasn't taking any chances." He laughed and leaned against his car, holding her gently.

"I think I'm going to enjoy being married to you."

"Yeah? How come?"

"Life will never be boring." She kissed him lightly. "Merry Christmas, love."

"Merry Christmas, sweetheart."

Someone came out of the drugstore and the music of "Hark the Herald Angels Sing" filled the air. Colin smiled and draped his arm around Michelle's shoulders as they started across the street. "And thank you, Lord Jesus, for a love even greater than ours."

Also by Sharon Gillenwater:

Love Story

Antiques

Look for her next release: Summer 1996

GIFT OF LOVE

AMANDA MACLEAN

Prologue

❧

The setting sun was just melting into Sapphire Lake when Sadie Grayson pulled her unruly thicket of blond hair into a ponytail. With a mischievous grin, she challenged Blake Adams to a race—just as she'd done every summer of their childhood friendship.

"This year I'll take you in seven-and-a-half minutes flat!" she tossed over her shoulder as she ran to the water.

"You do, and it'll be the first time—" Blake yelled, plunging in after her.

They splashed through the water, diving like porpoises, swimming madly to the far side of the cove.

A few minutes later Sadie emerged the winner, only to have Blake grab her ankle. She yelped, tripping him as he tried to gain a foothold in the sand. Laughing, he tumbled, then reached for Sadie's feet. She fell backward into the water, splashing and yelling.

Breathless, they finally collapsed on the sand, laughing into the sky, now ablaze in pinks and yellows and blues. Then Blake reached for Sadie's hands, pulling her to her feet. They strolled to a nearby dock and sat to watch the sky turn navy above the lake. Soon, a full moon rose in the east, casting a silver path across softly rippling waves. Emerging spangles of starlight formed a canopy above them, and Sadie thought she'd never seen such beauty.

"How about your dreams, Sadie?" Blake said suddenly, gazing up at the stars. "Still the same?" He turned to look in her face.

Sadie swallowed hard, his words reminding her that summer was almost over, that they would soon leave for their second year in college—at universities three thousand miles apart.

Studying his expression, she wondered if Blake felt the same sense of loss. They'd been best friends—and rivals—for as long as she could remember. In the moonlight, his clear green eyes were pale and bright. A brief shadow seemed to cross his face. "Yes," she finally said. "My dreams are the same."

"U.C.L.A. film school—?"

"Yes."

"Then Hollywood."

Sadie nodded. "Or New York." She considered his expression, then burst out laughing, trying to lighten their somber mood. "Blake, you've known forever about my plans. Don't look so pained. I don't do that to you when you talk about photographing the Amazon rain forest. And you've been dreaming of doing that since we were twelve."

He grinned, shaking his head slowly. "I know, Sadie. I know. But I'm going to miss you."

"It's not as if we won't see each other again. I mean, we can

190

write, visit each other from time to time—" Her voice broke off. Blake's family was moving to the east coast in three weeks. He would be at Dartmouth—a continent away from Cedar Creek, their little hometown in the Sierra Nevadas.

They fell silent, each lost in thought. After a few minutes, Blake stood and took her hand. Laughing softly as they spoke of shared memories, they walked slowly back around the cove, feeling the lapping water on their bare feet.

Blake suddenly stopped, turning Sadie toward him. He cupped her chin and tilted her face, his eyes searching hers. Then he kissed her lips, a gentle, lingering kiss.

Around them rose the night music of frogs and crickets and owls. But all Sadie could hear was the beating of her heart. When Blake released her, she gazed up at him in wonder. He touched her cheek with the backs of his fingers, smiling into her eyes.

"Sadie—" he began, then abruptly stopped. Drawing a deep breath, he stared at her in the moonlight, as if trying to memorize the look of her, as if unwilling to let her go.

Sadie had known Blake for most of her life. Together they'd caught frogs, climbed trees, hunted for Indian arrowheads—even danced at school dances—but never before had he kissed her. And never before had Sadie seen this expression on his face.

Bewildered, she gazed up into his face, fighting the urge to touch his chiseled jaw. She drew in a breath. No, it couldn't be love. They were best friends. Love would ruin everything.

Blake seemed to sense her confusion. After a moment, he put his arm around her shoulders, steering her toward the car.

Three weeks later, his family moved to Vermont. Blake

moved with them. Years later someone told her he had joined the Peace Corps. But Sadie hadn't heard from him again.

One

Sadie Grayson's violet eyes widened in dismay as she surveyed the set she'd so meticulously designed. Hurriedly, she closed the double doors behind her, tossed her parka on a hook, brushed the snowflakes from her hair, and headed down the aisle of the tiny mountain church.

On the stage—where the carpenter, his back to Sadie, still noisily hammered—stood an ugly, crooked, out-of-proportion stable. The manger was too small, the angel platform too high. Sadie let out an exasperated breath. When she agreed to write the pageant, Pastor Michael had promised her an experienced carpenter. Experienced? This man obviously hadn't even bothered to look at her plans.

He set down his hammer and reached for a box of nails. With his other hand he raked his fingers through a shock of dark hair that fell across his forehead. Then, as if sensing her presence, the man turned slightly, his green eyes meeting her gaze.

Sadie gasped. "Blake—" she whispered. "Blake Adams?"

A slow smile crept across his face. "Sadie?" He stood, dusting off his jeans. "Sadie," he repeated. He didn't seem surprised to see her.

Sadie quickly climbed the stairs to the platform. Blake caught her hand in both of his, laughing softly as he helped her to the top.

For a moment he just stood gazing into her eyes, and Sadie felt her stomach turn a flip. No, actually a cartwheel. But then, Blake Adams had always seemed to stir up a tumble of astonishing emotions inside her.

She smiled into his eyes. "Blake, how long has it been—" Retrieving her hand, Sadie tucked an errant blond curl behind an ear. "Ten years? Twelve?"

"Ah, let's see." He looked skyward for a moment, then back to her, grinning. "Ten years, six months and eight days."

Sadie chuckled. "You always were concerned with detail."

"And you always were as beautiful as you are right now."

Sadie felt herself blush—as if once again the teenage girl he referred to. "Ah, shucks..." she said, grinning. "You didn't turn out half bad yourself, Blake."

Sadie leaned against a sawhorse, crossing her ankles, and taking in everything about the man standing before her. He was powerfully built, with big shoulders, arms, and hands, though his tapered fingers looked more like those of an artist than a carpenter. His high cheekbones gave his face a chiseled look, and his eyes were as green as the pines just beyond the church windows.

"I had no idea you lived in Cedar Creek—" Sadie began.

"I don't." Blake settled onto a bale of hay near the manger.

He pulled a loose piece of hay from the bundle and chewed on one end.

She squinted at him. "Then what are you doing here?"

"I'm here on assignment."

"Assignment?"

"I'm a photojournalist."

"Then why—?" Her gaze took in the set.

"Oh, this? I was in Pastor Michael's office the day he'd been turned down by two carpenters and three handymen. I felt sorry for him and volunteered to help."

"And your assignment?" she prompted. She'd give him the bad news about rebuilding the set later.

"I freelance. *Contemporary Christian Women*—*CCW*—sent out word via Internet that they were looking for a journalist to cover this, ah—" He hesitated, a note of sarcasm creeping into his voice. "—this media event. I happened to spot the notice one night and shot off an e-mail. Of course I mentioned that Cedar Creek is my hometown—that my father actually helped build this church. My credentials plus my childhood connection with you cinched the assignment." He gave her a one-sided grin.

"So you knew that I'd be here?"

"It was in the posted notice: Emmy-winning screenwriter Sadie Grayson to journey back to her Christian roots—direct a Christmas pageant in the mountain village church of her youth—network TV in tow."

"Why would *CCW* want the pageant covered?"

"I assume for the same reason Hunter Shaw decided it was worthy of filming—human interest."

"Hunter Shaw had other reasons."

Blake cocked his head and narrowed his eyes. "How do you mean?" He still nibbled the piece of hay.

"He didn't want us to be apart for the holidays." She laughed lightly, though it was an effort. "He decided that a 'human interest' piece for network TV, live at Christmas, would tug at middle America's heartstrings. He's got connections. He pitched it to the right people. They jumped at the idea." She shrugged. "So here we are."

Was it her imagination, or did Blake look disappointed? "So the two of you are an—an item?"

"He would like for us to be." She thought about Hunter's lean, patrician good looks. Quite opposite from the brawny dark-haired Blake Adams.

"I see." The light in his eyes dimmed. Blake continued. "I know you're going to be busy during the next few weeks, but I'd like to stay on the sidelines, shoot you and the kids in rehearsal as the pageant progresses. Of course, there will be interviews—with you, the kids, the townsfolk. But I'll try not to be a nuisance."

"I've never known you to be a nuisance, Blake. Well, at least not more than a few times," Sadie added, smiling.

Sadie tilted her head, gazing at the man before her, and thinking about the last time she saw him. "You never told me goodbye, Blake," she said.

He lifted one dark eyebrow.

"I thought we were friends—and you simply disappeared."

He still didn't comment.

"We'd been part of each other's lives for years—and all at

196

once you were gone. You never called or wrote." Her eyes searched his. "I missed you, Blake."

For a moment neither spoke, then Blake dismissed her words with a shrug. "I was just eighteen. And, well, you know kids… who knows why they do what they do?"

"You were no ordinary kid, Blake—"

He interrupted before she could go on. "Tell me about your family, Sadie. Your sisters, your mom and dad."

For a few minutes they updated each other on their families' activities—Blake's still living in the East, and Sadie's now in Northern California.

"What about you, Blake? Are most of your writing assignments like this?"

He grinned. "Hardly. I took this for some very different reasons." He didn't elaborate.

Sadie waited for him to go on.

His expression sobered. For a moment he didn't speak but turned toward a nearby window. Sadie followed his gaze. Outside, clouds had settled to the ground, covering nearby pines with a ghostlike light. A light snow sifted a thin layer of white onto the bare oak branches and pines.

Blake turned back to Sadie. "My assignments are usually overseas," he began.

"Sounds glamorous."

"It's not." An expression of sadness, maybe despair, shadowed his face, then quickly disappeared. He smiled again. "More about all that later. I'd rather hear about the pageant. I've heard tryouts are tonight."

Sadie nodded. "If the weather doesn't keep everyone away."

Blake threw back his head and laughed heartily. "Ah, my dear. You've obviously not been in town long. This place has come alive with excitement—network TV on its way, big name producer Hunter Shaw, his son Alec, a TV star in his own right…not to mention the hometown-girl-who-makes-good, Ms. Sadie Grayson, screenwriter extraordinaire." Sadie noticed that a hint of disapproval had crept into his voice.

"You're being sarcastic, Blake."

"Oh, no, Sadie. I'm just letting you know how the townsfolk feel about it. People who haven't been in this church in decades simply want to be in the audience." He flashed her a lopsided grin. "They want to smile at Uncle Henry back East when the camera pans."

"Sounds like a circus in the making."

"Worse, probably."

Again Sadie wondered at his tone of disapproval. "But then, if it brings people out to church, what's the harm?"

"Maybe you're right," he said, now a bit humbly. "Pastor Michael says that church membership is lower than ever—twenty-five or so. Even less than that for Sunday services."

"See—" Sadie said triumphantly with a slight flip of her hair. "Maybe the pageant is just the boost the church needs—maybe the whole town will show up for the performance."

"I think you have no idea what you're in for, Sadie."

"And neither do you, dear Blake." She grinned at him.

"What do you mean?"

She crooked her finger. "Follow me, dear heart."

He stood, dusting off bits of hay from his jeans, and walked with her toward the set.

She drew in a breath, looking up at the ugly structure. "It's all wrong, Blake," she finally said. "It'll never work for the camera angles. The color's too drab. It just doesn't work."

"It doesn't work?"

Slightly annoyed that he didn't see her point, she hurried on impatiently. "It's got to pull in the audience—touching them with its simplicity and richness." Again she squinted up at the stable. "It just doesn't do anything for me...I don't think it will for anyone else either." Aware that Blake was staring at her, not the set, she turned to him. He seemed amused.

"You expect me to rebuild it?"

"Would you mind?"

"What makes you think it would turn out any better a second time?"

She shrugged. "Maybe this time you'll follow my design."

"You don't think I did the first time?"

Her eyes widened. "Did you?"

He laughed. "I couldn't make heads or tails of it—"

"I know that you're here on an assignment, and that I'm asking a lot of you, Blake. I don't even know if you've got the time..."

He touched her arm. "Don't worry about it, Sadie. I'll see if I can get some volunteers to help me. I know that we've only got a few weeks, but it should go fast." His eyes met hers. "Especially now that you're here to explain the plans in a little more detail."

"You're a gem, Blake. But then, you always were—"

Blake started to say something, when the double doors of the sanctuary swung open. They both turned as Hunter burst through, his handsome face brightening at the sight of Sadie.

"Darling…" He hurried down the aisle and bounded up the platform stairs two at a time to where Sadie stood with Blake. He kissed Sadie's cheek, then turned to greet Blake with a hearty handshake as Sadie made introductions.

Then Hunter spotted the stable. "What is this?" Disbelief shaded his voice. "Darling, where *did* you find the carpenter?" He laughed, shaking his head in disbelief. "You told me this was a one-horse town, Sade, but, really…this is too much."

"I'm afraid I'm the guilty party," Blake interjected dryly. "I built the set."

Hunter didn't have the grace to look embarrassed, Sadie noticed, or to apologize.

"Pastor Michael was in a fix. Blake volunteered to help him out," Sadie began. She could see Blake's big hands had curled into fists at his side. The veins in his forearms popped. She hurried on. "He's here on assignment—he's a photojournalist. He's actually here to cover the pageant."

"The media, eh?" Hunter peered into Blake's face as if seeing him for the first time. He looked back up at the stable. "Actually, it's not as bad as all that." He sighed. "I suppose it does have a sort of backcountry charm."

For an instant Blake's clear green eyes met Sadie's. Her breath caught uncomfortably. She turned abruptly to Hunter.

"Sade," he was saying, "we really should be on our way. I've found the little farm kitchen restaurant you told me about. If we hurry we can be there for supper and back here in time for the tryouts."

Hunter stuck out his hand to Blake. "Nice meeting you. No hard feelings about the set—we all have those areas where we excel. And—" His gaze again took in the stable. "Well, what can I say? Your genius must be writing and photography." He chuckled at his own joke.

Sadie suddenly wondered if Hunter had always been this rude, or if she was seeing him in a new light—a light that shone from being in this place, her little mountain hometown where life once seemed uncomplicated and love profound in its simplicity.

She glanced again at Blake; his eyes met hers with clear understanding. She felt her cheeks flush, before turning to step down the platform stairs with Hunter.

#

B lake watched Sadie leave the church. His delight at seeing her again had been crushed by the sight of Hunter Shaw.

Jamming his hands into his jeans pockets, he sauntered back to the set, squinting at his workmanship. Was it really that bad? Probably not, according to most standards. But then, Hollywood required something different.

Illusion, he decided, must be the key. Exterior was everything. Illusion—not reality—reflected theater's essence, whether a sitcom, play, or film. He pondered Sadie's world. How deeply caught up in illusion was she?

He gazed out at the sanctuary, now dim in the fading late-afternoon light. It was in this church—as it was being framed—that he'd first laid eyes on skinny-legged Sadie with her blond pigtails, sunburned nose, and dimpled chin. Their fathers had been part of a group of volunteers coerced by God-fearing wives into building the only house of worship in town.

Blake grinned at the memory. He and little Sadie had tagged along after their dads, picking up bent nails and scraps of wood, while their fathers had sawed boards and pounded nails.

He remembered the day their fathers had boarded up the baptistry, telling each other and anyone else who would listen that it wouldn't be needed. Religion was for sissies, he remembered them saying, for old folks, women, and weaklings. Not them.

Weeks later, when a traveling preacher spoke at the new little church's dedication, both men had found God—miraculously, joyously.

Blake looked down at the worn carpet at his feet. The baptistry lay hidden under the removable flooring. He remembered how he and Sadie had watched their dads pull out the same nails they'd hammered into the baptistry's cover. Then, during the first baptism, the two children sat side by side in the front pew, feet swinging, watching as Sadie's father stepped into the water, the first to be immersed. Blake's father was the second.

The sanctuary now was shrouded in darkness. Blake reached for a nearby switch and flicked on the light that illumined the stage. Looking down the rows of pews in the darkness beyond the single light, he suddenly had the eerie feeling he wasn't alone.

But he saw no one. After a moment he turned to pulling nails, thinking his imagination must be working overtime as it conjured up images from his past.

Blake's thoughts once again turned to Sadie as he worked. He wondered if even once during the years she'd been far from his consciousness. Sometimes he had caught glimpses of her on TV—at the Academy Awards, the Emmys. Her beauty on the small screen had left him breathless, but it didn't compare to seeing her in person.

When he'd seen her walk through the sanctuary doors, his heart had pounded wildly. Sadie's tumble of pale yellow curls fell to her shoulders, just this side of wild. And her eyes...those eyes that had haunted him for a decade, shimmering like mountain violets awash in morning dew. He drew in a deep breath. Seeing her again had stirred feelings inside him that he could no longer ignore.

It seemed that he'd loved Sadie Grayson forever. But only once had he held her in his arms—the last time he had seen her all those years ago.

That night by Sapphire Lake, Blake had wanted to tell Sadie that he would love her forever, that someday he wanted to marry her. But with stars in her eyes she'd spoken of her dreams. It had been plain that they didn't include him.

And Blake had known that he wanted no part of the show business world she'd described. He shared her love for writing. But he wanted to travel—live in the African bush or Asian swamps—bring attention to the urgent needs of the world's helpless with his writing.

He pulled another nail from a cross-support and removed another board. That night so long ago, as he watched Sadie's animated face, Blake had known that to save his dream—and hers—he had to leave. Perhaps he'd left without a word of goodbye as a gift to them both.

But now? He glanced out the window at the still-falling snow. He didn't know why he had picked this time to see her again. Perhaps it was simply a need for distraction from the trauma of his last assignments in Bosnia and Rwanda—both on the heels of the tragedy in Romania.

All he knew was that when he saw the Internet posting, a thousand wild horses couldn't stop him from trying to see Sadie again. He simply wanted to look into her violet eyes and touch her dimpled chin. He also knew that a journey back to the church of his youth would be a journey of love.

Looking around at the familiar knotty-pine walls, Blake smiled. It was good to be back. He began to whistle as he lifted the hammer to pull off another board.

Suddenly, he felt the hair on the back of his neck bristle. He looked up cautiously.

Someone was watching him. He could feel their gaze. He peered into the now dark sanctuary. The doors were still closed, and it appeared empty. He glanced at the windows on both sides of the rows of pews, but dusk and falling snow obscured his vision. Maybe it was his imagination.

He went back to his dismantling. But just as he lifted his hammer, a board creaked at the far end of the sanctuary.

"Who's there?" he called out.

Only silence answered.

Blake, still holding the hammer by his side, stood and stepped soundlessly down the platform stairs. He examined the rows of pews as he moved down the aisle.

The wooden floor creaked again as someone crept from behind the last row, and tried to make a dash for the doors. Even in the shadows, Blake could see the dull glint of a weapon.

He lunged forward to block the exit.

"Get outa my way." A boy no more than twelve tried to push Blake aside.

Blake grabbed the child's shoulder, then reached to the wall behind him and flipped on the overhead lights.

The boy narrowed his eyes menacingly. "Lemme go," he growled, twisting his shoulders defiantly.

Blake let him go, but stood firmly planted in front of the exit doors. "What're you doing here?"

The boy challenged Blake with a hostile stare. A headband was pulled down over straggly tufts of hair—hair obviously growing out after being shaved. An oversized tee-shirt and jeans larger than Blake's, covered a pathetically thin body. Gang attire. Blake had seen it before, but not on someone this young.

"What's your name?" Blake prodded.

"None of your business." The voice was low, surly. He swiped at his nose with the heel of his hand.

Blake looked into the child's dark eyes. They were too large for his pale, thin face. Combined with the short tufted hair, they made the boy look like a waif.

The kid suddenly jerked his arm back. Blake grasped the thin wrist before the boy could move it forward.

The boy's white-knuckled fingers were wrapped around a foot-long iron pipe. Blake squeezed his scrawny forearm until the pipe dropped with a clatter to the floor, then rolled under a pew.

"Now you weren't planning to use that, were you?" He stared hard into the boy's eyes.

The boy turned away. "No," he mumbled as Blake let his arm drop.

"Good, I didn't think so." Blake paused, still watching for signs of emotion in the child's face. "Now let's start over. Why are you here?"

The boy shrugged.

Blake sighed. "Let me guess. You wanted to get here early for the pageant tryouts."

A soft snort answered the question.

"Okay, then, let's try again. You're here to help me rebuild this thing." He jerked his thumb in the direction of the stable.

"Yeah, right." A practiced sneer curled the boy's lip. After a moment, though, he squinted toward the front of the church. "What do you have to do to it? Looks okay to me."

"Not according to the director. She says it's not right. Apparently, the size and color won't work for television."

"Yeah, like they had TV in those days—"

Blake grinned. "Yeah," he agreed. "You're right." For a moment the child's eyes met Blake's with a connecting flicker of emotion.

Blake went on, glad something had piqued the boy's interest. "So you know Cedar Creek's got a film crew coming...that the Christmas play's going to be on network TV?"

"Yeah, big deal." The bored expression had returned.

Blake heard car chains crunch through the snow and halt in front of the church. He glanced at the boy. A frightened look crossed his face as a car door slammed and the sound of hurrying footsteps approached the entrance.

A red-faced man with unkempt white hair burst through the doors. The boy stepped slightly behind Blake, as if to hide.

"Ren!" the big man roared, spotting the young man. "What're you doin' here? You've had your grandmother and me sick with worry. I should've known you'd be up to no good—"

207

The man looked wildly around, then rested his bushy-browed gaze on Blake. "Whadya catch him doin'—sprayin' graffiti on the walls, settin' fire to the place?" As he talked he pinched Ren on the collarbone to hold him in place. The boy winced.

Blake laughed lightly, at the same time drawing Ren away from the man's mean grasp. He patted the boy's shoulder as if they'd become friends. "No, sir," he said, smiling into the big man's face. "Ren just stopped by to volunteer to help me with the set here." Blake gestured toward the stage. "He's been telling me how he loves to work with his hands, how he's pretty handy with a can of paint. I said I sure could use a helper, with the film crews coming so soon and all."

Blake smiled down at Ren, noting the boy's surprised expression. "Isn't that right, Ren?"

Wide-eyed and speechless, the boy simply nodded.

The big man sputtered, and his red face turned a few shades lighter, probably in relief, Blake thought. "Well, well, now." He looked at the boy in approval. "That's a different kettle of fish. I'll run home and tell Grandma. She'll be pleased."

Then he stuck out his hand at Blake and they shook. "Name's Chandler," he said, "Will Chandler. This here's my grandson, Warren Chandler—but I guess he's already told you that."

Blake simply smiled and gave him a quick nod. "Glad to meet you, Will," he said. "You've got a good boy here."

The older man's brows shot upward. So did Ren's.

Blake grinned. "You'll be surprised at what he's about to accomplish."

Before Will Chandler's car had rattled away from the

church, Ren turned to Blake, another sneer sliding across his face.

"Don't think I'm glad for what you did," he mumbled. "'Cause I'm not."

Three

Sadie and Hunter sat at a small, gingham-covered table facing Sapphire Lake. A red-globed candle flickered between them. The snow no longer fell, and the glow of the moon backlit the clouds, casting a silver sheen across the lake.

The waitress, a plump, motherly woman, bustled to their table, setting two platefuls of fried trout before them on scalloped paper placemats.

"I don't know how you can advertise fresh rainbow, when it's not even fishing season," Hunter complained. "These obviously are frozen fish."

"As I said before, fresh from freezer to frying pan," the waitress said good-naturedly, wiping her hands on her red-checked apron.

"Ah-ah-ah…false advertising," Hunter needled, wagging his finger.

The waitress flushed, and Sadie suddenly wanted to crawl under the table. "Hunter," she finally said, exasperated, "what difference does it make?" She took a bite of the trout. "It's delicious—whether fresh or frozen. Try a bite."

When the waitress left for another table, Sadie narrowed her eyes at Hunter.

In the candlelight, his face looked more handsome than ever. Noticing her scrutiny, he dabbed at his mouth with the edge of a napkin. "Is something wrong, darling?"

"Why do you do that?"

"Do what?"

"Find fault so readily—in people who don't deserve it?"

"What are you talking about, darling?" He squeezed a wedge of lemon over the trout.

"The waitress. What difference does it make? She obviously can't serve fresh trout in the dead of winter."

He reached for her hand. "That's my point. Why should they advertise what they can't deliver?"

"We're not in Beverly Hills, Hunter. You can't expect—"

"Sadie, it seems you're picking at my faults—the very thing you're accusing me of doing to others. Is that true?"

Sadie sighed. The man was impossible. If he weren't so incredibly talented—and devoted to her—she probably would have stopped seeing him months ago. Shaking her head slowly, she smiled at him.

He rewarded her with a dazzling smile of his own. Then he took her hand between both his. "Something's been bothering you all afternoon, darling. What is it? I noticed your…ah, distance…immediately after leaving that little church of yours." He patted her hand. "I hope it doesn't have anything to do with the young man you introduced me to—what was his name again? Brady, ah—"

"Blake," she said patiently. "Blake Adams."

"Ah, yes. I noticed you seemed different, quieter somehow, on our ride to the lake."

"I didn't like the way you treated him, Hunter."

"Well, that's a relief."

She arched an eyebrow.

He laughed nervously. "I thought that maybe it was my snow driving that bothered you."

"This is serious."

"I know it is, dear. And so am I. I worry about how you see me in this—" He gestured toward the outdoors. "—this place where you grew up. I see the change it's brought in you. You're tougher here, more focused. Feet on the ground and all that."

"What's that got to do with your driving?"

"Even my Porsche is symbolic." He pushed back a thin strand of blond hair from his forehead, and reached for his coffee.

"What are you talking about?"

"Everyone here has a four-wheel drive." He picked up a french fry.

"What?" Sadie couldn't help it; she burst out laughing.

Hunter's aristocratic face split into a grin.

"You're serious?" Sadie asked after taking a gulp of water.

"It's true," he said, suddenly sobering. "When I drove up to the church, parked the Porsche next to a beefy old Land Rover, it struck me how alien this world is to me. I mean, I ski at Aspen as often as the next guy—but this is different." His expression lost the mask it so often wore. He looked longingly into her eyes. "Sadie, when I opened the door and saw you talking with that carpenter—"

"He's not a carpenter."

"Well, with that…whatever he is—I was jealous. Pure and simple. Jealous." His look of aristocratic arrogance was gone. "It was obviously his Land Rover outside—he looks the part…" His voice dropped off, then he began again. "If I were casting this as a play…I mean, you and him…" This time he didn't continue.

"That's why you treated him the way you did?"

He nodded. "I'm sorry, darling. I truly am."

Just then the waitress scurried to their table and told them about her fresh-baked apple pie. She grinned, looking pointedly at Hunter. "And this isn't false advertising," she said. "It's the freshest in the county."

They each ordered a slice with a scoop of ice cream. After they'd eaten, they lingered over coffee, and Hunter again took Sadie's hand in both of his.

"You know how I feel about you, Sadie."

She nodded.

"Alec needs a mother. I need you. Think of the team we'd make."

"We've talked about this before, Hunter. I've told you it's too soon—"

"I know what you said," he interrupted. "But here in this backwoods place of your childhood, I'm suddenly afraid the Sadie I know will disappear. And I can't let that happen. You're too precious for me to lose."

"You make me feel like a piece of antique china."

He laughed softly. "You do have a way with words, darling. One of the many things I love about you."

"Really, Hunter," she said gently. "I need more time. Please don't press me for a decision."

He lifted her hand to his lips, gazing into her eyes as he kissed her fingertips. "I'll give you all the time in the world, Sadie, as long as the answer is yes." His eyes seemed to mist. "And darling, wouldn't Christmas be a wonderful time to announce our engagement?"

Sadie tried to protest, but he shushed her by touching the fingers of his other hand to her lips.

By the time Hunter and Sadie pulled up in front of the church, cars had lined both sides of the street. People milled about the small outside porch entrance.

"Are we late?" Sadie checked her watch but couldn't make out the time in the dark.

Hunter turned the ignition key just far enough for the clock to light. "It's only six-thirty. Tryouts aren't due to start until seven."

She chuckled. "Blake was right—this is going to be a circus." She reached for the door handle.

"Wait." Hunter touched her arm. "You're still going to let Alec have the lead?"

She hesitated. "Of course. I've already talked with him about it. He's crazy about the idea."

Hunter chuckled. "The kid loves a camera."

"I'm a little concerned about him not practicing with the others. When will you be able to get him up here?"

"I'm leaving for home tomorrow morning, but I'll be back with Alec on the twenty-third. We'll caravan with the rest of the company—film crew, musicians. That'll give him a full day of practice before the performance."

He sighed, then smiled at her in the moonlight. "But I don't know if I can stay away from you that long, Sade. Don't be surprised if I squeeze in a trip or two before then."

"It's only three weeks till the performance, Hunter."

"I know. But it's going to feel like twenty."

She colored slightly. He'd misunderstood her meaning. "I meant we're really cutting it close for Alec's preparation—"

"I know, darling...but with your dynamite script and Alec in the lead, everything will be fine. You'll see."

"Just make sure he knows his lines."

Hunter's smile was a bit patronizing. "He's a pro, Sadie. Don't worry about the boy." He patted her gloved hand.

She nodded, then opened the car door and stepped into the crunchy snow. In an instant, Hunter had rounded the car and was escorting her into the church.

"Sadie." Pastor Michael rushed toward her in the foyer as she removed her parka. He grabbed both her hands, his round face wreathed in smiles. "I'm so glad you're here, dear. Blake told me you'd been by this afternoon. Tell me, when did you get into town?"

"Only yesterday." Sadie grinned at the man's exuberance. She had spoken with him several times on the phone—the first time right after he'd sent the letter asking for her help with the Christmas pageant, the last after she'd sent him the set design.

But this was their first in-person meeting. Looking into his twinkling eyes, Sadie was glad she'd said yes when he came up with the idea for the pageant.

"Pastor Michael," she said as Hunter stepped forward and took her arm possessively. "This is Hunter Shaw—"

Pastor Michael grabbed the younger man's hand in his, shaking it vigorously. "Glad to meet you, son. So good to have you with us."

"Actually, I'll only be here until tomorrow. I've got to get back to the city." Hunter smiled benignly. "But I'll be back in three weeks—just in time for the final rehearsal." He winked at Sadie. "Actually, the play can't go on without me—I'll have its star in tow. Not to mention the film crew, the musicians—"

Pastor Michael looked surprised; he glanced at Sadie for clarification. "The star—"

Sadie nodded. "Alec Shaw?" When the pastor looked blank, she hurried on. "Alec is Hunter's son. He stars in *Charlieville.*" Pastor Michael still frowned. "The new sitcom—?" she added quickly.

"But I thought local kids were going to fill the parts…"

"They are," she assured him. "All except Alec's role."

Pastor Michael's disappointment was clear. Sadie suddenly felt sorry she'd agreed to Hunter's request. But it was too late now. "Once we decided to film this live—I figured we needed someone with experience to pull the rest of the kids through."

The pastor nodded. "You also said something about professional musicians?"

"Yes. I've had a score written for keyboard, guitars, and flute. We're working on bringing in some strings and brass, too."

Again Pastor Michael looked disappointed. "I—I didn't know…"

Sadie tilted her chin, waiting for him to go on.

He cleared his throat. "I didn't know, so I—ah—asked Blake Adams to do the music."

Sadie swallowed hard. "You did?" Blake had once played guitar quite well and sang folk songs when they were in school. But that was years ago. What if his music was like his carpentry? "You asked Blake Adams?" she managed.

"Blake Adams?" Hunter echoed, his tone incredulous.

"Did I hear my name mentioned?" Blake's booming voice carried from inside the sanctuary. His gaze rested on Sadie as he strode toward them.

"Greetings, old man." Hunter stuck out his hand. "Pastor Michael here was just telling us that you've volunteered to play for the rehearsals. Awfully good of you. You'll get the kids worked up for the real thing."

Sadie glanced at him, confused. What was he saying? Out of the corner of her eye she could see bafflement in the others' faces.

"What do you mean?" Blake narrowed his eyes at Hunter.

"We have professionals coming for the performance." He looked pointedly at Blake. "But we're sure glad for your help, old man." He slapped him on the back. "Can't say how glad.

"Now," he said, beaming at each of the two men and Sadie. "We've got a pageant to put on. Let's get started, shall we?" And with his hand cupped under Sadie's elbow, he led her into the sanctuary.

Four

A ll right, kids," Sadie called out to the noisy audience. "Listen up! I need your attention. Now!"

Sadie stood on the platform, just to one side of the partially dismantled stable. She grinned, looking out at the sea of upturned, excited faces. Wriggling six- to twelve-year-old children had jammed themselves into the pews. They quieted, but excited whispers still carried from the back rows.

"Okay, that's better. But if you don't listen you won't know what's expected. You could miss out on a good time. You don't want that do you?"

"Noooo…" the children said in unison and grew still quieter.

Blake sat in the front pew near the baby grand. He gave her an encouraging smile, one eyebrow lifted in amusement. A boy sat next to him, a dark-haired, tough-looking kid. He glared at her welcoming smile.

She turned back to the rest of the group. "How many of you know the Christmas story?"

"I do…I do…" Little hands went up everywhere.

"Good," Sadie said with a smile. "Then you know that most Christmas pageants tell the story about Mary and Joseph heading by donkey to Bethlehem. About the shepherds tending their fields by night, the angels appearing, the kings arriving by camels to worship the Christ child."

"Yeeesss…" they called back, again in unison.

"Good," Sadie said again, then drew in a deep breath. "This pageant will be a little different." She gazed from pew to pew at the upturned faces. She could almost feel their excitement. "This," she began, "is the story of a shepherd boy. His name is Benjamin. He wasn't with the other shepherds when the angels came to tell them about Jesus being born in the stable."

The children watched Sadie intently. Some audibly scooted to the edges of their seats.

"Benjamin heard about it from some of the other shepherds. He heard a great King had just been born—the greatest King of all time. So he thought he couldn't go worship this baby King without a great and wonderful gift, a gift fitting the noble birth."

The children were silent, waiting for Sadie to go on.

"Imagine," she said, "what that must have been like. A little boy the same age as some of you—maybe ten, or twelve. He was a very poor boy. He had nothing of value. He wanted to see Baby Jesus, but he had nothing to present such a great King. So he began to look for the perfect gift. He didn't think he could go to the stable without it."

"What did he find?" A little boy in the back called out.

"Yeah, what will he do?" An older girl behind Blake asked.

Sadie turned the question to the kids. "What do you think he'll find for a gift?" she asked.

"Maybe a toy," a red-haired little girl in the front row said.

The girl next to her giggled. "Yeah, right, Jilly. What's baby Jesus gonna to do with a toy?"

"He'd play with it," Sadie answered gently. "At least he would when he was a little older. He was a real baby—and real babies love toys. I think a toy would've made a wonderful gift. But that's not it. Doesn't anyone else have any ideas?"

Several other ideas were called out, and finally Sadie held up her hand to silence the group. "I want you all to think about what you would give if you were the shepherd boy," she said. "We'll keep the real gift a surprise until a few days before the performance."

Moans of disappointment came from every corner of the room.

"I will tell you, though, that it will be the shepherd boy's most special possession."

There was more whispering, then Sadie again quieted the group. "Okay," she said, "Now to the part you've all been waiting for—tryouts for the speaking parts. Later on, we'll hold tryouts for the solos—there will be a few of those too. But first, I want you to know that there will be parts for everyone. And everyone's is as important as another person's. We need all of you to make this the best Christmas pageant ever seen in Cedar Creek."

More scuffling and whispering rose from the kids.

"First, I need at least twenty people for the angel choir. How many like to sing?"

Hands shot up. Some of the littlest children jumped up and down in their seats.

"All right, then. I need everyone under age ten who likes to sing to come up and stand beside me."

Pandemonium followed. Squirmy bodies crowded onto the stage. Sadie placed them in four lines of eight each.

Then she asked those who wanted speaking parts to come to the front of the sanctuary. After a few minutes listening to them read a few lines each, she picked the shepherds, the wise men, and Mary and Joseph.

"What about the shepherd boy, Benjamin?" Jilly twisted a red pigtail around her finger. She stood near Sadie with the rest of the angel choir. "Who's going to be him?"

Sadie smiled at Jilly, then turned to the rest of the group. "I have another surprise for you. How many have ever seen the TV show, *Charlieville?*"

Hands bobbed up and down. "I have! I have!"

"The boy who plays Charlie—Alec Shaw—is going to come to Cedar Creek just to play the part of the shepherd." Sadie caught Hunter's pleased look from the back pew.

Sighs of wonder filled the room. "Wow," several murmured in awe. Hunter beamed proudly, nodding to Sadie.

Then Jilly, still winding her pigtail, said, "But I want to be the shepherd."

Hoots of laughter made the child's face turn red. She stuck her chin in the air. "What's so funny about that?" she demanded. "I bet there were girl shepherds."

Sadie stepped quickly to Jilly's side and gave her a hug. "Angels are very important, Jilly. I need you here."

"But I want to give a gift for the King—can angels do that?"

"Of course they can." Sadie smiled at the child, wondering

221

how she would work it into the script. "Now," she said to them all, "before we go tonight, I want everyone to again take your seats. Here, close to the front." She gestured to the front rows. After much shuffling and scuffling, the children again quieted in their seats. "I want to try some of the songs for the play. Some you have heard before...and you probably know by heart. Others will be new."

Sadie had brought instrumental tapes the musicians had made to help the kids practice. But she looked across the room at Blake, meeting his eyes briefly. His guitar case lay at his feet. And suddenly, she wanted to hear him play.

"Would you mind?" She raised a questioning eyebrow.

Blake smiled. "Of course not. But the old standards are one thing...the new, quite another." He opened the case and lifted out the guitar, strummed a few chords to test the pitch, then made some adjustments.

"It's all yours, maestro." She introduced Blake, handed him a list of songs, and smiled as he pulled up a folding chair and sat down in front of the kids. The sullen boy who had been sitting next to Blake stood noisily and sauntered down the aisle and out the back doors.

"Let's start with some old favorites," Blake said to the kids, strumming a bit. "How about 'Bill Grogan's Goat'?"

"That's gonna be in the pageant?" a little voice giggled.

"Nah, this is just to warm us up—" He casually strummed a few more chords, then began to sing. The children joined in.

Sadie left the platform and settled onto the edge of the piano bench to watch and listen.

Blake's voice was warm and rich, somehow fuller than Sadie remembered. She found herself tapping her foot. The children clapped in unison as he began "Madelina Catalina."

Finally he glanced at the list. "We'd better move on to something more appropriate for the season. How many know, 'What Child Is This'?"

No one raised a hand. "Okay, I'll sing it once clear through, then we'll take it line by line. First I'll sing it alone—then you with me. Got it?"

Little heads nodded in understanding.

Blake strummed the simple melody quietly, simply. And when he began to sing, his voice was husky and gentle. She pictured him kneeling at the manger, seeing the Christ child for the first time. His voice was soft, as if not wanting to wake the baby, yet filled with the joy of being in the presence of the King.

Sadie felt the hot sting of tears behind her eyes. How long had it been since she had felt like kneeling in the presence of Christ?

For years Sadie had attended a church with a sanctuary that seated thousands. The choir alone was larger that most church memberships. The music, though inspirational, was a major production, full orchestra and stadium-sized video screen behind the platform. A far cry from the simple worship of a baby born to lowly, poor folks.

Sadie remembered one Sunday morning when she'd arrived early and slipped into a pew during preparations for the worship service. The soloist, a woman with a magnificent voice, was practicing with the orchestra. Sadie watched, disillusioned, as the singer choreographed her hand movements to the song—raising her hands in praise at a certain lyrical phrase, lifting her face heavenward at just the right time, and closing her eyes as if in ecstasy for a few moments at the end.

Feeling strangely empty, Sadie had quietly left her seat. She never could bring herself to return to that church.

Now, as she listened to Blake, the lullaby sounds of his guitar, his low, quiet voice, Sadie felt a sudden joy at being in God's presence. She gazed across the room at the children; they felt it too. Their faces were rapt with concentration, as if hearing someone who'd actually been present the night Jesus was born. When it was their turn to join in, their voices were soft, reflecting the same sense of awe.

After a few more songs, Sadie again moved to the platform, dismissed the angel choir, then asked those with speaking parts to stay while she handed out the scripts.

The little angels filed down the aisle amid shoving, giggles, and whispering. As soon as the sanctuary was quiet, Sadie turned to the rest of the group. There were about twenty children in all, ranging in age from nine or ten to twelve.

"I'll be giving you each a script with your part highlighted. You need to know your lines a week from today. Also before you leave, I need to send costume instructions home with you." Sadie began. "I'll need to meet with your mothers by—"

Suddenly, the back doors swung open with a bang. Everyone turned to look.

Jilly, who'd been dismissed with the angels, burst through, red pigtails flying. Her freckles stood out dark on her pale face.

"The bad boy just stoled a car," she yelled. "Right out here in front of everybody."

A moment of shocked silence followed.

"It's the Rover one," she shouted louder. "The land— land—um—land—"

"Land Rover," Blake finished for her, then bounded down the aisle.

"Yeah. The Land Rover one. You should see him go!" Then, grinning with pleasure at being the bearer of such important news, Jilly slammed back through the doors.

Shouts of "I wanna see! I wanna see!" rose from every pew, followed by pushing and shoving and more yelling as the children all tried to reach the exit at once.

"Wait!" Sadie shouted. "You need to take the costume patterns—"

But the children didn't stop to listen. Tryouts were over.

Five

B lake made it to the exit before the swarm of kids blocked his way. He pushed through the door, with Hunter Shaw close on his heels.

The two men sprinted from the church, following Jilly and the rest of the angel choir down the street, past the town square with its gingerbread style storefronts and twinkling Christmas lights. Then, huffing and puffing in the cold air, they made their way through the passel of excited and yelling children, and closed in on the Land Rover, now heading slowly up the winding road leading out of town.

The Land Rover suddenly slid crosswise, skidding on the ice-slick street. With each turn, the vehicle's rear end threatened to overtake the front.

Blake groaned as the Land Rover narrowly missed a pine near the road's edge and swerved onto a smaller road with an even steeper incline. Ren—by now Blake was sure he must be the thief—hit the gas hard, gunning the engine in an attempt to take the hill.

"That kid'll be...the death of me yet." Suddenly a puffing Will Chandler, Ren's grandfather, overtook Blake. "He's a hoodlum...just like his father was."

"Take it easy..." Blake panted as he ran, "he hasn't caused any harm yet."

The white-haired man snorted. "Easy for you to say—he's caused me and his grandmother more grief...than any one person deserves in a lifetime."

Just then the Land Rover began skidding sideways. Ren gunned the engine, but the back end fishtailed, swinging the massive vehicle hard to the right.

Blake caught his breath. "Not the brake, kid. Not the brake—" he muttered to himself.

Ren hit the brake. Now completely out of control, the Land Rover spun crazily backwards. Down, down, down the steep incline. Zigzagging the road three times, it finally headed over the berm and came to rest with a soft thud at the base of a small cliff.

By then, Blake, Hunter, and Will Chandler had overtaken the pack of running children. Clambering through the snow, Blake was the first to reach the Land Rover. Engine still running, it rested against a thick-trunked pine.

In the light of a nearby streetlight, Ren slumped across the steering wheel.

"Let me at 'im." Will tried to shove Blake out of the way.

"Wait—stand back," Blake murmured, opening the driver's side door. By now, children had slipped and slid down the small hill to the car. They stood around, speaking in hushed whispers. Will Chandler was muttering unintelligible swear words, and Blake thought he heard Hunter Shaw say something about being glad it wasn't the Porsche.

Blake reached over Ren and turned off the ignition. The boy moaned and opened his eyes.

"Easy now," Blake commanded as the child tried to remove himself from the car. "Easy…" He gently probed the lump on Ren's head.

"Ow!" Ren pushed Blake's hand away. At least the boy's hand was strong. A good sign.

Will Chandler pulled back the open car door to stand beside Blake, peering into the dark Land Rover. "Whadya think you're doin', pullin' a stunt like this?" His voice was gruff, though he sounded more worried than angry. He touched the boy's shoulder. "Answer me, boy, when I talk to you. Whadya think you're doin'?"

Ren groaned and tried to look away.

"Come on, now. Let's get you outta here." This time he tried to pull the boy from the car. Ren moaned again.

"Well, I, for one, think we need to get the sheriff—" Hunter, standing in front of the Land Rover, said to no one in particular. He produced a cellular phone. "Grand theft auto," he muttered as he punched in a number.

Blake moved away from the door, heading toward him. "You might as well put it away," he said.

Hunter looked up, surprised.

"Reason number one—there's no signal here," he said simply. "Reason number two—the Land Rover looks fine. And I'm not going to press charges."

Hunter scoffed. "After what he did? Are you kidding?"

"Hey, calm down…" Blake couldn't help himself. "I was

going to give Ren driving lessons anyway—he just beat me to it." In the car, Ren's eyes seemed to grow larger than his face. He stared unblinking at Blake.

"Just what the world needs—more bleeding hearts like you. That'll sure bring an end to crime..." Hunter snorted, shaking his head in disbelief.

Suddenly, Sadie moved toward them. She must have been with the group of children. "Come on, let's go," she said without looking at Blake. "We've got to get the kids back to the church. Their parents are probably wondering what happened to them."

There were groans of disappointment from the children, but they turned and slowly tromped up the hill with Sadie and Hunter.

Blake turned his attention back to Ren and his grandfather. The older man was helping him out of the car.

"Can you walk? See if you can walk."

The boy nodded, and placed his feet on the snow-covered ground. He nodded again. "I'm all right, Grandpa."

"Okay, then. Now I want you to lean on me." Will put his arm around Ren and slowly helped him up the hill. At the top, the white-haired man turned to Blake. "Thank you," he said gruffly. "I'll pay for any damage."

"No, sir, you won't," Blake answered. "That'll be up to your grandson."

Ren blinked, looking startled.

"Starting tomorrow."

The boy cocked his head.

"I'll be by to pick you up at ten."

Ren stared, his expression unreadable.

"I'll see to it that he's ready," the older man said, then turned to help his grandson to the top of the hill.

Blake climbed into the four-wheel drive vehicle, turned the key in the ignition, and backed away from the tree. The ancient Land Rover, having been through worse than this, proved its grit again. The engine hummed, taking the hill as if on a Sunday drive down a superhighway.

Grinning, Blake pulled onto the road and headed back to his room at Cedar Creek's only bed and breakfast.

Promptly at ten the next morning, Blake parked the Land Rover in front of an old frame house on Jackrabbit Road. The sun shone early-morning bright in a vivid blue sky. The snow of the previous day, though still pristine, dripped from the overhead pines. It had already turned to slush on the ground.

Will Chandler moved to the wide front porch and waved Blake in. "Boy'll be ready in a minute," he said as Blake strode up the gravel walk.

Blake nodded. "No hurry," he said. "How's he feeling?" He leaned against the porch rail.

"He's got a headache—from that bump on his head. But his grandmother's been fussin' over him. Givin' him aspirin. I think he'll be fine." The older man looked at his feet, embarrassed, then fixed his blue eyes on Blake. "I—ah—I'm sorry for what he did."

"I know. Don't apologize. It's not your fault."

"It's not been easy—since his father died. His mother was workin' two jobs just to make ends meet. Didn't have time for the boy. He got into the wrong crowd."

"Happens to a lot of kids."

"She sent him to live with us—thought we might straighten 'im out. But—" The old man shrugged helplessly.

Just then the screen door squeaked open. Ren sauntered across the porch, a bored expression on his face. The door slammed behind him. He wore his usual uniform—oversized tee-shirt and huge jeans. He stared sullenly at Blake.

"You're not dressed warm enough." Blake said quietly. "Go back and change."

"I'll be fine," the boy mumbled.

"We're heading into the backcountry. I suggest you grab a couple of sweaters and an insulated jacket. Longjohns wouldn't hurt either."

Ren shrugged and headed back into the house.

Will grinned at Blake and raised a white, bushy eyebrow. "Good luck," he said. "You're gonna need it."

Ren soon reappeared, his thin body swathed in heavy winter clothes. Only the unruly tufts of hair sticking out from beneath his hunting cap spoke of his usual attire.

A few minutes later, Blake nodded at the older man as he put the Land Rover in gear and pulled forward. Ren kept his eyes straight ahead. They drove through town, past the central square, and up the same hill Ren had tried to drive up the previous night.

As they passed the place where Ren had gone over the berm, the boy said nothing, just kept staring straight ahead, his mouth slack. Blake kept the Land Rover moving slowly forward, even after they moved out of town onto a narrow, unplowed road.

Within ten minutes he halted the Land Rover in front of a barrier made of two posts with a chain looped between them. To the right, a sign warned against trespassing.

"Okay, time for you to get out—" He looked at Ren.

The boy stared back.

Blake nodded at the barrier. "You need to unloop the chain while I drive through—then rehook it and get back in."

Ren's eyes widened for a moment, then he grinned. "Okay," he grunted, swinging his legs out of the vehicle. For a few minutes, he struggled with the heavy chain as he pulled it to one side of the road.

"That was cool," Ren announced, when he got back into the car. As they drove further up the winding, treacherous road, Ren became curious, animated. He swiveled around to check out the contents in the cargo space. "Wow," he said. "That a toboggan?"

"Haven't you ever seen one before?"

"Nah—only on TV. What're those other things?"

"What?"

"They look like see-through waffles."

"Oh, yeah. Those are snowshoes."

Ren gulped as he turned around. "We gonna be usin' that stuff?"

"Yep."

"Where're we goin' anyway?" His voice sounded small. No more Mr. Toughguy.

"I told you—the backcountry."

"That's pretty far, isn't it?"

"Yep. End of Blackpoint Road."

"I heard people died out there one time—got caught in a freak storm." Ren scrunched down to have a better look at the sky.

"Yep. Happened a long time ago. I was about your age."

"Where we're goin'—it's a pretty dangerous place?"

"Can be." Blake kept his eyes on the road. "If you don't know what you're doing."

Ren drew in a deep breath. "You been out here before, right?"

"Yeah. Lots of times."

For a few minutes neither spoke. The Land Rover moved slowly and steadily up the narrow incline. A solid granite drop-off fell from the driver's side, a steep bank jutted up on the other.

Blake glanced at the boy. His face was white, and he had clamped his lips together.

Soon the turnoff for Blackpoint Road appeared. Blake swung the Land Rover to the left, heading it into deeper snow. He slowed to a stop, putting it into low range four-wheel drive.

"Okay, Ren," he said suddenly. "It's all yours." He reached for the door handle.

"Wha—" The boy's dark eyes widened. His voice came out in a squeak.

"I said yesterday that I was planning to teach you to drive. Don't want to make me out a liar, do you?"

Ren swallowed hard then shook his head.

"Then get out and come around to the driver's side."

The boy took a shaky breath. "Right now? Here?"

"Yep. Let's get moving. We don't have all day."

Ren reached for the doorhandle with shaking hands. Blake pulled on the parking brake and hopped out, passing Ren in front of the car. Soon they'd both settled in their seats. Ren adjusted the driver's seat, and let off the brake.

"Nice and easy, now," Blake coaxed, and he led the boy through the procedures, cautioning him about speed and brake use.

Ren, a look of wonder on his narrow face, lurched the vehicle forward. It bucked a couple of times, then settled into a smooth slow grind through the snow.

"This is where I learned to drive," Blake said, ignoring the bumpy start. "Same age. Same conditions." He didn't add that he had had a father to teach him.

The boy, however, was concentrating on keeping the Land Rover on the road and didn't seem to hear. Ren drove on slowly, gaining confidence with each mile.

"Okay, pull 'er over here," Blake finally said. By now the sun was straight up. "How about lunch?"

Ren nodded, a tentative smile playing on his face. "Yeah," he said. "Cool."

"Good. We'll eat down there." Blake pointed to a clump of trees at least a mile down the mountain.

"There's no road down there," Ren observed.

"That's right." Blake opened the car door and stepped out.

Ren tilted his head, squinting, as he got out of the car. "Then how do we get there?"

"I'll show you." Blake opened the rear door and pulled out

the toboggan, the snowshoes, and a couple of sack lunches.

Ren swallowed hard. "We're ridin' that thing down there?"

"You got it."

"Cool," he whispered, taking a deep breath. "I think."

Blake placed the board on a flat place near the Land Rover. "Hold this while I tie on our gear."

The boy nodded.

"Okay, looks like we're ready to roll." Blake said after a few minutes. He showed Ren where to sit, then climbed on behind him. "You've got to remember," he said as they scooted to the edge, "we have to lean together. We can't steer it otherwise. Got that?"

Ren nodded, wordlessly. He licked his lips in fear.

"You ready?"

The boy nodded again, and Blake gave the toboggan a final shove over the berm. Ren screamed in delight as they bounced forward, picking up speed. The run was perfect, smooth, slick, and swift.

They sailed down the slope, still accelerating as they headed toward the grove of small pines.

"Turn," Blake commanded. "Lean to your left."

The boy seemed paralyzed.

"I said lean to your left," Blake yelled in his ear. Still Ren didn't move.

They were approaching the trees, dead on, with dangerous speed.

Blake grabbed him with one arm and leaned hard. The child's thin body yielded to the pressure, and he finally leaned with Blake.

They just missed the pines, whizzing by close enough to feel the sting of their branches.

After the toboggan came to a halt, Blake jumped off and grabbed the boy's arm. "Why'd you do that?" he demanded.

Ren's face was white; his chin shook. "I—I'm sorry," he said. "I—I didn't mean to. I just got scared." It was the first time the boy had expressed his feelings.

Blake drew in a deep breath. "It's okay to be scared, Ren. All of us are sometimes." Grinning, he gave the boy a bear hug. "Believe me—you just scared me to death."

After their bologna sandwiches and chips compliments of the B & B, Blake untied the snowshoes from the toboggan and tossed them one at a time to Ren. "Now for the real work," he said, strapping his pair over his boots. "We're going to find a Christmas tree for the church. You get to pick it out."

Ren rolled his eyes, but he looked pleased.

Blake carried the hatchet and Ren pulled the toboggan as they began their search through the forest. As they wandered in and out of the silvertips and white firs, Ren began to open up to Blake, telling him about his life in the city, how he missed his mother and his friends. By midafternoon, they'd found a perfect ten-footer, and Blake handed the hatchet to the boy. After he'd cut the tree and they'd tied it onto the toboggan, Blake nodded toward a couple of flat boulders nearby.

A few minutes later, they brushed the snow off and sat down to rest before trekking up the hill to the Land Rover. Blake pulled out a harmonica. "Ever seen one of these?"

"On Sesame Street once." Ren looked embarrassed. "A long time ago," he added quickly.

Blake grinned, ran it up and down his lips a few times. "You can't be in a place like this without one," he said. "Keeps a man from getting lonely." Then he began to play.

Ren watched him intently, a look of wistful wonder on his face. Gone was the defiance, the bitter chip on his shoulder.

"You want to learn how?" Blake asked.

The boy nodded. "Yeah. That'd be cool."

Blake pulled another smaller harmonica from his pocket and tossed it to Ren. The boy caught it and looked it over. "Like this—" Blake showed him the basics. Tentatively, Ren began to blow on the instrument.

He looked up with a laugh. "It doesn't sound like yours does."

"Time, my boy. With time." Blake blew a few more bars. The boy tried to copy him, his dark eyes wide with delight. He laughed and tried again, shaking his head.

After a while, Blake looked up at the fading sun. "Hey, my man. We'd better be headin' back, don't you think?"

Ren nodded reluctantly. He handed the harmonica back to Blake as he struggled to his feet in the snowshoes.

"No, you keep it, Ren. It's a gift."

The boy looked down at the ground for a moment, then back to Blake. "Will you teach me to play it—I mean, like you do?"

"Thought you'd never ask," Blake said with a grin.

"Thanks, man," Ren mumbled, looking embarrassed.

Blake wondered how long it'd been since the child had thanked anyone for anything. He threw his arm around the boy's thin shoulders. Ren grabbed the toboggan rope, and together they trudged in their snowshoes back to the Land Rover.

Three days later, Sadie arrived at the church just as a battered old pickup truck pulled away. A local rancher waved merrily from behind the steering wheel as he rumbled past.

Puzzled, she walked into the foyer and pushed open the sanctuary doors. The scent of the hay filled her senses, a smell somewhere between fresh fertilizer and old socks. Holding her breath, she flipped on the sanctuary light.

"Oh, no—" She touched her fingers to her mouth. Bales of hay had been stacked ceiling high on the platform—beside, behind, and in front of the partially dismantled new stable. Dozens of them.

Just then, the entrance doors opened. Blake stepped through, his eyes brightening as he came toward her. "How do you like it?" he asked, obviously pleased.

"Oh, Blake…" was all she could manage. Didn't he realize they would overpower the set? That the children's voices would be lost? That the audience would probably leave the performance because of the odor?

"You don't like it." Blake looked amused.

Sadie felt her cheeks redden in exasperation. He obviously didn't understand—no, worse, he didn't care—about creating the right "look" for the cameras. She tried to explain. "A few bales might lend themselves to authenticity if we could somehow cover the baling wires, but…" Her voice dropped off. She shook her head slowly. "It's just—a bit overpowering, don't you think?" Before he could comment, she hurried on. "We've got to send them back—all but two or three."

"We can't do that, Sadie." His voice was quiet.

They moved down the aisle closer to the set. "Why not? We obviously can't use them all."

"It's not that. It would be an insult. Jacob McGraw—the rancher who brought them—presented them as a gift. Said he wasn't much for churchgoing or even religion. But he's excited about what your play's doing for the community. He knew there wasn't much he could do, but still, he wanted to give something to help." Blake looked at her gently, his green eyes serious.

"A gift?" This might not be so easy to get out of.

Blake nodded. "When he unloaded the hay—helped me carry in the bales—it was the first time he'd ever been in here. You should've seen his face—especially when he saw the stable. Said he'd be glad to help with that, too."

Sadie drew in a deep breath, trying not to let it turn into a groan.

Blake went on. "He took the manger with him."

"He what?" That'd been the only part of the set that worked.

"Took the manger. Said it was all wrong. He thought it should look more like a cattle trough. Said that's what it was originally supposed to be, according to his recollection."

"The recollection of a man who says he's not much for religion or church-going?" This time Sadie groaned audibly. "You shouldn't have let it go this far, Blake. You had no right."

Now they were standing in front of the set. The bales of hay loomed large in front of them. The smell of must and mildew made Sadie slightly dizzy, nauseated. She gulped. "You should have waited to ask me, Blake."

Blake narrowed his eyes, suddenly appearing angry and disappointed at the same time. "The man is giving you a gift—of his time, his ideas. He's a rancher, not a set designer. But he wants to do something to help. And you're going to throw it back in his face?" He shook his head slowly. "You can't do that, Sadie, to him or anyone else in the community."

"I'm trying to put on a quality performance—not some homespun, hokey, backwoods comedy. I don't want people across the nation laughing at this, Blake. And they will if we're not careful."

"Laugh at you, or the performance, Sadie? Which are you afraid of?"

"Both," she said quietly.

Again, a look of disappointment crossed his face.

Sadie set her lips in a line, staring hard at him for a moment. How could he understand the fickleness of her profession? One moment a screenwriter is riding on top; the next, her phone calls aren't even answered. Of course she was scared that she'd be laughed at. But how could she expect Blake to understand? He'd never been part of that world.

Without another word, she turned to leave.

"Sadie, wait!" Blake grabbed her arm. She shook it loose and continued toward the door.

"Please, wait. I shouldn't have said what I did."

"No," she said, turning. "You spoke the truth, but it doesn't change anything." She glanced up at the set. "I want the hay out of here, Blake. I don't care what you've got to do—or say— to Jacob McGraw. Just get it out!"

A stunned expression crossed Blake's face, but Sadie didn't care. She whirled, then pushed through the doors, leaving Blake staring after her. She strode from the church, past the town square, and up the hill leading to her small rental cottage. After packing herself a sandwich and an apple, she grabbed a thermos of coffee, her backpack and parka, and headed out the door. She didn't need to be back until rehearsal tonight. And for now, she just wanted to clear her mind of the conflicting emotions that Blake Adams had stirred within her. When she was a child in Cedar Creek, hiking had provided a time of calm and reflection. She hoped it would provide the same tranquillity now.

Though a few clouds were building to the north, the vivid sky was mostly sunny. It was a perfect afternoon for an invigorating hike down the century-old railroad grade that wound into Cedar Creek. Even in her childhood it had been a favorite hiking trail—a few rusted tracks and rotting railroad ties and once in a while a water tower still filled with water from natural mountain springs.

She hurried past the town square, the church, and several cottages. Within minutes, she found herself on the old grade and set off at a brisk pace. The snow had melted to a thin layer, easy to walk through in her hiking boots. The winding route soon put her out of view of town.

Stepping onto a bridge about three miles down the trail, she suddenly stopped halfway across, moved by the beauty of the scene. Below her, the tumbling, singing Cedar Creek—after which the town had been named—cascaded down the mountain. The feel of the spray in her face exhilarated her; the gentle noise of the water, the sight of snow-dusted cedars and pines towering over ice-frosted boulders made her feel that she'd stumbled into a fairyland.

She lifted her face to the sunlight and closed her eyes, listening to the music of the creek. A rustle in nearby brush caught her attention. She looked up to see a mule deer, a doe, gazing at her with soft brown eyes.

Sadie didn't move, daring not to breathe for fear she'd frighten the magnificent animal. The doe moved from behind the manzanita, stopped, looked at Sadie again, then moved gracefully toward the creek. Behind her, two spotted fawns followed on thin, wobbly legs. Within moments, Sadie spotted them drinking from a still pool below the bridge.

Suddenly, she didn't want to leave the place. She looked up at the purple sky with its spattering of clouds, then let her gaze follow the deer as they bounded back into the forest. The sunlight slanted across the snow where they leapt, painting the ground with liquid diamonds.

Sadie felt the warmth of tears threaten her eyes. The beauty, the simple beauty of God's creation! How long it had been since she'd thought about it—or even noticed it. Somewhere through the years, perhaps while she was reaching for the top, life had gotten too complicated. And with those complications,

God's presence had been shoved into the darkest corner of her heart.

She took a shaky breath, suddenly thinking of her play, "The Shepherd's Gift." In it, the boy searched the countryside for a present fit for the newborn King. Then he discovered something that had been with him all along: his most precious possession was the only gift he had for the baby Jesus. And it turned out to be the most perfect present of all.

What do any of us have that is fit for our King? Sadie wondered. *Could it be simply those things, talents, that make up who we are—those very things with which God has gifted us?* And who was she to question another's gift no matter how simple, or seemingly inappropriate, when she had yet to give her own gift to the King?

Sadie thought briefly about Jacob McGraw. She'd been mean-spirited to order Blake to get rid of the hay. Picking up her backpack, she took a deep breath, drinking in the pristine beauty for another moment before heading back to Cedar Creek. She just hoped she could get there before Blake acted on her instructions.

Blake followed Sadie's footprints in the snow. An hour earlier he'd seen her pass by the church and head out of town. Impulsively, he grabbed a jacket and set out after her. He followed at least a mile behind, but he would have known where she was headed even without the footprints.

As he walked, he thought about the way they had parted. She was as stubborn as always. He grinned to himself. At least Sadie no longer threw things. He remembered too vividly being the target of at least three well-aimed pine cones and one dead gray squirrel before they reached age ten.

The squirrel incident happened after they'd found it dead—run over by a logging truck. She'd wanted him to help her build a barricade to stop log trucks from using the highway through Cedar Creek. He'd taken the loggers' side, teasing that there were too many squirrels in town anyway.

Exasperated, Sadie had glared at him fiercely, then quickly tromped over to the squirrel. She took careful aim, kicking the dead animal square in the middle, faster than a drop kick on a football field, straight at his stomach.

After hitting her mark, she'd tossed her yellow pigtails, stuck her little nose in the air, and stomped off, leaving him standing in the middle of the road, holding a dead squirrel.

He was still chuckling over the memory when he rounded a corner and saw Sadie sitting on the wooden rails of Cedar Creek bridge. For a few minutes, he didn't move, but watched as she seemed lost in thought.

Then as she stooped to pick up her backpack, he walked toward her.

She looked up in surprise. "Blake. What are you doing here?"

Her cheeks were pink from the cold. He fought the urge to peal off his gloves and warm them with his hands. He moved closer. "I have to confess. It's not by accident. I needed to see you, Sadie."

"After the way I acted?"

"I've been thinking—"

"So have I." she interrupted. She reached up to touch his face with her gloved hand. "I'm sorry," she began. "Sometimes

I act more like the child you once knew."

He grinned. "I've just been thinking about a certain dead squirrel."

She laughed softly. "Oh, dear…"

Blake pulled off his gloves and stuffed them in his pocket. "Sadie," he said, cupping her face in his hands. "Sadie, I'm sorry for doubting your motives. What I said about you—your fear of being laughed at. You've got a lot at stake here. I'm afraid I've not understood that."

She smiled softly. "But there was truth in what you said, Blake…about McGraw, about the community. It's only right that they contribute. When Pastor Michael asked me to write the pageant, it wasn't for network TV. That came up later—Hunter's idea."

With the mention of Hunter, Blake stepped back and shoved his hands in his pockets. He looked away from her shimmering eyes.

Sadie watched the cascading creek water for a moment, then touched his arm. "Blake?"

He met her gaze.

"What has made you different?"

"What do you mean?"

"I've noticed that you have a tenderness—a simplicity—about you that wasn't there before…" She seemed to be searching for words. "Maybe I'm saying it wrong. I don't know. It's just that you seemed changed."

He laughed quietly, and raked his fingers through his hair. "We can't help but change in ten years, Sadie. You have too."

"No. I'm not talking about just growing up." She frowned

at him. "It's different with you."

Again he looked out at the waterfall, but still he didn't speak.

"Something happened overseas, didn't it?" She touched his face again, gently turning it toward her. "I saw your pain the night you told me about your work."

"It's hard to talk about, Sadie. What I've seen—experienced—hasn't been pretty."

"I figured that—but I want to hear it anyway."

Blake gazed at her, knowing that he'd wanted to tell her. Maybe that's what had driven him to see her again. He took her hand and led her to the bridge rail. They perched on it together. She held his hand between both of hers, watching him intently as he spoke.

"I think I told you that most of my work is with Global Mission."

Sadie nodded. "The relief agency?"

"I write about their projects—profile the people involved, the workers, the victims of malnutrition, disease, violence, and war. Most of the time, the victims are kids."

Sadie drew in a deep breath. "So you go where the worst of humanity has left its mark."

He nodded. "One of my first assignments was in Romania. Talk about the worst of humanity…" He paused a moment, then continued. "Ceausescu—the former dictator—had mandated that all woman bear as many children as possible to create workers for the state. They were punished if they didn't comply. As a result tens of thousands of unwanted babies were born to families who couldn't afford them.

"Babies were abandoned on street corners, hospital steps, churches. They were placed in orphanages run by the state. Only there weren't enough caretakers. Many hovered on the brink of death from malnutrition and disease. No one ever touched them with love. They didn't learn to walk, to speak."

Blake held Sadie's gaze in his. "When Ceausescu was overthrown, relief agencies were finally allowed in. I went with the first wave of workers.

"Sadie, I'll never forget what it was like." He looked away, and Sadie squeezed his hand. He swallowed hard, then continued. "When the nurses tried to pick up the children, the babies shrieked in terror. They'd never been held. Even four-year-olds had never been out of their cribs."

"Oh, Blake…" Sadie felt tears build behind her eyes. "I'm so sorry. I didn't know."

"There was a child there, Sadie, who looked a lot like you—blond curly hair, big blue eyes. Her name was Emilia. She was about two, maybe three, when I saw her the first time. I taught her to smile. Imagine…a child three years old who had never learned to smile…

"Then I was transferred to Rwanda when massive starvation hit that country. Again, I saw tragedies that I can't even begin to describe to you…children starving, families separated, ten-year-old boys forced into military service…"

He put his head down, for a moment unable to go on. "I kept thinking of little Emilia. I made up my mind that I would go back and somehow get her out of Romania—give her the chance of a better life, with a family who loved her. That's all that kept me going."

"But you couldn't find her." Sadie's voice was soft.

"No. She'd disappeared. No one could tell me where."

"Oh, Blake. I'm so sorry." She looked into his face and Blake could see she understood. She lifted his hand to her face, kissed his fingers, then held them to her cheek.

"I came back to the States, discouraged, disheartened. I had begun my writing career thinking that I could bring change into the world—writing about causes to make people care. But in reality, what I did made so little difference.

"Did it change even one child's life in Romania, Ethiopia, Rwanda, Bosnia?" He shrugged. "Maybe. I don't know."

"That should've made you bitter. But you're not." She peered into his face. "I don't see a trace of defeat, or bitterness."

He smiled. "A very wise woman once said that God doesn't call us to be successful. He simply calls us to be obedient." He suddenly grinned, and took a deep breath. "When I heard that it was as if a huge sack of rocks had been lifted from my shoulders."

"Who was the wise woman?"

"Mother Teresa."

Sadie smiled with him, nodding. "Yes," she said. "There's no better."

"That's why, Sadie, I'm trying—just like your little shepherd boy in the play—to find those things in my life to give to God. It certainly isn't a changed world due to my efforts." He paused thoughtfully. "Maybe my gift is simply a heart of obedience."

Sadie slipped quietly into the back pew of the dark sanctuary. As usual, she was early for rehearsal. The baby angel choir wouldn't appear for another hour, and the others for an hour beyond that. They were well into their second week of practice, and she was pleased with the children's progress.

Parents, excited about their children's roles, had finished the costumes in record time. Jilly McGraw had been the first to show off her completed angel outfit—white flannel robe with silver tinsel wings and halo. She'd worn it to three rehearsals before Sadie convinced her it might get soiled before the performance. She finally took off the robe, but insisted on wearing the halo.

On the stage in front of her, Blake worked on the stable with the boy Ren. She smiled at their easy conversation. She'd noticed the boy still didn't speak to any of the other children and very seldom to adults. Even Pastor Michael could get little more than a sullen grunt from the dark-eyed child.

But when he was with Blake, Ren seemed to feel safe, cared

for. For several evenings now she had quietly watched Blake dealing with him. When Ren said he didn't know how to do something—from running a plumb line to mitering corners—Blake showed him once, then let him go at it himself. There was no hovering over the boy as if Blake thought he might mess up.

She'd watched as Ren daily became more confident, chuckling and joking with Blake as they dropped the Christmas tree into its holder and strung lights across its branches. Later, when they hoisted the hay bales into stair-step risers for the baby angel choir, Blake had grinned at the boy. "A perfect solution," he'd said as they lifted the final bale in place.

Now, Sadie settled back to watch what had become a ritual following their work on the set. Blake pulled out his harmonica and settled to the floor, his back against the bales of hay, his long legs crossed. He ran over some scales as Ren pulled his own instrument from a pocket and tried the same notes. Then together, they played "Silent Night." Blake gave the boy a pleased nod, and Ren tried a verse alone.

Sadie drew in a deep breath, leaning back against the pew. There was no place on earth she'd rather be. Her gaze took in the warmth of the sanctuary's knotty-pine walls, the deep green of the curtains and worn carpet, the twinkling lights of the Christmas tree. The look of the place hadn't changed since her childhood. And now, listening to the sweet sounds of Blake's harmonica and the off-pitch sounds of Ren's, and watching the tough, patient love in action—Sadie blinked away the sudden warmth of tears. She realized with hard-hitting certainty that she wanted it never to end.

Her gaze settled on Blake's face. In one week, the pageant would be over. Finished with his assignment, Blake would leave

Cedar Creek. So would she. How could she bear to say good-bye? How could she bear to return to her life in the city, her life with Hunter?

Hunter? She hadn't thought of him in days. She hadn't even returned the calls her answering machine had taken. She let out a breath, still watching Blake as he showed Ren another scale. How could she ever have considered marrying Hunter?

It was Blake she loved... wholly and completely. She'd never loved anyone else. She wondered, though, about Blake's feelings for her. He cared for her with deep affection, she could see it in his eyes. But love? Did he love her?

As usual, promptly at six o'clock, Jilly McGraw, red pigtails flying, halo askew, slammed through the doors and into the sanctuary. She was always the first to arrive for angel choir practice.

"Hey!" she yelled to no one in particular. "Where is everybody?"

"What do you mean? We're here," Blake joked, sticking his harmonica back in his pocket and standing to dust off his jeans.

Jilly ran down the center aisle and sprinted up the steps to the stage. Sadie flipped on the sanctuary lights, then followed behind her.

"My dad gave those," Jilly said, proudly lifting her chin in the air. The halo wobbled precariously. She pointed to the hay. "Those used to be in our barn."

Blake's eyes met Sadie's. She smiled back. "I don't know what we'd have done without them," he said, giving Jilly's pigtail a playful tug.

"My dad's gettin' everybody in town to come to the pageant—tellin' 'em that I'm gonna be on TV. He says hundreds are gonna be here." She looked up and down the pews, her eyes wide. "There's not gonna be enough room for everybody—what'll we do?" Frowning, she nibbled on the end of a pigtail.

"I'll bring in extra seats," said Ren. "I saw some folding chairs downstairs. I'll put 'em in back. Here in front, too." He squinted out at the pews as if measuring the numbers that could fit.

Again Blake's and Sadie's eyes met in brief understanding. Though he'd been at every practice, it was the first time Ren had spoken to one of the children.

Jilly narrowed her eyes at the boy, as if assessing him. She, as did most of the children, still referred to him as the bad boy. Suddenly, she smiled. "Okay," she said. "I'll tell my dad to invite some more."

Ren gave Jilly's red hair a brotherly tousle. Watching the brief interplay, Sadie found herself swallowing hard before she could speak. "All right," she finally said to Jilly and the rest of the angel choir now in place, squirming and giggling noisily in the front pews. "All right, kids. It's time to begin."

Blake pulled out his guitar, tuned it quickly, and began to strum.

Jilly hopped up and down in her seat, her hand in the air. The halo fell off, and she made a grab for it. "I have an idea! I have an idea! I want the bad—" She caught herself. "I want Ren to play his harmonica. I heard 'im playin' the other day. I want 'im to play, too." She looked proudly at Ren, who sat nearby, chewing on a piece of hay.

There was a jumble of excited talking from the choir members. "Unh-uh. He can't either," a little boy blond boy called out.

"Yes, he can. I heard 'im one time," somebody else yelled.

Blake looked up at Sadie, who had seated herself at the piano bench. She gave him a quick nod.

"How about it, Ren?" Blake directed his question to the wide-eyed boy.

Ren shrugged. "I dunno," he mumbled.

"Do it! Do it!" Some of the angels shouted, squirming up and down in their seats.

"Come on...pleeease," Jilly yelled louder that the rest. "Pleeease..."

The others pushed and shoved at each other, trying to see Ren's face.

Finally he sighed heavily. "Yeah, okay," he muttered and stood, still not looking at the children. He pulled up a chair beside Blake. The children cheered. He shrugged his thin shoulders again and adjusted the neck of his big tee-shirt, keeping his eyes on the floor.

Blake said, "Let's start with 'Silent Night.' Ready?"

The boy nodded, and Blake tapped a beat.

The guitar began, followed by the wavering and uncertain tones of Ren's harmonica. The children forgot to sing. Most sat with mouths open, watching Ren, who looked like he was straight off the streets of L.A., playing the soft and beautiful "Silent Night."

Ren finally looked up and saw the children's astonished gazes. "Well," he said gruffly. "Aren't you gonna sing? You don't sing—I don't play. Got it?"

The little mouths snapped shut. A few angels exchanged glances. Then Jilly, twisting her pigtail around her finger, started to sing with the guitar. Her wide eyes never left the boy's. Ren nodded, a smile playing at one side of his mouth as he again lifted the harmonica and began the carol. The rest of the children joined in just as Blake got to "Son of God, love's pure light."

The choir never sounded better. The best part of all, though, to Sadie, was the wavering tones of the off-pitch harmonica rising above the rest.

Later that night, after the children had left for home, Sadie stepped from the sanctuary, flipping off the lights. She grabbed her coat and turned to lock the church doors.

She looked up in surprise. Blake had waited for her on the outside porch. "Care for a walk in the starlight?"

"I'd love it."

He smiled and took her arm. They began walking toward town, their boots crunching in the snow. Now, only a week before Christmas, Cedar Creek had been strung with tiny white lights—lining the Victorian storefronts and steep-roofed cottages, circling the smaller pines and cedars. Here and there old-fashioned streetlights added a soft glow to the scene.

Sadie stopped and drew in a breath. "It's beautiful," she whispered. The snow-covered ground reminded her of sugar frosting on a gingerbread cake. She looked up at the sky, moonless with a million pinpoints of its own twinkling lights.

Blake nodded, though his eyes were on Sadie, not Cedar Creek. The expression on his face told her he had something important to say. But as they began walking again, he kept the conversation light, agreeing with her about the beauty of the night, then moving on to concerns about the pageant. They passed families sledding together, flying around the curves as they headed down the streets of town. Children's squeals of delight rang through the chilly air.

Arm in arm they strolled, away from the lights of the square, up Jackrabbit Road, past the Chandlers' place, to a rocky point at the end. A lone streetlamp cast a warm light onto a nearby iron-scrolled bench. Blake stopped under the streetlight and gently turned Sadie so that she faced him.

Without a word, he cupped her face in his bare hands and, for a moment that seemed to last an eternity, looked into her eyes, her soul. Sadie's heart caught as she met his gaze. She swallowed, unable to speak.

Then Blake touched her cheek with the backs of his fingers, letting his thumb brush the dimple in her chin.

She smiled up at him, softly. "So precious," he said. "You are so precious." His voice was low. Before she could respond, he tilted her face and kissed her lips. Sadie slid her arms around his neck, and he kissed her again, this time lingering with a passion that made her feel she was plunging into a pool of liquid sunlight—here in the darkest, most wintry night.

Then he pulled back slightly. "Sadie," he breathed. "I love you."

She looked into his eyes, still too moved to speak.

"I love you," he repeated, a look of wonder on his face. He gathered her fiercely into his arms. Even through their layers of clothing and woolen coats, Sadie could feel their hearts pounding in unison. "I don't ever want to let you go," he whispered. "I can't…" He didn't finish. For a moment, they stood in the lamplight, clinging to each other.

Then Sadie moved back slightly, and pulling off her gloves, she reached up to touch Blake's face, that strong, chiseled face she'd loved for years. His eyes seemed to burn with the same intensity as the stars overhead. She traced her finger along his cheek, his nose, his lips. He closed his eyes, catching her hand in his and holding it against his face. After a moment, she pulled his face close to hers, kissing his eyelids, his cheeks, then finally, his lips.

Sadie waited until he again looked into her eyes. "I love you, Blake," she said, her voice husky. Then she fell into his arms, holding him as if there were no tomorrow. She buried her face in his wool jacket. "Oh, my darling, how I love you!" she murmured, feeling she had at last come home.

For a long time they stood, arms around each other, with the stars blazing overhead. In the distance, faraway sounds of children laughing and the scraping sounds of sleds on icy runs carried toward them. Fainter sounds of a harmonica drifted from the Chandler house. It seemed to Sadie the most beautiful music she'd ever heard.

Finally, Blake bent to kiss her once more, and they turned to walk back to town. When he opened the gate to the picket fence at her cottage, he stopped, looking again into her eyes. "This changes everything, you know."

"I know."

"I'm not sure where we go now—"

"I know."

"Our lives are so different—"

She smiled gently, and touched his cheek. "We'll figure it out."

"All I know is that I love you and want to be with you the rest of my life." He touched her lips and kissed her again.

She smiled into his eyes, feeling her heart leap with a joy she'd never before felt. Then giving him a final hug, she stepped from his arms through the door and into her cottage.

Eight

The following afternoon, Sadie spent an extra three hours coaching the children with speaking parts. They met at her cottage, and she served cookies and hot cocoa while they recited their lines and walked through their parts.

The thin winter sun was just slipping into a gray horizon, when the last child left. Moments later, a quick rap at the door caused Sadie's heart to quicken. Expecting Blake, she dashed to the door, unlatched it, and threw it open.

There on her small porch stood Hunter Shaw, a bouquet of long-stemmed red roses in his arms. His eyes brightened when he saw her.

"Hunter—what a surprise!"

"Darling…" he hurried through the door and tried to pull her into his arms.

Sadie stepped backward.

He looked confused. "I told you, dear, that I wouldn't be able to wait until the twenty-third to see you again." He reached for her shoulders to draw her into an embrace.

She gently placed her hands on his chest. "We need to talk, Hunter. Something's happened—"

"Yes, darling. I agree." He smiled tenderly. "We've got a lot to discuss. I've been thinking things through—more seriously than you can imagine—"

She nodded, waiting.

"That's why I've made some special plans for us tonight—well, as special as can be made in this…place." He laughed lightly. "I'm taking you to dinner at our favorite place by the lake…actually, the *only* place by the lake. I stopped by and ordered your favorite meal. Brought up the ingredients from L.A."

Sadie couldn't help laughing. "You did what—?"

"I brought handmade penne pasta and New Zealand cockles—on ice, of course. Complete with detailed instructions for the chef."

"You're kidding."

He laughed at her surprise. "No, darling. I wanted the best for you tonight. Only the best."

Sadie bit her lip, watching him. He loved her. Or at least he thought he did. She would go with him and explain about Blake. She owed him that much. "Okay," she said softly. "But we've got to be back in time for rehearsal."

He nodded, a look of secret pleasure on his face. "My chariot awaits its princess, darling."

After Sadie quickly placed the roses in water, Hunter dramatically opened the front door and escorted her to the Porsche. Their conversation was sporadic as they drove the few miles to Sapphire Lake. Sadie kept searching for the words to tell him that their relationship was over.

They arrived at the small diner just as the final rays of sunlight melted into the indigo water. A table facing the lake had been set with a white linen cloth, silver, and china. It stood out among the plastic red-checked cloths and stainless flatware at the other tables. Sadie couldn't help smiling; it was so like Hunter to plan everything down to the last detail.

The waitress ushered the couple to the table. Hunter pulled out Sadie's chair, then seated himself at her side. A candelabra blazed at the table's center, and near Sadie's place a single rose stood in a crystal vase. She recognized the vase as Waterford, obviously brought earlier by Hunter. A card lay propped against it, her name scrawled across the envelope.

Her fingers shaking, she slid her thumb under the flap, pulled out the card, and read the note inside.

"Oh, Hunter—" she said, distressed. She touched his cheek affectionately. The card's sweet sentiment made her task even more difficult.

Hunter caught her hand and kissed her palm, holding it to his cheek as he examined her eyes. "No," he said softly. "Let me go first." He placed her hand in his, turning to gaze fully into her face. "Sadie, surely you know by now how I feel."

She nodded. "Yes, Hunter. But first you need to listen—"

He touched her lips, shushing her. "This can't wait, Sadie. I want to marry you. We've talked about it before. But the time is right. I've even talked to Alec about it. He wants you as his mother." He laughed softly. "He knows about tonight—wanted to come along. Can you imagine?" He laughed again.

"Alec?" She caught her breath. Why had she let their relationship go this far? Now a little boy would be hurt.

"Yes, Alec loves you nearly as much as I do, darling, and wants you to be part of our family. Isn't that wonderful news?" Hunter sounded triumphant, as if she'd already said yes.

"Hunter, dear." Sadie took both his hands in his, and looked tenderly into his face. "I've got something important to tell you." She swallowed hard. "I'm afraid things have changed drastically in my life. You've been so good to me, and it hurts me to tell you, but I must."

Hunter's gaze never left hers as Sadie explained why she couldn't marry him.

At a booth in the back corner of the same diner, Pastor Michael and Blake Adams lingered over their trout dinners, discussing Cedar Creek Church history, the coming pageant, and the growing excitement of the community. It had been Blake's idea to treat the elderly pastor to dinner. He wanted to thank him for generously allowing the pageant to take over his church— and especially, to thank him for asking Sadie to head up the effort.

He'd planned to confide in the man of God, telling him of the newly discovered love between Sadie and himself—how it must have been somewhere in God's sovereign plan for the two of them to return to Cedar Creek at just this time.

Blake had been about to speak of it when Hunter Shaw's Porsche roared into the parking lot just outside the booth's window. It was dusk, but not dark enough to keep Blake from watching Hunter open Sadie's door, then guide her into the restaurant, his arm firmly around her shoulders.

Then he watched with growing dismay as they sat engrossed in affectionate conversation. He'd watched Sadie's trembling fingers open an obviously intimate note. Then Hunter held Sadie's hand to his cheek, and took her hand in his. So engrossed was Sadie that she had no idea Blake was near her—not close enough to hear the words, but near enough to see every lift of her eyebrow, every tender expression crossing her beautiful face.

Finally, Blake turned away, unable to watch. How could he have been so wrong about Sadie?

He tried to continue his conversation with Pastor Michael, but found it difficult to keep the couple by the window from his mind. How could he have been so naive for not realizing before, for not seeing the actress Sadie had become? Perhaps she did feel some affection for him—even love for the childhood friend of her past. But she couldn't love him with all her heart, soul, and mind—the way he loved her—and sit with Hunter Shaw, engrossed in intimate conversation.

Sickened, Blake finally turned to Pastor Michael who was watching him, a curious expression on his lined face.

"We'd better get back to the church," Blake said grimly. "It's almost time for practice, and I've got to catch Jacob McGraw about the manger when he drops off Jilly."

Pastor Michael patted him on the hand. "I understand, son. You don't need to explain."

Blake nodded. Somehow he knew that Pastor Michael spoke the truth.

They walked from the restaurant without Sadie or Hunter Shaw so much as glancing their way. As Blake helped the elderly pastor into the battered Land Rover, he felt a sadness, a loss, deeper than any he'd ever experienced.

Sadie, his precious Sadie, had been merely a leftover dream

from childhood. He took a deep cleansing breath as he pulled onto the Cedar Creek highway. In a week this assignment would be behind him, and he could go on with his life. *But alone,* he thought bitterly. *So alone.*

An hour later, Sadie opened the doors to the church. Her heart was lighter than it had been in months. She'd known for a long time that her relationship with Hunter was leading nowhere, and now that she'd finally had the courage to tell him, she was hugely relieved. He'd taken the news with surprising grace. And he'd assured her, their relationship had nothing to do with the pageant. Film crews, musicians, producer and son, all would pull up in front of Cedar Creek Church as planned or December twenty-third.

She pulled her arms from her parka and headed into the sanctuary, looking for Blake. Her heart pounded in anticipation.

He was standing in front of the set with Jilly and her father. They'd just carried in the manger, and Jilly had brought a doll to try it out. The three turned when they heard her approach.

"Look here!" Jilly jumped up and down in excitement. "Look here what my daddy made—it's the manger!"

Sadie climbed the stairs to the platform. The manger was a work of art—rough-hewn wood, long enough to feed a few cows or donkeys, just as it should be, yet narrow enough to cradle a baby. It was perfect.

Relieved, Sadie looked over Jilly's head to meet Blake's eyes. But he turned away to speak with Jacob McGraw. His lips were drawn tightly, as if in anger.

Before Sadie could react, Jilly grabbed her hand and led her to the manger. "Kneel down here," she commanded. "Look at this. Look at how he made this." She pointed out how the wood slats fit together without nails. "You know they didn't have nails in them days," she said with authority. "And I painted it—my daddy let me help."

But Sadie barely listened. She nodded now and then, but kept her eyes on Blake, who still hadn't looked toward her.

Jacob McGraw gave Jilly a peck goodbye and headed for the doors, accepting their thanks for the manger—and the hay. Within minutes, the angel choir had gathered and, guitar in hand, Blake took his place on the folding chair.

Sadie sat in the front pew, watching Blake work with the children. He started out with camp songs, laughing and joking with Jilly and the others. After a while, Ren sauntered in playing his harmonica, and the angels lifted their pure, clear voices in song. Practice went on as usual. The children had no idea anything had changed.

But Sadie knew. Not once did Blake meet her gaze—or even glance in her direction. The warmth that had been so evident on his face last night—and even before—had turned to ice.

Finally, she stood and quietly left the room, her heart ready to break with confusion and pain.

Nine

❦

The following morning, Ren and Blake finished driving the final nail in the rebuilt set. After touching it up with gray-brown paint, they stood at the back of the sanctuary, admiring their work.

"Yeah, man. Looks real good," Ren mumbled, his head bobbing up and down. The boy still wore the oversized jeans and shirts. And he made a point of wearing the bandanna headband pulled over his forehead. His tufted hair, now a bit longer, stuck out in comical spikes. The tough look of the boy had changed little, but Blake had noticed a difference in his eyes, a small sign of life—and hope—in their dark luminance.

"Hey, how about a spin in the Rover?" Blake patted his back.

"That'd be cool." Ren flashed him a pleased grin. "Yeah, I'd like that."

"Good, let's go!"

Minutes later, they pulled the battered Land Rover away from the church and headed toward Blackpoint Road. Much of the snow had melted in town, but as they climbed, it grew deeper and deeper. Finally, Blake pulled over, put the vehicle in four-wheel drive, and set the emergency brake.

"It's all yours." Blake reached for the door handle.

"But we're not to Blackpoint Road yet."

"That's okay You can handle it."

Ren glanced at the steep drop-off to their left, then back to the narrow, winding road in front of them. He drew in a deep breath. "You sure, man?"

"I wouldn't risk my life if I wasn't."

Ren let out a soft whistle and reached for the door handle to exchange places. Within a few minutes, the boy had adjusted the seat and mirrors and slowly pushed down on the accelerator. They were off to a smooth start.

"Good job," Blake said quietly. "Very good job."

They wound up the mountain a few more miles, then turned onto Blackpoint Road.

"Okay, let's put this thing through a few paces." Blake glanced at the boy's white face. "You up to it?"

"Sure, man." His voice sounded small and scared.

"See that hill over there?"

"Yeah."

"I want to see if this thing can take it."

"You mean, you want me to drive up there?"

"Yep."

"There's no road, man." Ren adjusted his headband.

"I know."

"You want me to just drive right up that hill—no road, no nothin'."

"Yep."

Ren gulped hard, and with a shaky hand, put the car in a lower gear. The Land Rover lurched forward, heading toward the small incline. Blake could see that the boy was holding his breath.

Ren gunned the engine and the rear wheels slipped.

"Nice and easy now."

Ren nodded, letting out his breath as the Land Rover took the hill. Slowly they climbed, making fresh tracks in the snow.

"Okay, turn it around," Blake instructed.

"Here?" The boy's voice squeaked.

"Yeah—over there in that level spot."

Ren guided the car to the place and made a three-point turn. "Now what?"

"Back down the hill."

"Goin' down's harder."

"I know."

"You think I can do it?"

"No doubt in my mind."

Ren held the steering wheel so tightly his knuckles were white. "Okay," he muttered. "Here we go."

The nose of the Land Rover pointed straight down. It bounced through the snowy terrain, but the boy kept it moving straight and steady. In minutes, they were back on the Blackpoint Road.

"Wow," breathed Ren. "Wow."

"How about if we stop and play some mean harmonica?"

Ren nodded and pulled over near a lookout point. A few

minutes later, they were sitting on a boulder, looking out over Cedar Creek, fifteen hundred feet below.

Blake started playing tunes from the pageant; Ren joined in.

"You learn fast," Blake said when they'd finished.

The boy snorted. "You're the first one that ever told me that."

"That right?"

"Yeah."

"School probably hasn't been much fun."

"Nope."

"Maybe because it didn't seem to be leading you anywhere in particular."

Ren looked at Blake, frowning. "What'ya mean?"

"Ever thought about what you might want to do some-day—I mean when you're out of school?"

"Nah."

"You're good with kids."

"I am?"

"Yeah. Haven't you noticed how the kids love to have you join them when they're practicing? They watch you—try to do what you're doing."

"Yeah, I guess I noticed."

For a while they looked out at the scenery, talked about the pageant and the kids.

Then Ren looked at Blake. "You gonna be leavin' afterward, right?"

Blake nodded. "Yeah. I've got to get back to my regular work."

"What kinda work?"

Blake told him about his assignments with Global Mission, about the kids he'd seen in desperate conditions all over the world. The boy's solemn eyes didn't leave his. Ren seemed to hang on his words, swallowing hard, when Blake told him about the orphans he'd worked with in Romania, how they'd never felt the loving touch of someone who cared.

"You'd be good at working with kids like that." Blake had seen how Ren seemed to connect with the kids at church. There was a caring in him that shone through the tough exterior. Adults saw Ren's gang attire; kids saw something inside.

"Yeah, right. What could I do?"

Blake met his solemn gaze. "Sometimes we don't know what we can do until the opportunity comes up. Then all at once, the pieces come together—our caring, our gifts, our willingness to help."

Ren considered the words for a moment, then looked out over the snow-covered trees and boulders. Biting on his bottom lip, he suddenly turned back to Blake. "Why're you doin' this, man? Why're you botherin' with me?"

"You've got something special inside, Ren. I don't think you know it yet—but you're about to find it."

Ren stared at Blake for a moment, his dark eyes serious. "Yeah. Maybe," he said softly.

"Hey, we'd better be headin' down the hill," Blake said after a few minutes. Ren shrugged and pulled out his harmonica on the walk back to the Land Rover.

Blake drove back down the mountain to Cedar Creek, listening to "Sleep, Baby Jesus Boy" and "Silent Night." By the time they pulled into the town square, Ren had figured out the first few bars of "Bill Grogan's Goat."

That night after the angel choir rehearsal, Blake took a seat in the back of the sanctuary. Only a few days remained until the performance, and he needed to take notes for the *CCW* article. He'd brought the Nikon to get some shots of Sadie and the kids during practice.

He drew in a breath. At some point during the next few days, he knew he had to interview Sadie. Alone. The article wouldn't be complete without it. But he dreaded coming face to face with her. His pain was too fresh. He didn't know if he could gaze into her violet eyes, knowing that her affections lay with Hunter Shaw.

At the front of the sanctuary, Sadie called the children to their seats. She'd asked the angel choir to stay for rehearsal with Mary, Joseph, the innkeeper, the inn guests, and the shepherds. They sat together in the first few pews, squirming and whispering.

Jilly McGraw had started a trend. Now all the baby angel choir members wore their halos to rehearsals. Hovering by thin wires above their heads, the halos bobbed and wobbled in front of the rest of the children.

"Okay, kids," she called out. "I need your attention."

The children quieted.

"We're going to run through the entire play for the first time tonight. Think you're up to it?"

"Yeeesss!" they cried in unison.

Then Jilly raised her hand, jumping up and down. "Robbie Johnson doesn't know his lines," she yelled, then covered her mouth with a giggle.

"Busybody! Jil-ly's a busybody!" Robbie Johnson shouted and tried to grab Jilly's halo from three rows back. Jennifer Holt, who'd been chosen to play Mary, grabbed Robbie's ear and gave it a twist.

"Ow!" he screamed, holding his ear. "Ow!"

"I want it quiet—now!" Sadie called out. "Now!"

The din subsided.

"I said quiet." She lowered her voice.

The baby angels settled into their seats. Someone in the back row giggled and was shushed.

"All right, that's better." Sadie looked across the rows of children. "Now, we are going to go through the entire play. I want the baby angel choir to quietly—*quietly*—get up and move to the risers on the stage."

The angels, halos wobbling, climbed onto the stair-stepped bales of hay.

"My daddy brought these," Jilly whispered loudly as she took her place in the middle of the top row. "That too." She pointed to the manger.

"Big deal," Robbie Johnson muttered, still sitting in a pew with the shepherds.

"Okay, now I want the shepherds over here." Sadie pointed a place just below the platform. "Mary and Joseph, to the back doors—you'll walk up the aisle after the pageant starts." Then she nodded to the stable. "Innkeeper and guests—over here." The children scuffled and whispered and shoved each other into place.

"We'll begin with the angel choir." Sadie shaded her eyes from the overhead light and peered into the dark sanctuary. Earlier, she thought she'd seen Blake take a seat in the back row.

"Blake," she said quietly, "Are you still there?"

He stood, notebook in hand, and walked to the front.

"I know I didn't ask you ahead of time, but would you mind?"

"Not at all." He smiled at the kids, but not at her. Putting down the notepad and grabbing his guitar, he swung onto the platform and settled onto a bale of hay. Jilly giggled as he placed a piece of straw in his mouth.

Blake led the kids through the opening songs. They lifted their voices, singing better than ever before. During the third song, though, Mary and Joseph started down the aisle. Mary giggled when Joseph tried to help her walk, as he'd been instructed to do. He jabbed her in the ribs. She yelped, jabbed him back, but stopped snickering.

Sadie grew more and more dismayed. The play was a far cry from where it should be with the performance so quickly approaching. Mary and Joseph finally made it to the inn. The innkeeper and the guests said their lines without a hitch, then Mary and Joseph settled into the stable.

"This is where the lights will dim," Sadie said to the children. "When the TV crew gets here Saturday, they'll set up special lighting. All the lights will be out, except for a spotlight on the shepherd boy, Benjamin. He'll be standing over here by the piano."

Ren was sitting in the front pew near the place. "Ren," Sadie said, "would you mind filling in for the shepherd—just so the children have an idea how his part will go?"

Ren started to shrug indifferently, then glanced at Blake. Suddenly, the boy smiled. "Okay," he said, and walked slowly to the place.

Sadie led him through the actions and lines. He watched her intently, and followed her directions without a grumble.

"Benjamin," she explained to the children at one point, "is looking for a gift for the new baby King. He doesn't think he has anything of worth. He looks everywhere—" She instructed Ren where to move during the sequence. "—but he can't find any worthy of the King.

"A long time before, when Benjamin was a little boy, his father made him a little harp. Then he taught Benjamin to play it while he tended the sheep. Just like David in the Bible, Benjamin plays his harp and sings every night. Even after his father dies, the music brings peace to his soul. But the harp has been with him for so long that it seems very ordinary—not special at all."

Still, the children didn't utter a peep. Some seemed to watched Ren almost as if he were Benjamin.

"Then one night," Sadie went on, "the shepherd boy sits by his fire, sad because he has nothing for the King. He picks up his harp and begins to play. All at once, he realizes that the King, when he's a little older, might love the harp as much as he does.

"Suddenly, he knows that he has the perfect gift for the King."

Jilly raised her hand. "But won't he miss it?"

"Yes, Jilly, he will. But he figures that because he loves the harp so much, the baby King will, too. He's happy because it's a gift of love."

"But won't he be more lonesome after its gone?" Jilly sounded worried.

"He thinks about that too."

"He does?"

"Benjamin decides to write a song for the baby King and sing it to him when he presents the harp. That way, every time he sings the same song by his nightfire, he'll remember the King and the gift of love."

The children seemed in awe of the gift, and the rehearsal proceeded with new feeling. Afterward, several asked to see the harp.

"It will be here with the TV crews," she explained. "The boy playing Benjamin will bring it." Then she noticed Ren standing nearby, a look of longing in his dark eyes. He smiled softly, then turned to leave the church with the rest of the children.

Several minutes later, Sadie checked the pews, picking up stray scripts and pieces of tinsel from the halos.

"Sadie?"

She looked up. It was Blake.

"I need to interview you for the article."

"Really."

"My deadline's a week after the pageant is over. I figure it's better to do it now—before things get even more hectic closer to the performance." He brushed his dark hair away from his forehead. "If it's all right—I'd like to meet with you now for a few minutes."

She nodded, confused, not trusting herself to speak.

He nodded to the front pew. She sat, and he pulled up the folding chair and took out the notepad.

"Now," he said, all business, his eyes on the pad. "What

made you decide on a career in Hollywood?"

She ignored his question. "Why are you doing this, Blake?"

He looked up, his eyes full of misery.

"After what happened—after telling me you love me—you suddenly act as if you don't even know me? As if we're not even friends…"

He seemed to stare right through to her soul, but still he said nothing.

"Why? At least you owe me that."

Blake threw down the notepad, and stood, walking away from her a few steps. "Is that what you think we are, Sadie, friends?" He turned to look at her again, his expression a mix of anger, confusion, and pain.

She frowned, shaking her head slightly.

He suddenly moved toward her, pulled her to standing. "I loved you, Sadie—I was ready to ask you to marry me. I wanted to spend the rest of my life with you."

He'd used past tense. Sadie felt a chill travel down her spine. "Loved—?" she said, feeling she would choke on the word. "Loved?"

"Yes," he said fiercely. "I just had no idea it meant so little to you."

"I—I said I loved you, too." Her voice shook. "I—I—don't understand, Blake."

He took his hands from her shoulders, and stepped backward, his green eyes assessing her coolly. "To think, after holding you in my heart all these years, Sadie…" He didn't finish.

She held her fingers to her mouth. "Why, Blake? You still haven't said why."

275

But Blake simply gave her another cold stare, then turned and hurried down the center aisle, banging through the back doors.

For a moment, Sadie stood rooted to the spot, too stunned to move.

Suddenly, it was clear to her. Hunter's visit had been so brief—only a few hours. She'd thought no one had been aware of his presence. But what if—?

"Blake—" she cried, running for the exit. "Blake!"

Ten

B lake!" Sadie cried, running out the church doors and across the crunchy night snow. She could see him about to climb into the Land Rover.

He turned and watched and she ran to him.

"Blake! Oh, Blake—" She struggled to get the words out. "There's been a mistake—a terrible mistake."

"What do you mean?"

"Did you see Hunter?"

He cocked his head and narrowed his eyes.

"Did you? Please tell me, Blake. Did you?"

"Yes." His voice was cold.

She stepped back a step. "Together. You saw us together that night."

He nodded.

"Oh, darling—" She reached up to touch his face, but he removed her hand.

She swallowed. "I was telling him goodbye."

He snorted. "That was an elaborate goodbye—candlelight, silver..."

"You were there—at the restaurant?"

He nodded curtly as if he didn't want to remember.

Sadie drew in a deep breath. "You don't understand, Blake. He planned all that—he came up here to ask me to marry him. He'd planned it all, the roses, everything." Now Sadie was crying, afraid Blake wouldn't understand. She turned from him, unable to bear the sadness in his face. "Don't you see," she said softly, blinking back her tears. "I owed him an explanation—I told him about you, about us, that night. I told him it was over."

Sadie gulped a deep and shuddering breath. "I tried to be gentle—I owed him that." Then head down, she moved away from Blake, unable to look in his face. What if he didn't believe her? She couldn't bear to find out the answer. She didn't want to see it in his eyes.

"Sadie," he said, his voice low and gruff. "Forgive me."

Suddenly she felt his arms around her, turning her to face him.

"Sadie," he whispered again. "I shouldn't have doubted you. It's just that it looked like you...like he..." He didn't finish, but pulled her into his arms and held her fiercely. "I thought I'd lost you. After all these years of dreaming of you, wanting you, waiting for you—I thought I'd lost you. I couldn't bear it, Sadie."

Sadie put her hands on the sides of his face. "I'd planned to tell you that night after rehearsal what'd happened—but you didn't give me a chance." She bit her lip. "I didn't know you'd seen us together...Oh, Blake. I can imagine how it must have looked. I'm so sorry."

Blake touched her lips, then slowly traced a finger along her cheek and under her chin. With a smile that spoke of everlasting love, he tilted her face and covered her mouth with his. Then crushing her close, he kissed her yet again and again, more tenderly. He ended with a brush of his lips on her forehead.

Sadie's heart raced wildly. She slipped her arms around his neck, wanting to stay in his arms forever.

"Sadie—" he breathed, pulling back slightly and cocking his head. A tender smile played at his mouth. "You are so precious…"

She looked into his deep green eyes, suddenly feeling faint with the love she saw there. Taking his hands in hers, she kissed his fingertips. "I love you, Blake," she said simply. "I always have."

Blake wrapped his arm around Sadie's shoulders, and they walked through the town square and up the hill toward her cottage. After a few minutes, Blake pulled Sadie under the shelter of a towering pine. Turning, they watched the twinkling lights of the Cedar Creek storefronts glowing in the distance through the gently falling snow.

"We'll need to talk about the future, Sadie." Blake took a deep breath. "You've got your career—I've got mine. I don't know how—"

Sadie considered his words. "There's a lot I didn't get a chance to tell you after…" Her voice broke off. She couldn't bear to mention her dinner with Hunter. She began again. "After the first night we talked, I did some thinking—and a lot of praying. Mother Teresa's words have settled someplace in my heart…God doesn't call us to be successful—only obedient."

He nodded.

She squinted her eyes in thought, looking toward the glow of lights in the snow. "I still don't have all the answers about what lies ahead. But I've been thinking about 'The Shepherd's Song' and wondering about its message for me. What gift do *I* lay before the King?"

For a moment Sadie didn't speak. Then she looked again into Blake's eyes. "I guess what I'm trying to say is that I *don't* know any more about my career than I did a week ago, or a year ago, or a day ago. All I know is that it belongs next to the frankincense and myrrh—and the shepherd boy's love-worn harp—before the King."

Blake pulled her into a tight embrace. "That's all any of us can give him. Our hearts and everything we are."

She nodded, feeling the warmth of his love—and God's—surrounding her, as real as the strength of Blake's arms. "Yes," she sighed. "Our gift to the King."

The morning of December twenty-third dawned gloomy and gray. Sadie padded across the cold floor and peered from her window. Two feet of fresh snow covered the ground.

She bit her lip, and knew, even before the phone rang, who it was and what it was about.

"Sade?" There was static on the line.

"Hunter?"

"Sadie, I've got bad news."

"The snow. You can't get through."

"Honey, I'm sorry. We're at the bottom of the grade. The highway patrol has the roads blocked. No one can say when they'll be plowed—it's still snowing like crazy down here."

There was more static. "How is it up there?"

"The same. There's at least two feet on the ground and coming down hard. It looks like a blizzard."

"I don't know what to tell you—other than to go ahead with the dress rehearsal and hope for the best tomorrow."

"Hunter, what will we do if you can't make it even then? The performance will be ruined..." Her voice dropped.

He didn't answer right away. "I don't know, Sade," he said finally. "I don't know. The air time is purchased—I've got advertisers." He sounded distressed. "I can't just run *White Christmas* again."

"I meant about the pageant here. What do we do about that? The folks in town...the kids—they'll be so disappointed."

He didn't answer.

Sadie swallowed. Obviously, it was her problem. "Hunter," she finally managed. "We'll just go on as planned, until we know for sure you can't make it."

"Okay, Sadie."

She put down the receiver and turned again to the window. The snow continued to fall in rapid swirls.

It continued to snow through the morning. At noon Sadie met the children at church. The roads in town had been plowed, but the highways were still closed.

Jilly, waiting in the foyer, took Sadie's hand as they walked into the sanctuary. "When will Alec Shaw be here?"

Sadie smiled gently. "I don't think he's going to make it."

Jilly frowned. "How about the guys with the special lights?"

Sadie shook her head. "Maybe they can get through tomorrow. We won't know until we see how the weather is."

"And the music—the guys who're gonna play the special music you told us about?"

"I'm sorry, Jilly. They may not make it either."

Jilly let go of her hand and bounded for the stage. "Well, I don't think we need any of 'em anyway." She sat down on a bale of hay. "I like it just fine the way it is."

Within a few minutes, the rest of the children crowded into the pews. They all talked at once, excited about the snow, the film crews, and seeing Alec Shaw, admired TV star, whom they expected to see momentarily.

Jilly was first with the news, shouting above all the others. "He's not comin'," she said, sticking her little nose in the air. As always, she loved to be the bearer of tidings, both good and bad. She watched the others from the corner of her eye.

The children looked at her wide-eyed.

"I said, he's not comin' today," she repeated. "Can't get here 'cause of the snow."

"Liar-liar-pants-on-fire!" yelled Robbie Johnson. He sounded ready to cry.

"Children—children!" Sadie called for their attention. "Jilly's right." There were groans of dismay before she could finish. "Please," she said quietly, understanding their disappointment. "Listen up!"

Dozens of pairs of worried eyes stared at her. "Jilly's right. The film crew, Alec, the musicians—all of them—are waiting at the bottom of the mountain. As soon as the roads are cleared, they'll start for Cedar Creek." She paused, nearly unable to bear their sad little faces. "We just don't know when that will be."

"We're not gonna be on TV, then, are we?" Robbie Johnson scooted down in his chair. "Are we?"

"It depends..." Sadie looked out the window at the near-blizzard conditions. "Actually," she continued. "I don't think so. It will take a miracle for them to get through today."

Jilly bobbed up and down in her seat, her hand raised. "How about tomorrow? What if they can't get here by tomorrow?"

Sadie swallowed hard. She was about to answer when the back doors swung open. In walked Blake with Ren. They moved to the front of the sanctuary and sat in a pew behind the children.

"I was about to say," Sadie continued, her eyes briefly meeting Blake's, "we may have to cancel the pageant."

"It doesn't *have* to be on TV," Jilly said, her voice subdued. "We could still do it." Several of the children said, "Yeah, it doesn't," but their voices were sad.

Sadie smiled gently. "That's true, it doesn't."

"And music—we don't have to have keyboards and all the stuff you told us about."

Sadie nodded. "You're right."

"I have an idea! I have an idea!" Jilly jumped up and down in her seat. "Listen to this!" She twisted her red pigtail until she had everyone's attention. "I have an idea," she yelled once more for emphasis.

"Yes, Jilly?"

"Ren can be the shepherd boy."

"Yeah, he can be the one," Jennifer Holt called out.

"Yeah, that'd be cool," Robbie Johnson yelled, then twisted

around to look at Ren. Everyone else did the same thing.

"He'd be better than Alec Shaw any ol' day," another boy said under his breath.

All eyes were on Ren. He swallowed hard, then looked at his feet without speaking. Blake's eyes met Sadie's. She nodded with a slight smile.

"Ren?" she said softly. "How about it?"

The boy still didn't look up.

"I think you'd do a beautiful job. You've been walking through the part for the kids' sake all along. You'd be great. Really."

"I dunno," Ren finally mumbled, then looked up shyly. "I dunno if I could do it."

"Pleeease," Jilly yelled, hopping in her seat. "Pleeease."

The others joined her with another long, drawn-out, "Pleeease."

Ren suddenly grinned, his dark eyes brightening. "I guess," he said. "Yeah, I guess so."

Sadie gave him a wide smile. "Good, then it's settled. The show will go on."

The children cheered, then climbed over, around, and under the pews to race to Ren's side as he moved to the aisle.

"It was all my idea," Jilly said, yelling louder than everyone else.

Ren grabbed her pigtail and gave it a tweak. She made a grab for his bandanna headband, snatched it from his head, and raced from the sanctuary. Amid shouts and yells and giggles, pushes and shoves, the children scrambled after the two.

"This is going to be some pageant," Sadie said to Blake,

shaking her head in wonder.

"Probably the best that's ever been—just as you told the kids in the beginning." He grinned, then draped his arm around her as they walked from the sanctuary. "The best ever."

Eleven

The snow continued off and on through the night. By morning another foot lay on the ground. Wide-eyed, Sadie stepped from her house to see Blake shoveling her walk.

He grinned, his warm breath showing in the cold air. "Oldtimers are calling this the snow of the century," he said, laughing. "Three feet on the ground, and the possibility of more on the way."

"I wonder if the roads are cleared."

"I doubt it. I talked with the road crews earlier. There's too much snow at the higher elevations—four feet in some places. They think it may take days to plow it."

Sadie smiled, a bit sadly. "I didn't think the crew would make it." Glancing down the road to town, she frowned. "The plows haven't even started on the roads in town." She looked back to Blake, narrowing her eyes. "What if no one comes? Most of the people were more excited about being on TV than anything else. Now—" She let the word hang limply. "Now—?"

He gave her a hug. "We'll do what we can for the kids,

Sadie. Besides, I ran into Jacob McGraw on the way up here. He was already out with his plow—a blade on the front end of his pickup—but he said he was on his way to clear the roads so the kids can get to church."

Sadie laughed. "Jilly was probably by his side making him do it."

"Come to think of it, she was riding with him."

Heavy dark clouds slid across the sun and blotted out the pale sky by midday. Sadie's plans for dress rehearsal disappeared as snow again swirled to the ground. The recently plowed roads soon turned white again. Even cars equipped with tire chains stayed safely tucked in their garages.

Cedar Creek settled into a silent and snowy Christmas Eve. Smoke twisted up from chimneys, and twinkling lights glowed bright in a premature dusk.

At five o'clock, Blake ventured out in the Land Rover. After picking up Sadie, he drove them to the church. Pastor Michael had just finished shoveling the walk. The three entered the warm sanctuary together, stomping the snow off their boots at the doorway.

"I'm so sorry," she said, taking the pastor's cold hands in hers. "We had such grand plans—"

"Don't worry, child." His eyes were merry. "God moves in mysterious ways. When I contacted you about doing the play—I thought it was a grand idea for bringing new life into the church, into the community." He glanced out a window at the blizzard and shrugged. "I prayed about it...gave it to God. Thought I was onto something good." He shrugged. "I found out a long time ago, though, God's ways are often different than mine." He smiled wryly. "In fact, they nearly always are."

The children began arriving a few at a time. Jilly, arriving in Jacob McGraw's heavy pickup, was first. She bounded into the church, her worn parka zipped over the angel robe and, as always, the now-tattered halo bobbing.

"Where is he?" she demanded to everyone as she ran down the aisle.

"Where's who?" Sadie was at the front of the church, going through the script to make adjustments for fewer kids.

"Ren, that's who! Where is he?"

"There's plenty of time, Jilly. Don't worry." Blake looked up from where he sat, tuning the guitar.

Jilly shrugged and whispered and giggled with the other children as they arrived. Sadie noticed, though, that she couldn't keep her eyes off the back doors.

By six o'clock the children were in their places in the front pews—thirty-two baby angels, Mary and Joseph, shepherds, the innkeeper and the inn guests, and the wise men. Sadie glanced at Blake, smiled and shook her head. She couldn't believe they had ventured out in the storm. She just hoped they wouldn't be disappointed because of the turnout. Though even if just their parents came, the church would be half full.

"Okay, kids," Sadie called out. "I need your attention."

The giggling and squirming died down.

"We've got nearly an hour to go over our parts, warm up our voices—"

"But where's Ren?" Jilly interrupted, her normally exuber-ant voice subdued. "What if he doesn't come?"

"He's got plenty of time, Jilly," Sadie said confidently,

though she cast a glance at Blake. She could see a shade of worry in his face.

Jilly sighed loudly and scrunched down in her seat while Sadie led the others through their speaking parts. Then Blake led them through their songs. From time to time the little girl cast a furtive glance at the doors.

At six-thirty Sadie was as worried as Jilly, and by six-forty-five, she wondered if Ren would show at all. At six-fifty, Sadie led the children to a Sunday school classroom downstairs to await their entrance.

As they were leaving, Pastor Michael dimmed the overhead lights, lit candles that had been placed in an arrangement of holly atop the baby grand, then plugged in the twinkling white lights of the Christmas tree. Blake, sitting near the stage, began to strum Christmas carols on his guitar.

Downstairs, with Blake's sweet carols in the background and the voices of people entering the sanctuary, Sadie told the children that the play would have to proceed without Ren. "We'll work around his part unless he comes within the next few minutes," she said sadly.

There were moans of disappointment.

Jilly looked ready to cry. "Maybe it's 'cause he didn't have a costume," she said quietly.

Sadie's heart sank. Hunter had said he'd get Alec's costume from the studio wardrobe department, and beyond that, she hadn't given it a thought. Maybe Jilly was right. Though she pictured that tough little boy in his oversized tee-shirt and jeans and couldn't imagine him donning a shepherd's robe.

"But I want him here," Jilly said, sniffling loudly. She chewed on the end of one red pigtail.

"We all do, Jilly." Murmurs of agreement rose from the rest of the children.

"Hey, guys!" Sadie said cheerfully. "We can't put on a joyous Christmas story with sad faces and voices. Come on—I want to see some smiles."

A few tried, though halfheartedly.

"That's a little better—"

Upstairs, Blake began playing "O Come, All Ye Faithful," their entrance cue.

Sadie straightened a few halos and robes, and gave some quick hugs as she placed them in a double line. "Okay, this is it. Are you ready?"

A few angels nodded, others shrugged, still looking downcast. Sadie took the hands of the two little angels at the front and led them upstairs and through the doors.

The children gasped audibly as they entered the sanctuary. The church was full of people, so many that some were standing at the back and along the sides. The effect on the children was immediate: little shoulders squared and wide smiles appeared as the children paraded down the center aisle to Blake's music.

Within a moment, the baby angel choir had climbed into place on the hay-bale risers, Jilly grinning at the center back. Mary and Joseph and the people of the inn took their places. The shepherds stood just below the stage and off to one side, pretending to watch their sheep. Sadie took her place near the piano where she could see and help the children with their lines.

Blake nodded to the angel choir, and began to sing. The children chimed in, their voices rising clear and loud. At the end of the third song, a noise at the back of the sanctuary caused the children to stop mid-note, astonished expressions lighting their faces.

Sadie turned to look. So did everyone else.

Ren stood just inside the backdoors, taking in the room full of people. He was dressed in his grandfather's green plaid robe and his grandmother's sandals. A white cloth—Sadie thought it looked like a floursack dishcloth—fell in folds over his head, shepherd-like, with his gangland bandanna headband holding it in place. He looked small, scared, vulnerable.

There wasn't a sound in the sanctuary as the child stood rooted to the spot, his large dark eyes showing his fear.

"Hey, everybody!" Jilly suddenly yelled. "He's here! Ren's here." Pushing and shoving the other baby angels out of the way, she scrambled off the hay risers and bounded down the aisle to where Ren stood.

Grinning, she reached for his hand and slowly led him to the front of the church. "This is our shepherd," she said to the audience, her halo bobbing. "He's our star, you know."

After Ren was in place at the foot of the stage, Jilly sat by him, elbows on knees, chin cupped in her hands. Blake led the angel choir in another song, and Jilly sang along from her place with Ren. She didn't budge from the spot during Mary and Joseph's journey to Bethlehem, during the scene at the inn, during the angels' appearance to the shepherds, or even during the Magi visit to the stable.

Then it was Ren's turn. He stood uncertainly, his eyes downcast, and waited for the spotlight he'd helped Blake rig days before. He seemed so small and scared. How would he make it through the pageant, the speaking parts, the songs?

Suddenly, the boy Ren disappeared, and the shepherd boy Benjamin took his place. Ren lifted his shoulders tall and tilted his chin upward, looking every bit the part of the shepherd Sadie had envisioned when she wrote the play.

With a clear, steady voice, Ren began to speak, bringing his part to life as he searched for the perfect gift for the baby King. Not a sound rose from the audience. Even the normally squirmy Jilly sat transfixed, her eyes never leaving the boy.

The play moved into its final scene. The shepherd boy sat down by his cellophane nightfire to play a lullaby from his love-worn harp, his most precious possession.

Ren lifted his harmonica to his lips. He closed his eyes, and in beautiful simplicity, played "Silent Night." The music seemed to flow from someplace inside the boy's soul. Sadie glanced at Blake, who met her gaze, his eyes moist.

As the final sweet notes of the song died away, Ren stood and faced the audience.

"The shepherd boy looked everywhere for a perfect gift. He wanted to give the baby King something special. It turned out he had that special gift with him all along.

"It was his harp—something his dad made for him before he died years before.

"I know what it feels like not to have a dad." Ren paused, swallowing hard. "If my dad had given me something before he died—it would've been the same as the harp was to Benjamin—the most special thing in the world."

He looked down, as if trying to find the words. Then drawing in a deep breath, he looked over to Blake, still sitting with the baby angel choir. Blake met his gaze, smiling gently.

Ren raised his chin, and when he spoke, he looked at the

manger, seeming to speak to Someone unseen. "I don't have a harp. I only have this—" He held out the harmonica. "—but it's the best thing anybody ever gave me."

He sniffled softly. "And I want to give it to the baby King." He walked slowly up the stairs and laid the harmonica by the manger next to the gold, frankincense, and myrrh.

By now sniffling could be heard throughout the sanctuary. After a moment, Blake began strumming "What Child Is This." The baby angel choir joined in, Jilly singing louder than everyone else. Then Ren headed down the stairs, reached for Jilly's hand, and the two of them moved down the center aisle.

"Ren's the best shepherd we ever had," Jilly said as they walked, her little chin in the air. "And it was all my idea. I found him."

After the children, their parents, and the rest of the audience left the church, Blake and Sadie turned for a last look at the sanctuary before flipping off the lights.

"You were right—this was the best pageant that ever could've been," Sadie said, still feeling awed by Ren's performance. "I came back to Cedar Creek with grand plans for a professional production. None of them worked out—and it turned out better than if they had." Her voice softened. "And Ren…that child gave us all quite a gift of love—all the kids did."

Blake nodded. "Especially Jilly," he added with a smile.

"And she's the one who asked if angels could give gifts."

Sadie gazed at the stable, the bales of hay, the Christmas tree in the corner. She wanted to tuck away the memory of it in her heart. For a moment she didn't speak.

Blake considered her gently, seeming to understand her thoughts before she spoke. "Something happened here tonight—a kind of miracle…"

She gave him a quick smile, nodding. "We came to celebrate the birth of Jesus, the greatest gift the world—any of us—could ever receive. Yet tonight I saw firsthand that God's giving didn't stop there. He cares about every detail of our lives.

"Think about the transformation we've seen in Ren—the growth in him." She smiled softly into Blake's eyes. "You saw something in him that none of the rest of us did. You reflected God's compassion…and he responded to that love. It changed him."

She tilted her head in thought. "And us, Blake—" Her gaze lingered on the knotty pine walls, the pews, the worn oak floor, the platform where the baptistry was hidden. "To think that God brought us together after all these years in the little church that our fathers built…in the place where we tagged along behind them, helping and making mischief."

"I helped. You made mischief." Blake grinned as he pulled her closer and draped his arm around her shoulders. Then his voice quieted. "Tonight it seems like this is a place of miracles, Sadie—all brought about by love—God's for us, and ours for each other. And not just because it's Christmas Eve…"

Sadie nodded as Blake helped her into her coat, and after a moment they walked slowly from the church.

"Christmas Eve…" Sadie murmured as their footsteps crunched through the snow. They turned toward the twinkling lights of the town square. In the distance carolers lifted their voices in song, and above them spangles of stars shone brightly in the now cloudless sky. "I'd almost forgotten what a night of miracles it was," Sadie whispered, looking up at the sky.

"And still is," Blake said. He suddenly stopped, pulling Sadie close. In the soft glow of the streetlight, his eyes shimmered as brightly as the stars. Gently, he kissed her lips, then moved back a bit, his face filled with love. "Sadie, do you have any idea how much I love you?"

"Oh, Blake—" Sadie breathed, struck by a sudden sadness, by the intrusion of something she hadn't let herself think about for days. "I'm going to miss you." They'd spoken of a future together someday. But when would it be? With their careers... She frowned, not wanting to continue the thought. How could she bear to let Blake walk out of her life again? Warm tears filled her eyes. "When are you leaving?" Her voice was barely a whisper.

Blake drew in a deep breath, studied the heavens for a moment, before again looking back into her eyes. "I can't yet," he said.

She tilted her head. "Why not?"

"I haven't finished the article."

"Oh." Her voice was small.

"I have a number of questions to ask you." His eyes twinkled.

"You do?"

He nodded. "Yes." Again, he grinned. "Although there's one question the *CCW* readers won't be as interested in as I am."

"And what question is that?"

He smiled softly, gently brushing an unruly curl from her forehead, his gaze never leaving hers. "Will you marry me?" His voice was low, intense. "Sadie—" He tilted her face toward his. "Please say you'll marry me."

A wide smile spread across her face. She wrapped her arms around his neck. "Yes! Oh, yes!" she whispered. "I'll marry you, Blake!"

With a whoop of joy, Blake grabbed her into a giant bear

hug, his arms lifting her feet from the ground. Around and around he twirled her, the snow crunching under his boots. She laughed joyously with him as they whirled.

Finally, he set her down. "Now the other questions."

She lifted an eyebrow. "For the article?"

He chuckled. "Readers might be interested—but again, not as much as I am."

"Go on."

"When shall we marry, fair maiden—and where?"

Sadie cocked an eyebrow toward the church. "I don't think there's any question about where. But I suggest we wait until the snow melts…"

He laughed, pulling her into his arms and kissing her joyously. "I agree, though I don't know if I can wait that long." He hugged her again exuberantly.

After a moment, Sadie looked up at him. "Now, I have a question."

He waited for her to continue.

"We haven't talked much about my screenwriting, your traveling…about what we'll do…"

"I've got an idea, Sadie, that we might consider." His handsome face was earnest. "There's an assignment coming up this summer. I've been asked to cover a children's choir in Africa. It's made up of orphans. They're tremendously talented—travel all over the world giving concerts."

She watched him intently, touched by his enthusiasm and love for his work.

"I thought—the way the pageant turned out, the way you work with children—it might be something we could do together." His brows knit into a frown. "I know it's a lot to ask. I know it's completely alien from your world. It's probably completely unfair of me—"

Sadie touched his lips with her fingers. "Ssssh." She said, smiling happily. "I love the idea. I'll go."

"Just like that? You'll go?"

She nodded. "But there's something else we ought to consider."

"What's that?"

"Ren."

He raised a brow. "You think Ren should go with us?"

She nodded again. "He'd be great with the kids."

Blake broke into a wide smile. "We'll tell him in the morning—it'll be our Christmas gift to him."

Then Blake took Sadie's hands in his. "One more thing," he said, his voice husky.

"Another question for the article?" She laughed softly, somehow knowing it wasn't.

He shook his head and reached into his pocket. Smiling, he placed into her open palm a tiny velvet box tied with a delicate gold ribbon.

With trembling fingers, Sadie unfastened the bow and lifted the lid. For a moment she didn't speak, then she raised her eyes to Blake's. "It's perfect," she whispered as he slipped the ring onto her finger. "A perfect gift of love."

Also by Amanda MacLean:

Westward

Stonehaven

Everlasting (Summer, 1996)

You may write to:
Peggy Darty
Sharon Gillenwater
Amanda MacLean
c/o Palisades
P.O. Box 1720
Sisters, Oregon 97759

Palisades…Pure Romance

Refuge, Lisa Tawn Bergren
Torchlight, Lisa Tawn Bergren
Treasure, Lisa Tawn Bergren
Secrets, Robin Jones Gunn
Whispers, Robin Jones Gunn
Sierra, Shari MacDonald
Westward, Amanda MacLean
Stonehaven, Amanda MacLean
Glory, Marilyn Kok
Love Song, Sharon Gillenwater
Antiques, Sharon Gillenwater
Cherish, Constance Colson
Angel Valley, Peggy Darty
A Christmas Joy, Darty, Gillenwater, MacLean

Treasure, Lisa Tawn Bergren
ISBN 0-88070-725-9
She arrived on the Caribbean island of Robert's Foe armed with a lifelong dream—to find her ancestor's sunken ship—and yet the only man who can help her stands stubbornly in her way. Can Christina and Mitch find their way to the ship *and* to each other?

Secrets, Robin Jones Gunn
ISBN 0-88070-721-6
Seeking a new life as an English teacher in a peaceful Oregon town, Jessica tries desperately to hide the details of her identity from the community...until she falls in love. Will the past keep Jessica and Kyle apart forever?

Sierra, Shari MacDonald
ISBN 0-88070-726-7
When spirited photographer Celia Randall travels to eastern California for a short-term assignment, she quickly is drawn to—and locks horns with—editor Marcus Stratton. Will lingering heartaches destroy Celia's chance at true love? Or can she find hope and healing high in the *Sierra?*

Westward, Amanda MacLean
ISBN 0-88070-751-8
Running from a desperate fate in the South toward an unknown future in the West, plantation-born artist Juliana St. Clair finds herself torn between two men, one an undercover agent with a heart of gold, the other a man with evil intentions and a smooth facade. Witness Juliana's dangerous travels toward faith and love as she follows God's lead in this powerful historical novel.

Glory, Marilyn Kok
ISBN 0-88070-754-2
To Mariel Forrest, the teaching position in Taiwan provided more than a simple escape from grief; it also offered an opportunity to deal with her feelings toward the God she once loved, but ultimately blamed for the deaths of her family. Once there, Mariel dares to ask the timeless question: "If God is good, why do we suffer?" What follows is an inspiring story of love, healing, and renewed confidence in God's goodness.

Love Song, Sharon Gillenwater
ISBN 0-88070-747-X
When famous country singer Andrea Carson returns to her hometown to recuperate from a life-threatening illness, she seeks nothing more than a respite from

the demands of stardom that have sapped her creativity and ability to perform. It's Andi's old high school friend Wade Jamison who helps her to realize that she needs inner healing as well. As Andi's strength grows, so do her feelings for the rancher who has captured her heart. But can their relationship withstand the demands of her career? Or will their romance be as fleeting as a beautiful *Love Song*?

Cherish, Constance Colson
ISBN 0-88070-802-6
Recovering from the heartbreak of a failed engagement, Rose Anson seeks refuge at a resort on Singing Pines Island, where she plans to spend a peaceful summer studying and painting the spectacular scenery of international Lake of the Woods. But when a flamboyant Canadian and a big-hearted American compete for her love, the young artist must face her past—and her future. What follows is a search for the source and meaning of true love: a journey that begins in the heart and concludes in the soul.

Whispers, Robin Jones Gunn
ISBN 0-88070-755-0
Teri Moreno went to Maui eager to rekindle a romance. But when circumstances turn out to be quite different than she expects, she finds herself spending a great deal of time with a handsome, old high school crush who now works at a local resort. But the situation becomes more complicated when Teri meets Gordon, a clumsy, endearing Australian with a wild past, and both men begin to pursue her. Will Teri respond to God's gentle urgings toward true love? The answer lies in her response to the gentle *Whispers* in her heart.

Angel Valley, Peggy Darty
ISBN 0-88070-778-X
When teacher Laurel Hollingsworth accepts a summer tutoring position for a wealthy socialite family, she faces an enormous challenge in her young student, Anna Lisa Wentworth. However, the real challenge is ahead of her: hanging on to her heart when older brother Matthew Wentworth comes to visit. Soon Laurel and Matthew find that they share a faith in God...and powerful feelings for one another. Can Laurel and Matthew find time to explore their relationship while she helps the emotionally troubled Anna Lisa and fights to defend her love for the beautiful *Angel Valley*?

Stonehaven, Amanda MacLean
ISBN 0-88070-757-7
Picking up in the years following *Westward*, *Stonehaven* follows Callie St. Clair back to the South where she has returned to reclaim her ancestral home. As she works to win back the plantation, the beautiful and dauntless Callie turns it into a station on the Underground Railroad. Covering her actions by playing the role

of a Southern belle, Callie risks losing Hawk, the only man she has ever loved. Readers will find themselves quickly drawn into this fast-paced novel of treachery, intrigue, spiritual discovery, and unexpected love.

Antiques, Sharon Gillenwater
ISBN 0-88070-801-8
Deeply wounded by the infidelity of his wife, widower Grant Adams swore off all women—until meeting charming antiques dealer Dawn Carson. Although he is drawn to her, Grant struggles to trust again. Dawn finds herself overwhelmingly attracted to the darkly brooding cowboy, but won't marry a non-believer. As Grant learns more about her faith, he is touched by its impact on her life and slowly begins to trust.

A Christmas Joy, MacLean, Darty, Gillenwater
ISBN 0-88070-780-1 (same length as other Palisades books)
Snow falls, hearts change, and love prevails! In this compilation, three experienced Palisades authors spin three separate novelettes centering around the Christmas season and message:
By Amanda MacLean: A Christmas pageant coordinator in a remote mountain village of Northern California is reunited with an old friend and discovers the greatest gift of all.
By Peggy Darty: A college skiclub reunion brings together model Heather Grant and an old flame. Will they gain a new understanding?
By Sharon Gillenwater: A chance meeting in an airport that neither of them could forget...and a Christmas reunion.

Refuge, Lisa Tawn Bergren
ISBN 0-88070-621-X
Part One: A Montana rancher and a San Francisco marketing exec—only one incredible summer and God could bring such diverse lives together. *Part Two:* Lost and alone, Emily Walker needs and wants a new home, a sense of family. Can one man lead her to the greatest Father she could ever want and a life full of love?

Torchlight, Lisa Tawn Bergren
ISBN 0-88070-806-9
When beautiful heiress Julia Rierdon returns to Maine to remodel her family's estate, she finds herself torn between the man she plans to marry and unexpected feelings for a mysterious wanderer who threatens to steal her heart.

NOTE TO DEALER: CUSTOMER SHOULD PROVIDE 6 COUPONS AND YOU SHOULD RETAIN THE COUPON FROM THE FREE BOOK (#7). WE WILL SEND YOU A REPLACEMENT COPY OF THE PALISADES NOVEL YOU GIVE AWAY VIA SPRING ARBOR, CONSOLIDATED FREIGHT. (IN CANADA, CONTACT BEACON DISTRIBUTING.)

PLEASE FILL OUT:
(ON PAGE FROM FREE BOOK ONLY)

FREE BOOK TITLE _____

ISBN _____

STORE NAME _____

ADDRESS _____

_____

SPRING ARBOR CUSTOMER ID# _____
(VERY IMPORTANT!)

BEACON DISTRIBUTING ACCOUNT # (CANADIANS ONLY) _____

STAPLE THE 6 COUPONS TOGETHER WITH #7 AND THE INFORMATION ABOVE ON TOP.

YOU MAY REDEEM THE COUPONS BY SENDING THEM TO:

PALISADES CUSTOMER SERVICE
QUESTAR PUBLISHERS, INC.
P.O. BOX 1720
SISTERS, OR 97759

CANADIANS SEND TO:
BEACON DISTRIBUTING
P.O. BOX 98
PARIS, ONTARIO
N3L3E5